Praise for Miche

Endangered

"What a unique and interesting story. Good for fans of urban fantasy and shapeshifters. This was fun, and funny, with a great cast of characters. Plenty of action and great chemistry between the main characters. Loved the world building and can't wait to read more."—*Kat Adams, Bookseller (QBD Books, Australia)*

"When X-Men meets Twilight, the outcome is this wholly enjoyable paranormal fantasy. Grab this book, suspend disbelief and cosy in for feel-good impossibilities."—*reviewer@large*

"This was a very impressive novel. It was a skillfully crafted story, and one does not have to look too far to see parallels in today's America."—*Kitty Kat's Book Review Blog*

"*Endangered* by Michelle Larkin is a delightful novel with some heavy moments but enough lightheartedness to keep you thoroughly entertained."—*Romantic Reader Blog*

"What I liked most about this novel was its tone, mostly linked to Aspen's sense of humor and the banter between the characters in times of danger…[T]he rhythm, the humor, the interesting and endearing characters were enough to keep me hooked…"
—*Jude in the Stars*

Unexpected Partners

"There is a lot of action in this story that will keep you interested and sometimes on the edge of your seat as you read…I liked the main characters and could see the chemistry between the two, and enjoyed the way the romance was treated throughout the story. The secondary characters were also well-developed and made the tale better."—*Rainbow Reflections*

By the Author

Mercy

Unexpected Partners

Endangered

Sylver and Gold

SYLVER AND GOLD

by

Michelle Larkin

2020

THIS TRADE PAPERBACK ORIGINAL IS PUBLISHED BY
BOLD STROKES BOOKS, INC.
P.O. BOX 249
VALLEY FALLS, NY 12185

FIRST EDITION: AUGUST 2020

CREDITS
EDITOR: RUTH STERNGLANTZ
PRODUCTION DESIGN: STACIA SEAMAN
COVER DESIGN BY TAMMY SEIDICK

Acknowledgments

Endless thanks to my editor, Ruth Sternglantz, for her steady guidance, humor, and support.

A standing ovation goes to the very talented Tammy Seidick for designing yet another beautiful book cover.

Heartfelt gratitude to my writing confidant and sounding board in life, Deb Roberts-Arthur, who has become one of my dearest and most cherished friends.

A sincere thank you to Della for her quick wit, wry humor, and wonderful feedback.

And, finally, I'm deeply appreciative of my sons, Levi and Jett, for anchoring me in the precious moments of our day-to-day lives and teaching me that pinkie promises are worth more than gold.

This book is dedicated to Ruth Sternglantz—the best literary compass an author could ever want.

CHAPTER ONE

Detective Reid Sylver stepped inside her captain's office and tossed him an oatmeal muffin. He caught it one-handed and set it on a paper plate. She pulled up a chair on the other side of his desk and took a swig from the mug of coffee he'd prepared for her—black, with just a pinch of cinnamon.

"Was beginning to think you wouldn't show," Cap said without looking up as he peeled the paper from his muffin.

Reid glanced at the clock on the wall behind his desk: 4:38 a.m. Eight minutes late for their breakfast and workout routine was a new record for her. "Bakery opened late," she lied. The owner of the hottest bakery in Boston always handed her a bag with two oatmeal muffins as she passed on her morning walk to work. She returned the favor by making sure his car never got towed from the one-way street where it was illegally parked.

Chewing, she took one last look around the captain's office before finally meeting his gaze. They held eye contact for long seconds in silence. Reid had briefly considered not showing up at all this morning, but she didn't roll like that. Cap deserved better.

"Should I congratulate you or offer my condolences?" he asked, breaking the moment.

She threw a glance at Mugshot, who cocked his head and returned her gaze from his dog bed in the corner, an old tennis ball lodged firmly in his mouth. "He worked hard for that title," she said proudly. They'd spent the weekend competing in Petaluma, California. Mug had won first place in the World's Ugliest Dog contest.

"Had a feeling the votes might swing in your favor." He opened a drawer, withdrew a red gift bag, and slid it across the desk.

"What's this?"

"Just open it." He set a second gift bag on the floor and called Mug over.

Reid reached inside and pulled out a gray sweatshirt. *I'm with ugly* was stitched in navy blue across the front. She watched as Cap slid a sweatshirt over Mug's head that read *Ugly and damn proud*. He worked Mug's front paws into the small holes provided, for a perfect fit, digging into the gift bag again to hand Mug a new tennis ball.

Mug spit out the old tennis ball and trotted over with the new one. He set the ball in Reid's lap and gazed up expectantly with his one remaining eye. Some asshole biker had set him on fire as a pup. Ironically enough, Mug's breeding papers listed him as pick of the litter—a show-quality brindle bullmastiff. But nobody in their right mind would believe that now because he was a wrinkly, scarred, nearly furless mess. His ears were burned to nubs. One eye was sunken and sealed shut, damaged beyond repair by the flames.

"We'll play fetch later," she promised. "Thanks, Cap." Finished with her muffin, she stood and extended her hand across the desk, her vision blurred by tears.

Cap stood from his chair and returned the gesture with the calloused grip of a hardworking cop. "Catch up with you later, Sylver."

With Mug on her heels, she walked to the door. From this point forward, Reid would be heading to the gym alone.

From behind her, Cap said, "You really think there's something on the other side?"

"I don't *think*, sir." She turned to face him. "I *know*."

He studied her. "All these years, and we've never really talked about what you do. I didn't want to know the details because, well, it scares the hell out of me." He slid his hands in his pockets, shrugged, and looked at the floor. "I'm real sorry about that."

"No need to apologize, Cap."

"You deserve an apology. I just…" He looked her square in the eye. "I just want you to know, I think what you do is amazing. Gift or no gift, you're one hell of a detective, Sylver. Don't ever forget that."

All she could manage was a nod as she stepped out from his office and shut the door.

Mug followed her to the gym, happily chewing his new tennis ball as he kept pace on the treadmill beside her. They'd just finished mile three when the sound of a gunshot cracked like a whip through the air. She powered down both treadmills, withdrew her earbuds, and wiped the sweat from her face with the towel around her neck.

This was the part she was dreading the most. No way around it. Someone had to find the captain and call it in. As a homicide detective, she'd certainly seen more than her fair share of bodies. But this one was personal.

She'd been working under the captain's leadership for thirteen years. It hadn't taken him long to figure out something was up when she breezed through her own cases and then dug up cold cases, solving those in record time, too. She thought back to the day he'd called her into his office, closed the door firmly behind her, and instructed her to take a seat.

"What the hell is going on here, Sylver?" he asked.

"Boyle's being a whiney little dickwad, Cap."

He set his hands on his hips, towering above her. "Did you just use dickwad *to describe a fellow detective to your commanding officer?"*

"I could throw out some alternative descriptions if you want," she said, unapologetic. "Dickwad is the only G-rated word I could come up with on short notice."

Shaking his head, Cap took a seat behind his desk. He leaned back in his leather chair and pierced her with a look of disapproval, bewilderment, and just a hint of admiration—an expression with which she was already well acquainted. He finally shook his head and chuckled, surprising her. "Off the record, I don't disagree with your assessment of said dickwad."

Boyle had held the record for cases solved six years in a row. She'd effectively ousted him from his throne. Now his nose was out of joint, and he was stomping around like an angry toddler.

"I've read your reports, Sylver. Things just aren't adding up. I need you to be frank with me. How the hell are you solving these cases?"

"What's on the line, sir?"

"Your ass. My ass." He threw his hands up in frustration. "The communal ass of this department."

She thought for a long moment before warning him. "You won't like it."

"Does it involve you being corrupt?"

She shook her head.

"Then lay it on me."

She sighed. "I can talk to the dead, Cap."

He laughed heartily and slapped his desk.

But she said nothing more and looked away, embarrassed.

He stopped laughing. The room was quiet, save for the ticking clock behind his desk. "Jesus Christ. You're not joking, are you?"

"I'll hand in my resignation first thing tomorrow," she said, standing. Conversations like this would only lead to mandatory sessions with the department shrink. She refused to go down that road.

"Just hold on a minute." Cap ran a hand over his face. "I'm not done with you yet, Sylver. Sit down."

She did.

"So you're telling me—"

"I can talk to dead people," she finished for him. "Spirits. Ghosts. Apparitions. Whatever you want to call them."

"Christ. Really?"

"Really." She watched as he struggled to come to terms with this new information. She made a point of never telling anyone about her ability. She knew from experience it changed the way people looked at her. "By the way, your mom says you should never use the Lord's name in vain."

The captain narrowed his eyes. "You could've just pulled that out of your ass."

"She also wants you to know she's grateful you've kept her rosebush alive all this time. She loves the roses you leave at her grave every year."

"Christ almighty." The captain glanced at the ceiling. "Sorry, Ma." He stood and paced the length of the room before turning to her. "How long's this been going on?"

"As long as I can remember."

"So, what, you interview a homicide victim, and they tell you who killed them and where to find the evidence?"

She nodded. That was pretty much the gist of it.

"Do you actually see them when they talk to you?"

She nodded again. "They look just like regular people. The only difference is—"

He held up his hand. "Forget it. I don't want to know." He paced the room some more, visibly stressed. "You can't breathe a word of this to anyone."

"Want me to cancel the press release I had scheduled for this afternoon?"

He stood in front of her, leaned against the front of his desk, and crossed his arms. "We need to find a way to plug up the holes in your reports before someone else figures this out."

"We?" she said, taken aback. "As in...you and me?"

"I'll keep you on Homicide. You keep...doing whatever it is you do. We'll meet here every morning before shift and write your reports together. I'll help you cover your tracks."

She hesitated. "What's the catch?"

"No talk about anything otherworldly."

Sensing there was more, she waited for him to go on.

"After we're finished dotting our i's and crossing our t's, we'll hit the gym. You can help me get back in shape." He patted his ample gut. "Wife's on a health kick and wants me to lose some weight."

Reid squinted. "That's it?" she asked, suspicious.

"That's it."

She stood. They shook hands to seal the deal. As she turned to leave, Cap called out, "Zero four thirty. Sharp."

"But, Cap, shift doesn't start till seven."

"Those are the terms." He returned to his leather chair. "Take it or leave it."

And that was how thirteen years of muffins, cinnamon coffee, and workouts began—the best mornings of her life, by far. When Cap revealed he'd been diagnosed with an inoperable brain tumor and that his neurological demise was imminent, he'd informed her of his plan to take his own life. He couldn't bring himself to do it at home or in his car—too painful a reminder for his wife. Sitting behind the desk from which he'd supervised countless detectives for nineteen years was where he wanted to be during his final moments.

She swallowed the lump in her throat as she realized her only friend in the world was now gone. He was the first person—the only person, ever, in her life—to have her back.

Reid left Mug in the gym and then waited by Cap's side until the medical examiners arrived.

Dr. Fred Grady, Chief ME, stepped inside and locked eyes on Reid. They'd sent the big gun for this one. No one messed around when it involved the death of a cop. "You found him?" Fred asked.

She nodded.

"Did he leave a note? Anything like that?"

"None that I found."

"You see him this morning?"

She nodded again. "We usually work out together. Said he wasn't feeling well, that he'd catch up with me later." Always best to stick with as much of the truth as possible.

Fred shook his head. She knew he and the captain went back a long time. His sadness was palpable. "Sorry you had to see him like this, Sylver."

"You, too, Fred." She cast one last look at the captain. "Take good care of him, huh?"

"Will do."

With a heavy feeling in her chest, she retrieved Mug from the gym, exited through the rear of the building, and drove home in an unmarked car. She set her duffel on the kitchen table, unzipped it, and stared at the two red gift bags inside.

As if sensing her grief, Mug leaned against her leg in his characteristic show of support. She'd been wrong to think she'd lost her only friend. Mug was still here. She reached out to give him a reassuring pat on the back. Ever her faithful companion, he was her rock in life.

Reid slipped the sweatshirt over her head and grabbed a dry tennis ball from a bin near the back door. She played a long game of fetch with Mug in the backyard as a cold November breeze dried her tears.

❖

Reid's cell vibrated noisily on the nightstand. Tennis ball in mouth, Mug pawed at her from his place on the bed until she leaned over and picked it up. "Sylver," she answered, yawning.

"You coming in today or what?" Boyle asked.

She sat up and threw a glance at the bedside clock: 5:22 a.m. "What the hell, Boyle? Why're you calling me so damn early?"

"Because nobody's seen you in over a week. Better get your ass in here. Today."

She rubbed her temples, trying in vain to stave off the imminent hangover. "Or what?"

"Or you'll have the entire squad running lights and sirens to your house and breaking down your door."

Shit. She hung up on Boyle without another word.

Reid gazed longingly at the empty beer bottles on her nightstand. Looked like her plans with Sam Adams would have to be postponed until tonight. She swung her feet over the side of the bed, waited until the room stopped spinning, and headed to the shower.

Detective London Gold opened the closet door and took one last look at herself in the full-length mirror. Her long navy-blue blazer, heather-gray scoop-neck tee, charcoal slacks, and navy square-heel boots were the very definition of business casual. This was the big day. Everything had to be perfect.

She reached behind her neck and fastened a gold chain with a small cross pendant—the one her parents gave her for her first communion. Even though she hadn't seen her parents in over a decade—their choice, not hers—she wore this necklace, faithfully, every day. Part of her was sad they weren't here to celebrate with her. Someday, maybe they'd change their minds.

With eight years under her belt as a patrol officer, she'd finally been promoted to detective. The timing couldn't be better. A spot had just opened up in Homicide.

Becoming a homicide detective had been her dream since she could remember. But she was even more excited about the opportunity to learn from Reid Sylver. The woman was legendary. Not a single homicide case that crossed her desk in the last thirteen and a half years had gone unsolved. Those statistics were simply unheard of.

Reid was confident, intelligent, beautiful, and—if London's gaydar was functioning properly—gay.

London's heart picked up speed at the thought of spending her first few months as a detective with this incredible woman. Rubbing the cross between her fingers, she shook her head and sighed. *Don't mess this one up, London. Keep your crush in check.*

CHAPTER TWO

Armed with her favorite travel mug, Red Sox ball cap, and the darkest pair of sunglasses she could find, Reid stepped off the elevator and made a beeline for her desk. The World's Ugliest Dog followed at her heels. With any luck, no one would even notice they were there.

"Hey, guys," Marino bellowed. "Look what the dog dragged in."

"What's with the sunglasses, Sylver? Tie one on last night?" Boggs winked.

"We can make these lights a little brighter if you want," Garcia said, jumping on the bandwagon.

"Talk a lot louder, too," O'Leary added at a volume that made her wince and wish she had earplugs.

"Fess up, boys." Reid calmly set her mug on the desk, took a seat, and spun around in her swivel chair to face the barrage of comedic detectives. "You missed me."

"Right." Marino scowled. "Missed you like bad BO."

"Yeah." Boggs laughed and gave Marino a high five. "Missed you like a plumber's ass crack."

"Like a kick in the nuts," Garcia pitched in.

Everyone looked at O'Leary and waited as he crossed his arms and stared at the floor in thought. Long seconds ticked by.

O'Leary finally looked up. "We missed you like a maggot-riddled cadaver on a hot summer day," he said, beaming and clearly proud of himself.

No one said a word as they continued to stare at O'Leary.

"What?" O'Leary shrugged. "I've been taking that creative writing class, you guys. C'mon. That was the best one!"

Undoubtedly, word had spread that she'd found the captain's body. She'd worked alongside these detectives for over a decade. Perverted as it was, this was their version of a warm welcome back. The more you were razzed, the higher their respect for you. She shook her head. Like it or not, this was the world she lived in.

Reid slid open her desk drawer and reached inside for a new tennis ball. Only five balls left. She made a mental note to replenish her stock soon. She picked up her trash can and held it under Mug's chin.

He looked at her suspiciously.

"Don't worry—I'll give you a new one," she assured him.

With a few more chews for good measure, he spit out the old ball and accepted the new one.

Boyle stepped out from the captain's office. "Sylver, a word?"

What the hell was Boyle doing in *there*? She took a swig of coffee, stood, and made her way across the room.

With Mug at her side, she stepped inside the captain's office. Boyle closed the door behind them. The smell of fresh paint slapped her in the face and made her hangover-induced nausea swell to seismic proportions. In stark contrast to the white walls that had yellowed with age, Cap's office was now a distinguished and very masculine dark blue.

She looked around, stunned. Everything was different. New desk, new chairs, new leather couch, new cherrywood file cabinet. Even the wood floors looked different. She'd never seen them so…shiny.

The only two things that remained the same were the clock and Mug's dog bed in the far corner of the room—Boyle's way of saying that she and Mug belonged here. The realization hit her hard. She was thankful for the dark glasses as her vision clouded.

Boyle took a seat behind the desk as Reid reached forward to pick up the new nameplate: *Lieutenant Adam Boyle*.

He watched her as she studied it. "Cap hounded me for years to take the exam. I finally did"—he shrugged—"just to shut him up."

Reid nodded but said nothing. She couldn't bring herself to speak just yet.

"Listen, Sylver. I'm not claiming I can fill Cap's shoes—"

"Good. Because you can't." She felt a surge of righteous anger.

He fell silent and studied her once again.

The concern in his expression pissed her off even more. "Jesus, Boyle. What's done is done. So if you're finished with this kumbaya shit"—she stood—"I have cases to solve."

"I know what Cap asked you to do," Boyle said gently. "He told me."

Shocked into silence, she sat back down.

"That's why I took the exam. Cap wanted me to step in for him, when the time came."

Cap's old walnut clock ticked in the resultant quiet. Curiosity got the best of her. "What else did he say?"

"Said you're the best detective he ever knew. Made me swear I'd have your back, no matter what."

"And?" she asked suspiciously, waiting for the other shoe to drop.

"Made me promise to quit smoking. Said to tell you I'm taking his place for the morning workouts."

She laughed. Like *that* would ever happen. Boyle had been smoking a pack a day for as long as she'd known him.

He shrugged out of his suit jacket and rolled up his sleeve to show her the nicotine patch on his arm. "Oh, and I like oatmeal muffins just fine," he added with a knowing smile.

Damn. She wasn't even that crazy about Boyle. "Fine. Be here at six a.m. tomorrow."

"He told me you'd try that. Schedule stays the same. See you at zero four thirty. Sharp."

"But shift doesn't start till seven."

"Rules are rules, Sylver. I'm not about to go back on my word to a dead man."

"Fine." *Damn you, Cap.* "But don't come crying to me if you keel over from a heart attack after the first lap."

Boyle called Mug over, pointed to a stainless-steel dual-compartment trash can, and stomped on one of the pedals. The lid on the left side popped up, revealing a treasure trove of bright yellow tennis balls. "Anytime you need a new one, pal, you just come in here and help yourself." He showed Mug how to step on the pedal with his paw. "And if you run out, there's always a backup supply." When Boyle stomped on the right-side pedal, the lid lifted to reveal an equally well-stocked compartment.

Prancing in place excitedly, Mug poked his head inside, plucked a tennis ball from the lot with his mouth, and hurried over to deposit it in Reid's hand. He promptly returned to the trash can, stepped on the pedal like a pro, and reached in for seconds.

Six years ago, Boyle had taken an instant liking to Mug. If Reid hadn't adopted him, she knew Boyle would have.

She and Boyle had been on their way back to the precinct, stopped at a red light at the corner of Mass Ave. and Melnea Cass. They'd watched from across the busy intersection as a heavyset man with a tattooed head and long beard poured gasoline over a puppy and set him on fire. They'd bolted from the car—Boyle tackled the bastard to the ground while Reid worked frantically to douse the flames with the fire extinguisher she'd grabbed from the trunk.

When patrol officers arrived, they turned over the handcuffed perp and drove to Angell Animal Medical Center with lights and sirens the whole way. She and Boyle enlisted fellow detectives to take shifts at the hospital. From the time he was admitted, Mug was never without a BPD detective by his side. They held his paw as he whimpered in pain, spoke soothingly in the once-floppy ears that were burnt to nubs. That's when Mug's tennis ball obsession had started. He held the ball in his mouth like a pacifier. It stopped him from whimpering. It kept him calm.

Reid had had no intention of keeping Mug. She'd never even owned a dog before. Boyle—along with everyone else on the planet—wanted to adopt him. It was Mug who chose *her*. His bandaged tail thumped loudly against the sides of his metal crate whenever he heard her voice. He wouldn't eat for anyone but Reid and wouldn't allow anyone else to change his bandages.

She'd always wondered if Mug somehow sensed they'd been through something similar. As crazy as it sounded, she'd lay down her life for this dog. She knew he'd do the same for her.

Boyle pointed to the trash can. "I'll keep the right side stocked," he told her. "You take the left." He grimaced as Mug deposited a slimy ball in his hand and went back for thirds. "You could probably feed a small country with all the money you've spent on these things." He handed the ball to her and wiped his hands on his pants. "Figured the least I can do is share the expense."

"Thanks," Reid said, touched by the gesture. She stood, called Mug to her side, and turned to leave.

"One more thing, Sylver."

"What?"

"Fundraiser's this weekend."

Every year around Thanksgiving, organizations representing Boston's police and firefighters hosted a weekend-long softball tourney to raise money for Christmas gifts for homeless kids. She'd been pitching for Cap's team for the last thirteen years. They'd never lost a single game. "I'm not playing this year," she told him. It just wouldn't feel right without the captain.

"Maybe this'll change your mind." Boyle yanked open a desk drawer, pulled out Cap's old glove, and tossed it to her. "He left it in his locker."

"So?"

"Turn it over."

She did. In black marker, Cap had crossed out his name and added hers.

She felt the tears well up and spill down her cheeks against her will.

"Left this, too. Gave us each one." Boyle stepped over and held up two navy-blue T-shirts. One had Boyle's name and team number on the back. *Team Captain* was printed on the front breast pocket.

"Good for you. You deserve it," she said sincerely, her cheeks still wet.

"Read yours."

With her name and team number on the back, hers looked the same as always. She flipped it over and read the fine print on the left breast pocket: *Co-Captain, aka Boyle's muscle. Watch out, she'll kick your ass if you don't listen to Boyle.*

Laughing through the tears, Reid finally removed her sunglasses.

Boyle grinned and slapped her on the back. "Practice is Wednesday. Same place and time." He returned to the other side of his desk. "One more thing, Sylver."

"You already said that."

"Then…one more thing in addition to that other thing."

She slid the well-worn leather glove over her hand, grateful to the captain for leaving it to her. "What?"

"You'll call me *Lieutenant* from now on."

"Fuck." She wrapped the T-shirt around her neck and pretended to strangle herself. "You can't be serious."

"Dead. And I'm assigning you a trainee."

"That's not one more thing. It's two." If the new lieutenant couldn't add, then they were in serious trouble. "Boyle, there's no way in hell—"

"Lieutenant," he said, a biting edge to his voice. He set his hands on his hips. She'd seen that look before. He meant business. "You'll address me as Lieutenant from now on."

"With all due respect, *Lieutenant*, I'm not cut out to be anyone's babysitter."

"Her name's London Gold. She was just promoted to detective. Exemplary record. Solid cop. We're lucky to have her. You'll show her the ropes. Teach her everything you know."

"And if I refuse?"

"Then I guess another spot just opened up in Homicide," he said, unflinching. He threw a glance over her shoulder at the window facing the squad room. "She's sitting at your desk. Go make nice."

London watched as Detective Sylver stepped out from the lieutenant's office and marched straight toward her. She stood from the wooden chair. "London Gold," she said, extending her hand with a smile. "It's nice to finally meet you, Detec—"

"Can you run in those things?" Reid made no move to return the handshake.

"Run?" she asked, frowning.

"Those things you call shoes." Reid glared at her square-heeled leather boots. "Can you run in them?"

"Oh. I…" London followed her gaze. "I don't know. What do you mean by run?"

Reid sighed impatiently. "Can you do three miles on a treadmill?"

She looked up. Reid was even more beautiful up close. Short

black hair accentuated piercing, bright green eyes. Even in flats, Reid was taller by at least a few inches. She looked strong, fit, and in control. "Probably not."

"Then why the hell would you wear those here today?"

"Are we running on a treadmill?" she asked, confused. "Because I have workout clothes in the locker room."

Reid set her hands on her hips. "If I have to chase after a suspect, will you be able to keep up during a foot pursuit in *those*?" Without giving London a chance to respond, Reid extended her index finger. "Lesson number one on how to be a good detective: dress for the job."

London glanced at Reid's sweatshirt. *I'm with ugly* was written across the front. She raised an eyebrow. "I was told business casual was appropriate."

"Sure, if you're working IA. Did you *want* to work for IA? Maybe you're in the wrong place."

She met Reid's green-eyed gaze. "I'm exactly where I'm supposed to be. And I'm excited to work with you, Detective Sylver." She picked up her leather briefcase—the one she'd splurged on when she got the call about the opening in Homicide. Her initials were monogramed on the side. "Give me a minute. I'll go change into my sneakers."

She headed off to the locker room, determined not to let Reid's lack of enthusiasm diminish hers. Fellow officers had already warned her about the detective's abrasive temperament, but London couldn't be knocked off course. Her mission to be the best homicide detective she could be was already locked and loaded in her mind. The surest path to being the best was to learn from the best. She'd had a feeling this partnership would start out rocky. She was prepared to deal with whatever Reid dished out.

She tossed her boots into the locker, laced up her Adidas running shoes, and headed back to the squad room. Reid was nowhere to be found. The dog that went everywhere with her was also gone. Out of the corner of her eye, she saw the elevator doors slide shut. She watched as the indicator to the floor below lit up. Reid, it seemed, had used the shoes as an excuse to duck out and ditch her.

Without bothering to grab her coat, she headed to the stairwell and jogged down the four flights of stairs to the rear parking lot where detectives kept their unmarked vehicles. She already knew which vehicle was Reid's. It was impossible to miss—the only black 1980

Camaro Z28 in the lot. London was already leaning against the car with her hands in the pockets of her blazer by the time Reid and the dog sauntered over.

Keys in hand, Reid looked up and sighed. "You again?"

"Me again."

"Thought I left you upstairs."

"You did. But I'm fast in these." She gestured to her running shoes. "If you were trying to lose me, you should've kept me in the boots and sent me on a bogus coffee run."

Reid shook her head and sighed. "I'll keep that in mind for tomorrow. Get in." She opened the car door and pushed the passenger's seat forward.

London stepped aside for the dog to jump in, but the dog merely sat beside Reid and looked up at her quizzically. Nobody moved. They all just stared at one another.

"You getting in or what?" Reid asked.

"In the back?"

"Where else? Front's only big enough for two."

Without argument, London climbed in and contorted her body to fit in the tiny space. Reid released the front seat, and it sprang back and pressed painfully against her knees. The dog jumped in and promptly turned to stare at her. *Whatever it takes*, she reminded herself.

Reid walked around the car, slipped behind the steering wheel, and started the engine. London was about to ask where they were headed when Reid turned on the radio, surfed some local rock stations, and finally settled on "Another One Bites the Dust." She cranked the volume to high.

Not missing the irony of the moment, London rode in the back seat, silent. She only hoped her eardrums would still be intact when they reached their destination.

CHAPTER THREE

Reid tapped her thumbs on the steering wheel to the beat of the music as she drove. She couldn't believe the rookie had figured out her plan so quickly. Looked like this one was smarter than the average bear. She'd make a point to remember that moving forward.

London Gold. Maybe that's why Boyle had insisted on torturing her with this rookie. Sylver and Gold. Wasn't that just cute?

Who the hell named their kid London, anyway? Talk about a snobby, highfalutin name. Sounded like she was born with a silver spoon in her mouth. Reid glanced in the rearview mirror as London gazed out the window. Ramrod straight, silky blond hair was cut in a perfect bob. She was the epitome of the wholesome all-American girl next door—large brown eyes, high cheekbones, full lips, and a petite nose with a sprinkling of freckles across the bridge. Manicured nails. Obviously smart, professional, well-mannered. Reid thought back to the Italian leather boots and expensive monogrammed briefcase. The rookie had Ivy League written all over her. Classic overachiever. What the hell was she doing at the BPD?

Reid turned down the music but kept her fingers on the knob. "Where'd you go to college?"

Chestnut-brown eyes met hers in the rearview mirror. "Why do you want to know?"

She shrugged. "Curious."

London looked away. "Harvard."

Figured. "How long were you in patrol?"

"Eight years."

She raised an eyebrow, surprised the rookie had lasted that long.

A few weeks in homicide should be enough to send her packing. Homicide was a very different world—much too dark and sinister for a wholesome, doe-eyed rookie.

"What about you?" London piped up from the back. "How long were you—"

Ignoring her, Reid turned up the volume, tapped her thumbs against the steering wheel to "Livin' on a Prayer," and focused on the road once again. She had no intention of sharing any information about herself whatsoever. Nothing. Nada. Zilch. Her storefront was closed for business and had been for quite some time. Which is why she worked best alone.

With no cases to work and no clear destination in mind—her sole mission had been to make a quick getaway—she headed for her favorite coffee shop near the Common. She'd just banged a right on Tremont when she saw the old woman in the middle of the road.

Nobody was stopping or even slowing down. Vehicles rushed past, completely disregarding the disoriented elderly woman in her pale green bathrobe and fuzzy slippers. For all intents and purposes, the woman looked real enough. But Reid knew she wasn't.

Her body had perished and was most likely somewhere nearby. What Reid now saw standing in the road was merely the old woman's ghost.

Damn. With the rookie underfoot, this one could prove to be tricky. She pulled to the side of the road and switched on the emergency light bars in the front and rear windows. She grabbed her travel mug from the cup holder, turned in her seat, and held it out to London. "Can you grab me a refill?" She dug in her pocket for some cash and nodded toward Peet's Coffee. "Grab yourself one, too. On me," she said, holding out a twenty-dollar bill.

"You won't get any points for originality if you drive away while I'm on a coffee run. Remember, that was my idea."

"Car stays here. You have my word."

London accepted the cash and narrowed her eyes. "Where will you be?"

"Just right there. Tadpole Playground. Mug needs to do his business," she lied. Reid had a feeling that's where she'd find the old woman's body.

"At a kids' playground?" London asked, her tone disapproving.

Reid reached inside the glove compartment and held up a plastic grocery bag. "I always pick it up."

Just two weeks out from Thanksgiving, there was now a frosty chill in the morning air. She glanced at her watch: 8:42 a.m. It was still too cold this early to bring kids to the park, but the sun was out and it was supposed to warm up soon. Their arrival was imminent. She had no intention of letting a child stumble upon the old woman's corpse.

She opened her car door and stood, walking around to the passenger's side to let Mug out. "Meet you back here in fifteen," she said as she held the seat forward for London.

"You never told me."

"Told you what?"

"How you like your coffee."

London climbed out from the cramped back seat space with considerable grace, Reid noted, impressed. "No need. They know me there."

"Right. But I'm not you," London replied, looking at her like she was missing the obvious.

Reid pointed to the travel mug in London's hand. "They'll know that." The mug had been with her since her days at the academy. It had survived countless tumbles to the pavement from the roof of her car as she drove off in a hurry. The original blue color had mostly peeled away. With countless scratches and dents, it looked like it had once been the target of a mallet-wielding psychopath.

London held the mug up for inspection and grimaced. "You like this thing so much you named your dog after it?"

"His name is Mugshot." She attached the leash to his collar as he sat and waited patiently. "Mug for short." Without another word, she turned and headed toward Tadpole Playground.

Thankful to be out of the rookie's company, Reid let out a breath. No one had ever guessed that before. She had, in fact, named Mug after her lucky mug. It was lengthened to Mugshot by default when Cap and the other detectives assumed that was his full name.

Looked like this rookie was even smarter than a smarter-than-average bear.

She made sure no one was around when she cupped her hands

around her mouth and called to the old woman in the middle of the road. "I can see you. There. Standing in the road."

The old woman gazed back at her with a look of surprise.

"Yes. You." She waved the old woman over. "Walk with me."

She watched as the old woman shuffled across the street in her pale green bathrobe and fuzzy slippers, oblivious to the cars that passed right through her. Hazel eyes were now focused on her.

Reid fought to keep her feet firmly in place on the sidewalk. Once she acknowledged a spirit, she felt drawn to them like an industrial-sized magnet to iron. It had taken her years to resist the urge to go to them. Instead, she now waited until they came to her. It was safer that way, particularly when a spirit was standing in the middle of a busy road.

The old woman stepped over the curb and stood beside her on the sidewalk. She gazed up, her face stitched with concern. *Something awful happened, dear.*

"I'm here to help," Reid assured her. "Let's go for a walk."

The old woman nodded. *This way*, she said, already leading Reid through the gates of the playground.

They walked in silence. Reid glanced over her shoulder to make sure London wasn't following. Satisfied the rookie was stuck in a long line of coffee lovers by now, she turned back to the old woman. "Can you tell me your name?"

It's Beatrice, dear. Beatrice McCarty.

"Nice to meet you, Beatrice. I'm Detective Sylver. This is my partner, Mug." Mug wagged his tail at the mention of his name and looked directly into the old woman's eyes. Reid knew from their years on the streets together that Mug saw spirits just as clearly as she did. As far as she could tell, this wasn't the norm for dogs. She had an inkling Mug's close brush with death as a pup had something to do with it. But she would never know for sure.

Kind of an ugly mug, wouldn't you say?

"He's beautiful, once you get to know him."

Before she knew it, they were standing in front of the old woman's body. She'd been duct taped to one of the park's sand-colored slides, clad in the same pale green bathrobe and fuzzy slippers. She was lying down with her arms raised above her head and her eyes closed. Her face had been molded into an expression of joy. Whoever did this had staged the scene to make it look as though the old woman was enjoying herself on the playground slide.

The staging was obviously significant.

Careful not to touch anything, Reid ordered Mug to stay put and stepped over to get a closer look. Judging from the sunken-in cavities below the frontal bone, it appeared the old woman's eyes had been removed and her eyelids sewn shut. There were no other visible wounds on Beatrice's body. "Can you walk me through what happened?"

I was taking my mail out of the mailbox and felt a sharp pain in my back. Then another. And another. I fell down on my porch. She looked over at Reid. *That's all I remember.*

Sounded like Beatrice was stabbed in the back, which would explain why there were no visible wounds on the front of the body. But she'd have to wait for the ME's report to know for sure.

She stood, careful not to disturb the mulch underfoot as she returned to Beatrice's side. "Did you see who did this to you?"

Beatrice shook her head. *I'm afraid not. The last thing I remember seeing was a yellow envelope from my granddaughter. I think there was a birthday card inside.* She smiled proudly. *Meghan always remembers my birthday.*

Reid suspected the murder had occurred sometime in the past twenty-four hours. Rigor mortis was in full swing. Beatrice's body was as stiff as a tree trunk. Most people weren't aware that there were two stages to rigor mortis: the rigor stage, where the muscles stiffened gradually over a period of about twelve hours and maintained that rigidity for another twelve hours, and the flaccid stage, where the muscles gradually became more relaxed over the next twelve hours. A corpse could effectively go from a state of unyielding rigidity to squishy pliancy in a thirty-six-hour period.

Reid cleared her throat. "Do you remember what day it was when you checked your mail?"

Of course, dear. It was Saturday. I play bingo every Saturday at Saint Mary's. It's in Waltham, she added as an afterthought. *I checked the mail that night as soon as I got home.*

"Around what time was that?"

I'm not sure, exactly. Beatrice thought for a moment. *Around ten, I think.*

If Beatrice was, in fact, murdered Saturday night, her body should have entered the flaccid stage by now. She frowned. Something wasn't adding up here. Maybe the ME would shed some light on the time discrepancy. "Do you remember your address?"

Well, I should hope so! I've lived in that house for over half a century. Beatrice recited her address without skipping a beat.

Instinct told Reid the killer was on the outer periphery of Beatrice's life—someone with whom this woman was probably unfamiliar. She couldn't explain how she knew this, but her instincts were usually right. At times, she wondered if these feelings were just thinly veiled psychic abilities. She was often tempted to open her mind to other information, but she fought it. There was simply no room in her life for more weird shit. Communicating with dead people was where she drew the line. "Can you think of anyone who'd want to hurt you?"

Beatrice shook her head as she gazed down at her body. *No one I know would ever do something like this.*

"Is there anything else you can remember?" Reid asked. "Anything at all that might help me find who did this to you?"

Beatrice thought for a moment. Her face lit up as she met Reid's gaze. Even spirits could have an aha! moment. *Someone left a single white rose on my porch a few days ago,* she recalled. *It was the most perfect flower I'd ever seen.*

"Was there a note?"

No note. Just the flower. I thought it was odd. I never did find out who left it there.

Interesting. "Did you keep it?"

The old woman nodded. *I put it in a vase and gave it some water. It's on my kitchen windowsill.*

Reid made the call to dispatch, reported the body, and requested patrol officers for a perimeter around the park. With any luck, the park would be locked down before long. She ended the call and slipped Mug a biscuit from her pocket.

Will you catch him? Beatrice asked. *Before he does this to someone else?*

She shared Beatrice's concern. Instinct kicked in once again, warning her there'd be more victims. "Truth be told, you're not giving me a lot to go on here, Beatrice. I'll do the best I can." She cleared her throat self-consciously as she saw London approach from the corner of her eye.

London handed her the battered mug and froze, wide-eyed, as she stared at the old woman's body. "She's dead?"

"Looks like that Ivy League education paid off."

Ignoring her, London quickly surveyed the park. "Who reported it?"

"Me."

She turned her attention to Reid. "You sent me for coffee when you knew there was a body?"

"I didn't *know* anything," Reid said in her own defense. "I found her like this."

"You expect me to believe you pulled to the side of the road on a whim and just, what, stumbled upon this crime scene?"

Reid shrugged. "Believe whatever you want."

London narrowed her eyes as she took a sip from the disposable cup in her hands. "Who were you just talking to?"

"Dispatch. I called it in."

"No. I saw you end that call and put your phone in your pocket. Then you said something to someone named Beatrice."

Shit. Reid tried to think on her feet but came up empty. Best way out of this one was flat-out denial. Before she could open her mouth, two BPD bike officers raced toward them, braked in unison, and gaped at the body.

She held out her badge. "Detective Sylver," she said, grateful for the well-timed rescue. "Block off all entry points. Make sure no one gets in."

The female officer glanced over her shoulder. "Channel Four News was right behind us."

The last thing she needed was help from an ambitious reporter. She already had her hands full with an ambitious rookie. Reid sighed. "Just keep them the hell away from my crime scene." The minute local news learned a killer was targeting the elderly, all hell would break loose. Frightened senior citizens would be banging down the precinct doors.

Nodding, the patrol officers mounted their bikes and raced toward the park's entrance.

"We're taking this case?"

"*I'm* taking this case. It's in my jurisdiction and obviously a homicide."

"But what if it's not?"

"Not what?"

"A homicide," London said, studying the body.

"You think the victim just duct taped herself to the slide, removed her own eyes and stitched her eyelids shut, and then—what—died of natural causes?"

"What if she died of natural causes and *then* someone brought her here?"

"Why the hell would someone do that?"

"I have no idea. My point is, we won't know it's a homicide until the ME decides cause of death."

"Cause of death was—" She stopped herself, realizing she'd almost gone too far.

"Was what?" London prompted, stepping toward the body for a closer look. "No signs of external trauma, from what I can see. Am I missing something?"

"We'll know soon enough." She watched as the forensics team unloaded their equipment from a white van and carried it over.

"So"—London started to shiver—"what now?"

For the first time since they'd left the precinct, she realized London wasn't wearing a coat. She'd no doubt left it behind in her attempt to beat Reid to the car. "We wait," she replied calmly, unaffected by the cold.

CHAPTER FOUR

L ondon had no idea why Reid was trying to pull the wool over her eyes. Reid had parked on the street and sent her on a bogus coffee run so she could check out the park by herself. At least that much was clear. But how did Reid know there was a body in the playground? Had someone tipped her off? None of it made any sense.

She flashed back to Reid's conversation with someone named Beatrice. Something told her the name was important. Reid had ended the conversation in a hurry as soon as she'd approached. Like she was hiding something.

London intended to find out exactly who Beatrice was. Maybe Beatrice was in on this somehow—whatever *this* was.

Still shivering, London piped up from the back seat, "Where are we going now?"

"To the precinct. To get your coat."

"How did you know?"

"The blue lips and violent shivering gave it away."

"No, not that." London sighed. "You were so sure it was a homicide before they even flipped the body over. What did I miss?"

"Nothing. Just a gut feeling."

"Does that happen a lot? You get a gut feeling, and it turns out to be right?"

This was one nosy rookie. "Any cop worth their weight in salt gets gut feelings after the first few months on the job," she said evasively. She pulled up to the BPD, climbed out, and walked around to the passenger's side. Mug scooted over to the driver's seat as she reached inside and held the passenger's seat forward.

London looked up but made no move to exit the car.

"Coat. Remember?" Reid prompted.

"Are you coming inside, too?"

She shook her head. "Mug and I will wait here." But she had no intention of waiting. She and Mug would be peeling rubber in about ten seconds.

London sat back in her seat and refastened her seat belt. "No."

"No?" Reid repeated, incredulous.

"I am *not* getting out of this car without you."

"I'm already out of the car. It's you who's still inside the damn car."

"You know what I mean."

"I don't. Enlighten me."

London locked her chestnut gaze on Reid. "I'm not going inside that building without you."

"And why the hell not?"

"Because as soon as I walk in, you'll drive away and leave me here." She paused, searching Reid's face. "You have a plan up your sleeve, something you're itching to do that's relevant to the investigation. I intend to be there to see it. I'm here to learn from you, Detective Sylver. Not read about how you solved the case later in some report."

Damn. London was on to her. "Suit yourself." She pushed the seat back, and Mug returned to his rightful place.

Having this rookie around asking endless questions and scrutinizing her every move would only slow things down and hamper the investigation. How the hell was she supposed to work under these conditions?

She walked to the driver's side and slipped behind the wheel once again. For the time being, it seemed they were glued at the hip. The way she saw it, she had three choices—find more creative ways to lose the rookie, keep working the case with the rookie underfoot without giving anything away, or leave the job altogether. She'd just reached her twenty-year mark a few months ago. Retirement was always an option.

London leaned forward from the back seat and was promptly rewarded with a quick lick to the nose from Mug.

Traitor.

London smiled and gave him a scratch under the chin. "Where are we off to now?"

"Making a pit stop in Waltham."

"What for?"

Reid shrugged. "Just something I want to check out."

"Related to the investigation?"

She met London's eyes briefly in the rearview mirror, neither confirming nor denying.

"I knew it," London said, grinning broadly. "What's the plan?"

"Bingo."

London frowned. "Come again?"

"The vic was old. Old people play bingo."

"Oh." London looked like someone had let the wind out of her sails. "I'm risking hypothermia to interrogate senior citizens?"

"The risk wasn't worth the payout, I assure you."

"There must be dozens of spots around town that host bingo. Why are we driving all the way to Waltham?"

"Shit. Do you always ask so many damn questions?"

"I do when the best detective in Homicide—the one I'm supposed to be learning from—keeps everything close to the vest."

"Nice one. I see what you did there. Flattery to get me to open up and share."

"Did it work?"

"Solid effort." She met London's gaze briefly in the rearview mirror before returning her focus to the road. "But no."

Not in the least bit ruffled, London persisted, "At least let me in on how you chose this particular location."

"Easy. They have the biggest jackpot." But she had no idea how big their bingo jackpot was, or even if there was one. Her knowledge of the game was limited to someone shouting *Bingo!* upon winning. Money had to be involved, right? Why else would anyone play? She should've asked Beatrice more questions when she'd had the chance. From now on, she'd be more adept at covering her tracks with this helicopter rookie.

Reid pulled into the parking lot behind Saint Mary's and cracked the windows. She climbed out and called Mug to follow her out her door. Ignoring London, she slammed the door and started toward the church entrance.

London called out through the cracked car window, "Hey, you forgot someone back here."

She halted in her tracks, returned to the car, and leaned over to talk into the crack. "I didn't forget. How could I possibly forget the rookie who insists on making more work for me by asking a million questions? Way I see it, you need to start thinking about ways to pull your own weight around here. Least you can do is figure out how to let yourself out of the car."

Reid straightened and walked briskly to the church entrance with Mug at her side. She smiled, pleased with her own aptitude for thinking outside the box. The passenger's side lock was childproof and could only be opened from the outside. The seat on the driver's side didn't push forward—it had been stuck in the same position for years.

That should buy her at least a little time alone.

She stepped through the doorway and gazed around the near-empty church. A solitary nun was praying at a pew near the front. She took a deep breath and let the quiet wash over her, a luxury she'd be sure never to take for granted again.

The stillness was short-lived. She and Mug spun around as the door swung open behind them.

London strolled over with a grin, evidently proud of herself.

Reid sighed. "You again?"

"Me again."

"How the hell did you get out so fast?"

London looked down and lifted her foot. "These sneakers give me superpowers, allowing me to escape from even the most challenging childproof locks."

"If you broke a window to get out, so help me—"

"I broke a window to get out," London blurted.

Reid felt her blood pressure skyrocket. "Seriously?"

London took a step back and nodded. "I'll pay for it," she added quickly.

"You bet your goddamn ass you'll pay—"

"Pardon me?" the nun asked as she marched toward them, rosary in hand. Her habit framed a plump wrinkled face with intelligent blue eyes. "You're not using the Lord's name in vain *here*, are you?" She crossed her arms and cast a stern, tightlipped glance at Reid.

"No, Sister." It occurred to Reid that telling a lie here, of all places, was probably a bad idea. "I mean…yes, Sister. But it's a good thing my old boss isn't here. He used the Lord's name in vain *way* more than I do." Nuns had always made her uncharacteristically nervous and prone to babbling. "He's dead now," she added, giving herself a mental dope slap.

"Maybe that's why," the nun said coldly.

The three of them stood together awkwardly.

The nun winked. "That was a joke. A very bad one, I'm afraid. Forgive me." She put her hands together and bowed her head. "I'm very sorry for your loss."

Reid would have laughed if she wasn't busy feeling so damn intimidated. "Detective Sylver," she said, extending a clammy hand. "This is…this is…" she stammered, suddenly at a loss as to how to refer to the rookie beside her.

"Detective Gold," London finished, offering a well-manicured hand to the nun. "You'll have to forgive my partner. I've been standing on her last nerve since we met."

The nun reached back. "Sister Margaret Mary," she replied with a genuine smile. "How long have the two of you been partners?"

London flicked her wrist and checked her Apple watch. "Six hours and twenty-two minutes," she said in a chipper tone.

Reid shook her head and sighed. "Longest six hours of my life."

Sister Margaret glared at Reid in the same faultfinding, hypercritical way that all nuns seemed to have mastered. She'd been rubbing nuns the wrong way as far back as she could remember. It all started back in kindergarten at the Catholic school she'd attended. Her first teacher, Sister Nancy, had made it her life's mission to convert Reid from a tomboy into a proper young lady. Needless to say, it hadn't gone well. Seeing Sister Nancy's face after she stole a pair of buzz cutters and shaved her head in second grade still ranked in the top ten of her favorite memories.

Reid ran her fingers through the hair that she kept short, like her fingernails. She'd never grown her hair long again after that.

Sister Margaret's expression softened as she studied London. "That's a beautiful cross."

Smiling, London reached up to rub the cross between her fingers. "My parents gave this to me for my first communion."

"Do you still attend mass?"

London shook her head.

"And your parents?" Sister Margaret asked. "Do they attend?"

"Honestly, I'm not sure." London let her hand fall away from the cross as she returned the nun's gaze with a palpable sadness. "They haven't spoken to me in ten years."

Reid's curiosity was piqued. Why in the world would two parents cease contact with this perfect rookie?

"I'm sorry to hear that." Sister Margaret stepped closer to London and took both her hands. "We're all children of God, learning, growing, forgiving—"

"If you'll excuse us for a moment, Sister." Reid grabbed London by the elbow, led her away, and whispered, "When you're done with family therapy, can you ask her if she recognizes our vic?" She retrieved Beatrice's photo from her phone and held it out to London.

"Why don't you ask her?" London whispered back.

"Because she's giving me the evil eye."

"You're afraid of a nun because she *scolded* you?"

"I'm not afraid. Let's get that straight."

"Then go ask her yourself." London handed the phone back.

"Come on, this is your chance to shine. Besides, you've built a rapport with her. She likes you."

"Only if you admit it."

"Admit what?"

"You're afraid of the nun."

"Fine." Reid sighed. "Maybe I find her a little intimidating."

"And you won't beat me up when we get to the car and you see the broken window."

"Don't push it."

London extended her hand. "Fine. Give it here."

Reid handed over the phone and stayed put as London returned to the nun. Pulling Beatrice's name and address out of thin air obviously wasn't an option with her new sidekick in tow. All they needed was an identity so she could drive to Beatrice's house and get this investigation officially underway.

With Mug at her side, she watched London and Sister Margaret from across the room. Sister Margaret made the sign of the cross when London held up the phone with Beatrice's photo. They talked for several minutes and then shared a warm embrace. Sister Margaret stepped to the front of the church, lit a candle, and promptly knelt in prayer.

Reid frowned. No nun had ever hugged *her*.

London returned and held the phone out but said nothing.

She followed London to the back of the church. She could be mistaken, but the rookie seemed suddenly angry. "Well?" she asked as they stepped outside. "Did she recognize our vic or what?"

London nodded.

Reid could all but see the steam coming out of her ears. "And?"

London set her hands on her hips. "What game are you playing?"

"Huh?" The busted window on her prized Camaro Z28 granted her exclusive rights on the pissed-off cop face that London was now wearing.

London started pacing. "What I don't understand is why you dragged me all the way out here if you already knew the victim's name."

Oh. That. "I didn't know our vic's name. Still don't. So?" Reid tossed her hands up in frustration. "What the hell is it?"

London stopped pacing. "*Beatrice*," she said sarcastically.

Reid kept her poker face. "Does Beatrice have a last name?"

"You're just going to stand there and pretend you didn't know?"

"Know what?" Reid asked, still playing dumb.

"That the vic's name was Beatrice!" London shouted.

"How the hell would I know that?"

"I heard you, Sylver. I heard you say that name clear as a bell when I brought you your coffee this morning. Which I spat in, by the way."

"You did?"

"No. But I wish I had."

That was the last time Reid would send the rookie on a coffee run. "I assure you, *that* name did not come out of *my* mouth this morning."

"So you're saying I imagined it?"

"I don't know." Reid frowned as she studied the ground and pretended to give the question serious thought. "Are you psychic?"

"What?"

"Psychic."

"Of course not. I don't believe in that stuff."

"What other explanation is there?"

"The only plausible explanation is that you're playing some kind of prank on the newbie."

"Rookie," Reid corrected. "And no. In case you haven't noticed, I'm not the type."

London laughed dryly, apparently unconvinced. "Whatever you say."

They were standing in front of the car now. To Reid's surprise, all of the windows were intact. "Thought you said you broke a window to get out."

"I was joking."

Now it was her turn to get all angry and indignant. "Well, isn't that the pot calling the kettle black?"

"You deserved it after you locked me in the car like a prisoner."

"At least I left the windows cracked."

London opened the passenger's door, climbed in the back seat, and returned the seat to its upright position for Mug.

Reid slipped behind the steering wheel once again. "You going to give me the vic's last name or what?"

"Like you don't know."

"I don't."

London gazed out the window. They sat in silence.

"Are you seriously forcing me to face the scary nun again?"

"It'll be good for you. Sister Margaret will set you on the righteous path of honesty."

Damn. London was calling her bluff. "Fine. I'll be right back. Don't break any windows while I'm gone."

Chapter Five

L ondon watched Reid jog back to the church. No matter how hard she tried, she couldn't—for the life of her—figure out what game Reid was playing. Had it all just been some kind of test? If she hadn't seen the ME zip up the body bag, she'd be wondering if there was really even a body at all. The more likely explanation was that Reid had staged everything for her benefit. But that obviously wasn't the case, either. The body was real.

Why would Reid not only deny knowing the victim's name but drag her all the way out here pretending she didn't know? This trip had been a giant waste of time.

She shook her head and sighed, frustrated with Reid's reticence to share information. To get what she needed, she'd have to be more creative and think outside the box from now on.

Reid stepped quietly inside the church. Sister Margaret was still kneeling, deep in prayer. Fairly certain it was a cardinal sin to disturb a praying nun, she leaned against the wall and waited. She didn't really need to talk to the nun—Beatrice had already shared her last name when they'd talked earlier that morning. All she had to do was stay put for the few moments it would take to acquire such information.

Straightening to leave, she turned and bumped into the holy water font near the church entrance. The copper bowl toppled, spilling its precious contents all over the front of her jeans and sneakers. It landed on the marble floor with a thunderous *clang*.

She cringed. *So much for sneaking out.*

Sister Margaret was at her side in seconds, scowling. "Spilling holy water on oneself is an act of sacrilege."

Reid felt her eyes grow wide.

"Another bad joke, I'm afraid." Sister Margaret winked. "To what do I owe the honor of two visits in one day?"

"Just one more question, Sister. What was Beatrice's last name?"

"I already told your partner."

"I realize that. But she…"

"Forgot?"

"Not exactly." Reid hesitated. "She just…won't tell me."

"And why is that?"

"She thinks I already know."

"Do you?"

Reid's knee-jerk reaction was to lie. But she stopped herself, wondering if she'd be forever cursed if she lied. In church. To a nun.

"It's a simple yes or no question, Detective Sylver. Do you already know Beatrice's last name?"

Reid hung her head. "Yes, Sister."

"Then why are you here asking me a question you already know the answer to?"

"Because I can't tell the other detective how I found out."

The nun frowned. "Exactly how *did* you find out?"

"I was kind of hoping you wouldn't ask about that."

"Well, I did." She crossed her arms and tapped her black shoe impatiently on the church's marble floor. "I'm waiting for your answer, Detective Sylver."

Reid hesitated, bracing herself. "The victim told me."

"Beatrice?"

She nodded.

"But your partner said she's dead."

She sighed. "Thus, my dilemma."

Sister Margaret's expression remained unchanged. "You can communicate with spirits."

Reid said nothing and simply waited for the onslaught of scorn and judgment. She'd been down this road before in her youth. Which was why she stayed as far away from the Catholic church as humanly possible. "Go ahead," she prompted.

"Go ahead and what?" Sister Margaret asked, looking genuinely baffled.

"Judge me. Harshly. The way only a nun can. Then tell me I'm doing the devil's work and implore me to schedule an exorcism with the reverend father."

"I beg your pardon? I'll do no such thing."

"Another joke, right?"

"God gave you a gift. You're using that gift to help thy fellow man."

Reid pretended to unplug her ears. "Come again, Sister?"

"You heard me. Our job as mere mortals isn't to pass judgment. It's to help our fellow man realize and execute the plan that God has set forth for us. You're already doing that. God would be proud."

Few situations in her forty years on earth had rendered her speechless. This definitely ranked as one of the most surreal moments of her life.

"Come back to the Church." Sister Margaret reached over and gave her hand a gentle squeeze. "You're welcome here anytime, Detective Sylver."

Reid shook her head and took a step back. "The Catholic church won't welcome me." She felt her guard slipping back in place. "I'm gay."

"Well, in that case"—Sister Margaret crossed her arms and frowned—"I'm afraid I must rescind the invitation."

Reid nodded, surprised to discover she was actually a little disappointed as she turned to leave. "Thanks for your time."

Sister Margaret called out from behind her, "Have you completely lost your funny bone, Detective?"

Reid glanced back and watched as the nun's stern expression broke into a beautiful smile. "You have a very dark sense of humor, Sister."

"So I've been told. I expect to see you at Sunday mass. Nine sharp. And bring your partner. I get the feeling she was driven from the church for the very same reason."

"You think she can talk to dead people, too?" Reid asked, confused.

"No. The other reason," Sister Margaret said, shaking her head. "And you call yourself a detective?"

It took her a moment to realize what Sister Margaret was saying.

London was a lesbian? How the hell could a nun's gaydar be better than hers?

Back inside the car, Reid met London's gaze in the rearview mirror. "Hope you don't have any plans for Sunday."

"What's on Sunday?" London asked suspiciously. "Another prank?"

"Sister Margaret invited us to mass."

London leaned forward, her eyes wide with surprise. "She invited *you*?"

Reid turned in her seat. "Is that so hard to believe?"

"As a matter of fact, it is."

London's face was uncomfortably close to hers in the confines of the car. For the first time since they'd met, Reid realized how beautiful London was. "Sister Margaret even held my hand," she admitted proudly.

"Congratulations." London sat back and gazed out the window. "But I can't go back to the Catholic church."

Was Sister Margaret right about London? She couldn't tell for sure one way or the other. She felt the first stirrings of curiosity and suddenly found herself craving more information on this rookie. "When she invited me to mass, I told her I was gay. Figured that would earn me a lifetime exemption."

London stared at her. "And?"

"No such luck. It appears the Catholic church—or, at least, this one—is finally coming out of the Dark Ages."

"No way. You're still invited?" London looked just as shocked as Reid felt. "Even though you're…"

"Gay? You can say it, you know. It's not contagious."

"Too late." London rolled her eyes. "I already caught it."

Reid pulled up to Beatrice's quaint ranch-style house and parked on the street. She cracked the windows and told Mug to stay as London climbed out of the car. They were entering a crime scene now, and Mug wasn't allowed.

"He's okay in the car?" London asked, looking doubtful.

"Mug's better behaved than most humans. He'll be fine." She and Mug went everywhere together. After six years, he probably knew their routine better than she did.

Reid realized she depended on him as much as he depended on her. Communicating with spirits on a daily basis was draining and, at times, overwhelming. Most days, it left her totally depleted. Mug's constant presence in her life kept her grounded. The upside to their relationship: no talking—or listening—was required. She preferred it that way. In her eyes, Mug was the embodiment of the perfect partner.

Which was another reason this rookie was grating on her nerves. The endless stream of questions made it difficult to focus and diverted her attention from the case. It was like trying to play the cello while having a conversation. She knew from experience it was possible to do both at the same time, but the quality of the music inevitably suffered.

Beatrice appeared the moment she set foot on the porch. The old woman smiled in recognition. *You made it.*

"We made it," Reid replied.

"Made what?" London asked from behind her.

Beatrice pointed to the outdoor area rug under Reid's feet. *That's where it happened.*

"Hold up a minute," she said, halting London on the steps behind her. She reached inside her coat pocket and withdrew two pairs of latex gloves. She handed a pair to London. "From this point forward, we don't touch anything with our bare hands. Take care to preserve everything exactly as is." Slipping the gloves on, she squatted down and lifted one corner of the rug.

"Is that dried blood?" London asked, pulling on her gloves as she squatted down beside her.

"Looks like this is where our vic was stabbed." Reid carefully lifted the rug the rest of the way to reveal telltale brown stains and droplets along the wooden planks.

Told you, Beatrice said matter-of-factly. *But I'm not sure how the rug got there. It's not mine.*

The killer must have put it there to cover the evidence. Interesting. Either he brought it with him—which meant the murder was entirely premeditated—or he stole it from a neighbor's porch after the fact. She dismissed the idea that he returned after moving the body just to cover the bloodstains—too risky. Sticking a mental Post-it in her mind, Reid withdrew her cell and dialed Forensics.

"How'd you know to look under the rug," London asked as soon as she hung up.

"When you're working a crime scene, you start from the bottom and work your way up. No stone unturned."

"But we weren't even sure this *was* the crime scene. For all we knew, our vic was abducted from her home and stabbed elsewhere."

Reid shrugged. "Well, now we know she wasn't. Let's suit up and get a look inside." London followed her to the car.

"Protocol says we're supposed to refrain from entering the premises until Forensics—"

"One thing you'll learn about me is I don't follow *all* the rules. Just the important ones." She handed London a sealed plastic package with a white Tyvek suit and booties inside.

"But waiting until Forensics clears the crime scene is a pretty important rule."

"It is if you don't know what you're doing." Reid stepped onto the sidewalk and pulled the suit over her clothes, leaning against the car as she slipped the booties over her sneakers. "Follow my lead, and you'll be fine. Do *not* mess up my crime scene. Understood?"

London nodded.

She waited for London to gear up before leading the way back to Beatrice's porch.

You have to wear all that just to go inside my house? Beatrice asked.

Ignoring the question, she met Beatrice's gaze. "If I were a key, where would I be hiding?"

"Under the mat?" London offered, kneeling to take a peek.

Beatrice led her to the side of the porch and pointed to the corner. *Right there, dear.*

Reid reached between the wooden railings and lifted the key from the nail it was hanging on. "Found it," she said, holding it up for London to see.

London stood. "How'd you do that?"

"Do what?"

"Find the key. What made you think to look way over there?"

"You get pretty good at finding things when you've been doing this as long as I have." She unlocked the front door, and they both stepped inside.

Reid took in her surroundings. The house was cozy, sparsely decorated, and very clean. Living room to the right. Office space to the left. Eat-in kitchen off a short hallway, dead ahead. Bedrooms were probably on the other side of the house.

Beatrice stood beside her. *He left a note for you in the kitchen.*

"Where do you want to start?" London asked.

Asking Beatrice to elaborate wasn't exactly an option at the moment. "Kitchen," Reid replied, already on her way.

There, in the center of the countertop breakfast bar, was a handwritten note in bold black marker: *Sylver—I know your secret.*

The note was held in place by a clear glass vase containing what had once been a single white rose. All that remained in the vase now was a flowerless stem. The rose itself had been cut off and placed, upside down, on one corner of the note.

London frowned. "The killer left you a note?"

Reid thought for a moment and shrugged. "Could be a weird coincidence." Maybe she shared the surname of the note's intended recipient. Seemed unlikely. But the alternative was even more strange. Why would the killer leave a note for her? And how'd he know she'd be the detective working this case? She was assuming the killer was male. Statistically speaking, chances favored a man.

She caught Beatrice's eye. If there was ever a time when she needed to ask questions, this was it. But her hands were effectively tied at the moment.

Beatrice had said the note was for her. Spirits always spoke the truth. At least, that had been her experience to date. Instinct told her Beatrice was no different from the countless other spirits who'd found her in their time of need.

Careful not to disturb anything, Reid and London toured the remaining rooms of the house but found nothing of interest. They stepped down from the porch and onto the sidewalk as Forensics arrived.

Reid slipped out of the Tyvek suit and, in a replay of her earlier movements, leaned against her car to remove the booties.

"Already been inside?" Cabrera asked, suiting up.

Reid nodded. "Heads." She tossed him the key, which he deftly grabbed in the air. "Vic was killed on the porch. There's a note on the kitchen counter." She doubted they'd find any prints. The killer seemed too meticulous.

Cabrera nodded. "Mug with you today?"

Mug barked from the car at the mention of his name.

Cabrera reached inside the van and withdrew a can of tennis balls. There was a small red bow stuck to the can's lid. "Congrats on the win," he said, tossing it to her. Everyone knew about Mug's addiction. "And sorry about your captain."

"Thanks. Have you met Detective Gold?" she asked in an effort to change the subject.

"Sylver and Gold?" Laughing, Cabrera stepped forward and extended a hand to London. "Never known you to take on a partner, Sylver."

"We're not partners." London corrected him. "She's training me."

Cabrera raised an eyebrow. "Never known you to take on a rookie, either."

"Boyle's just flexing his muscles," she said. "Let me know if you find anything."

"Will do." He shut the van door and started toward the house.

CHAPTER SIX

Seated in the car once again, London decided riding in the back had its perks. Sure, it was uncomfortable and a little humbling to be taking a back seat—literally—to a dog. But, back here, she could gaze at Reid's profile without being noticed. She'd never had the chance to study her up close.

Reid was stunning from every angle. The raven hair that she kept almost as short as a military crewcut only enhanced her beauty. Without a drop of makeup and exhibiting zero effort in the fashion department, it was clear that Reid put very little time, effort, or thought into her appearance. London doubted Reid was even aware of just how beautiful she was. Her bold confidence and take-it-or-leave-it attitude made everyone around her accept her for who she was. She had clearly worked hard to make a name for herself and was readily respected by colleagues.

London took a deep breath and realized her crush was getting the best of her. Even Reid's brashness somehow added to her appeal. But there was something deeper in Reid that drew her attention—something she hadn't noticed before now. Pain.

There was a distinct vulnerability in Reid that lay, at least partially concealed, underneath her thorny attitude. It was well camouflaged but definitely there. London couldn't help but wonder what it was.

The note inside the victim's house sprang to mind. If, indeed, the note had been meant for Reid—as London suspected it was—she wondered what the secret was. Could that secret somehow be connected to the pain she sensed in Reid?

She cleared her throat, surprised Reid hadn't resorted to blasting the radio the moment she'd started the car. Perhaps no radio was an invitation to talk. "What did you win?"

"Huh?" Reid asked, clearly jolted from her thoughts.

"Cabrera congratulated you."

Reid gazed proudly at the dog beside her. "Mug here won first place."

"In what?"

"Ugliest Dog."

She laughed, waiting for the real answer. None came. "Oh."

"I always say, if you've got something unique going for you, own it and be good at it." Reid reached over to pat Mug on the back. "Just so happens he's really good at being ugly."

London couldn't help but smile. Now their matching sweatshirts made sense. The love Reid had for Mug was clear. There was a soft side to this detective, after all.

"Where to now?" London asked from the back seat.

"Back to the precinct to get your coat."

"We've been over this. I am *not* going inside without—"

"Mug and I will escort you inside, Your Highness." This time, Reid didn't have anything up her sleeve. It was simply too cold outside to make the rookie traipse around in a blazer. London's periodic shivering was starting to make her feel guilty.

"Then what?" London persisted.

"We'll return to canvass the neighborhood. See if anyone saw or heard anything on Saturday night."

"Why Saturday?"

"Because that's when our vic was murdered."

"ME's report came back?" London met her gaze in the rearview mirror. "Already?"

Damn. She'd slipped. Again. "Hasn't come back yet, no," she replied nonchalantly.

"Then how do you know she was murdered Saturday night?"

Reid shrugged. "Educated guess." Keeping up with London's questions and covering her tracks while working the case was proving near impossible.

"Let me guess. When you've been doing this as long as you have, you get pretty good at these things."

Reid sighed, grateful for the save. She couldn't stop thinking about the note in Beatrice's house. It was taunting her now. The only thing she kept secret was her ability to talk to the dead. And there were only two people in the world she'd ever confided in: her grandmother and the captain, both of whom were now dead.

She pulled into the BPD's parking lot, climbed out of the car, and led the way upstairs with Mug at her side and London behind her. She took a seat at her desk and picked up the phone, intent on calling the ME for an update.

London stood beside the desk and held out her hand.

"You hoping for a tip?"

"Keys."

"To what?" she asked, balancing the phone on one shoulder.

"The car. What else?"

"No. Keys stay with me."

"Fine. Then I get the dog."

"Over my dead body."

"Come on, Sylver." London sighed impatiently. "I have to use the bathroom."

"And you need my dog to help you?"

"I need something for insurance."

She replaced the phone on its cradle, annoyed beyond measure at these constant interruptions. "What the hell are you talking about?"

"Insurance," London repeated. "So you won't bail on me again."

It'd be a miracle if she got through the rest of this shift without losing her temper. Fuming, she opened her desk drawer, stood, and handed over the keys.

"Nice try. But these aren't them," London said without even looking down.

"How the hell do you know that?"

"I saw you put them in your pocket."

"Shit." She felt herself soften a little. "You might be in the right line of work, after all."

London took Reid's hand and placed the imposters firmly in her palm. They locked eyes the moment their hands connected. "Thanks. I'll take that as a compliment."

Reid drew in a breath, surprised by the sudden chemistry between them. Not only was London not backing down, this rookie was holding her own. She found that incredibly alluring.

She was close enough now to notice how good London smelled. Her blond hair looked silky-soft. Large brown eyes were intelligent and probing. There was a fresh-faced beauty about her. In that moment, Reid knew she was in trouble. She withdrew her hand and took a step back, her gaze still on London's.

"Right pocket," London prompted, breaking the moment. "Hand them over so I can pee."

"Fine. Here." She dug into her pocket, sat back down, and set the keys on the corner of the desk to avoid further physical contact. Watching London walk away, she didn't have the heart to tell her that she had a spare set. Every good cop did.

Back in the car and alone for the first time all day—finally—Reid took a deep breath, started the ignition, and peeled out of the parking lot. She started toward Beatrice's neighborhood and had driven for about five minutes before her conscience kicked in. Cursing, she pulled to the side of the road.

She wanted nothing more than to lose the new baggage that had been forced upon her, but she just couldn't bring herself to do it. *Shit.* She beat the steering wheel and cursed aloud as Mug peered at her quizzically.

Since her transfer to Homicide, knowing her secret could be uncovered at any moment by a nosy reporter, colleague, or boss, she'd kept early retirement in her back pocket. Her plan B was to start her own private-eye business. Was it finally time to put in her papers?

Mentoring London meant she'd have to find a way to solve cases without revealing her secret. Limiting her conversations with the dead and keeping her secret under wraps would likely more than double her workload.

Even with her best efforts, there was always the risk she'd be discovered. If anyone could figure out her secret, it was London. The one thing Reid had in her favor was London didn't believe in that stuff.

She'd said as much when Reid deflected the rookie's suspicion by asking if *she* was psychic.

Reid shook her head as she slowly came to terms with this new arrangement. Looked like her days of solitude were over, at least for the next six months. Boyle had better not saddle her with anyone else after that.

Her mind made up, she put her blinker on, swung a U-turn, and returned to the precinct.

London couldn't believe it. Reid had left her. *Again.* She set her hands on her hips and took one last look at where the black Camaro should have been parked.

Had Reid given her the keys to another car? She fished them out of her coat pocket to take a closer look. These were Reid's car keys all right. She was sure of it. The slippery detective must have had a spare set.

She shook her head, remembering when their hands had touched upstairs as she'd pressed another set of keys into Reid's palm. Something had changed between them in that moment. Something had ignited. She'd felt it with every cell in her body. Reid was attracted to her. *That's* why Reid had fled.

"Have you seen the rookie?" Reid asked as Garcia rounded the corner with his daily hot dog from the cart across the street. London was nowhere to be found.

"Yup."

"Well?" she asked. "Where is she?"

"What's in it for me?"

Sighing, she cast a glance at Boyle sitting behind his desk on the phone. She couldn't let on that she'd lost the rookie on day one. "Tomorrow's hot dog—my treat."

Garcia sat down, propped his feet up on his desk, and casually took a bite. "Let's see. One hot dog in exchange for saving your ass with our new lieutenant." He shook his head and looked up at her. "No deal."

"Fine. Two hot dogs. Final offer."

He took another bite and proceeded to answer around a mouthful of hot dog, "I'm thinking more along the lines of a month's worth ought to do it."

She set her hand over the Glock at her hip and unsnapped the holster.

Garcia's eyes grew wide. "Two hot dogs it is. A very generous offer."

Reid snapped the holster shut and let her hand fall away. "So?"

"She took off a few minutes ago." He threw a glance at Mug. "Said the car wasn't big enough for the three of you."

"Where the hell is she now?"

"Up your ass, picking daisies. How the hell should I know?"

Hoping to find London waiting near the car as she had earlier, Reid returned to the parking lot. No luck. The rookie had mysteriously vanished.

Had she driven London off after less than a day on the job? Instinct told her the rookie had more tenacity than that. She'd turn up. Eventually.

Well, rookie or no rookie, Reid had a case to solve. She glanced at Mug. "The crime-fighting duo is back in business," she said, leaning down to give him a high five. She held the car door open for him and then settled behind the steering wheel, determined never to take her solitude for granted ever again.

Reid parked, curbside, across the street from Beatrice's house. Forensics was still inside. She climbed out of the car, and Mug followed suit behind her. She surveyed the surrounding houses as he sniffed at some brown grass on the sidewalk.

This was an upper-middle-class neighborhood. Some of these residents were bound to have security systems with video cameras. Maybe she'd get lucky and find a recording of the suspect loading Beatrice's body into a car.

As if on cue, Beatrice appeared. *Where have you been?* she asked.

"Working your case," Reid answered.

Have you caught him yet?

"No, but it's still early." She looked around to make sure no one was watching her have a seemingly one-sided conversation. "Do you know any of your neighbors on this street?"

All of them, dear. Why?

"Do you know if any of your neighbors have security cameras?"

Beatrice pointed to the house directly across from hers. *That's Paul and Marge's house. When Paul died a few months back, Marge had a security system installed. It's quite state-of-the-art.*

Mug finished his business and accompanied her to Marge's front stoop. Reid rang the doorbell. She knocked loudly, without waiting. Since London's whereabouts were still unknown, she was feeling a wee bit impatient.

An older woman—presumably Marge—opened the door and scowled at Reid. She held out a tiny biscuit for Mug. He gingerly plucked it from her grasp. "You must be Detective Sylver," she said, still scowling. She set a hand on her hip and opened the door wider to reveal the missing rookie. "Detective Gold here was just telling me how you mistakenly left her behind at the police station."

With a glass of milk in one hand and a cookie in the other, the rookie looked right at home.

"You two know each other?" Reid asked.

"We do now," Marge replied. Her expression softened as she gazed adoringly at London.

What was it with London and little old ladies?

"You wait right here, honey," Marge said, withdrawing farther into the house. "I'll wrap up your cookies so you can take them with you."

"Mrs. Rugers, you don't have to do that."

"Nonsense. It'll take but a minute. Be back in a jiff."

London's smile vanished as she met Reid's gaze and joined her on the stoop. Mug greeted her with a quick lick to her hand. His scarred, furless tail wagged exuberantly.

They stood, side by side, in awkward silence. Reid couldn't stand it anymore. "How'd you get here?" she finally asked.

"Wouldn't you like to know?"

"What, are we in fifth grade, and you're mad, so you're pitting an old lady against me?"

"I can't help it if she likes me. That's usually what happens when you're a courteous human being. With *manners*." She crossed her arms. "You might want to try it sometime."

Touché.

Marge returned with a giant baggie of oatmeal cookies. Smiling, she handed them to London. "Let me know if there's anything more I can do to help."

"We'll be in touch. Thanks for your time, Mrs. Rugers."

Reid eyed the baggie with envy. Oatmeal cookies were her favorite. She'd skipped lunch and was starving. "Do I get cookies, too?"

With one last disapproving glare, Marge slammed the door in her face.

"Guess that's a no?" Reid called out.

London turned, jogged down the steps, and hurried along the sidewalk.

CHAPTER SEVEN

"Hey, where're you going?" Reid ran to catch up.

London stopped in front of a massive black truck with tinted windows. "Need a ride?"

She felt her eyes grow wide. "Is this Boyle's truck?"

London nodded.

"Holy shit. Did you steal it?" Boyle would have her head on a platter.

"Of course not."

"Is Boyle dead?"

"Not the last I checked."

"Then how the hell did you convince him to give you the keys?"

"I didn't convince him to do anything. He offered."

"No way." The Boyle she knew would never part with his beloved Ford Super Duty F-450 King Ranch.

"When he saw me outside, all abandoned and alone, he handed me the keys."

"So it's a pity truck."

"Pity truck or not, it's mine for the duration of our training."

Perfect. Boyle and London were now working together to make her life miserable.

"See you later, Sylver." London pressed a button on the key chain to disengage the alarm and unlock the truck door.

"Hold up." Clearly, this rookie needed some guidance. "We still have the rest of the street to talk to." She waved a hand in the air. "Both sides."

"No, we don't."

"Yes, we do."

London slipped her cell out of her coat pocket and held it aloft. "I have everything we need right here."

"You have all the vic's neighbors tucked inside that tiny phone?"

"No one saw or heard anything on the night in question, but they all have security cameras."

Failing to connect the dots, Reid waited impatiently.

"They've given me access to video surveillance from Saturday night."

"All of them?"

"The whole street." London nodded. "Beatrice has been organizing a neighborhood potluck for the last forty years. They want this guy behind bars more than we do."

Not bad for a rookie.

"I'm heading back to the precinct now to review the footage," London went on. She opened the baggie and held it out to Reid. "Just one," she warned. "The rest are mine."

Without hesitation, Reid plucked a cookie from the bag and took a big bite. "I shouldn't have left you like that," she admitted, chewing. "My bad." Whoa. This was, by far, the best oatmeal cookie she'd ever tasted.

"Apology accepted."

Reid popped the last delicious morsel in her mouth and eyed the remaining cookies in London's hand.

London reached inside the bag, broke off a small piece, and slipped it to Mug. "I like South End Pizza on Tremont."

"Are we sharing random facts now?" she asked, wiping her hands on her jeans.

"It'll take hours to go through all of the footage from Saturday." London checked her watch. "If you happened to swing by and pick us up a pizza for dinner—green peppers, black olives—I could probably hook you up with another cookie."

Reid frowned. "Just one cookie for a whole pizza?"

Reid stepped off the elevator, pizza box in hand, hoping for more than one cookie.

"Good. You're here." London stood, whisked the box away, and plopped it down on Reid's desk. She set two pizza slices on a paper plate and handed the plate to Reid with a napkin. "I already started," she said, pointing to an iPad beside Reid's computer. "I split the videos down the middle and sent you yours."

"Sent them where?" Reid asked, taking a bite.

"You're all set up. Just press enter, and the first video will start playing automatically."

"How'd you get the passcode to my computer?"

"Easy." London rolled her eyes. "Anyone who's known you for five minutes would've guessed *Mugshot*."

They ate together in silence. With perfect posture, London was perched on the edge of an old foldout chair. Reid almost laughed aloud when she saw the neatly folded napkin on London's lap. This rookie's manners were impeccable. Reid leaned forward and steadfastly made her way through each video, her stomach full. But she was finding it more and more difficult to focus with London sitting so close. She smelled *amazing*.

Reid paused the video. Nothing of interest so far. She needed a break. Working this case the old-school way, without any help from the other side, was taxing. "What're you wearing?"

"Clothes?" London answered without looking up from the screen.

"The perfume. What is it?"

"Oh. Egyptian Goddess. But it's not a perfume. It's an oil."

"It's nice."

"Thanks," London replied, her focus unwavering.

"Can you stop wearing it?"

This got London's attention. She paused the video and met Reid's gaze with a look of bewilderment. "Why?"

Reid shrugged. "Homicide has traditionally been filled with smelly men, who burp and fart a lot."

"You want me to smell bad just to fit in better?"

"If it wouldn't be too much trouble." She glanced at London's lap. "Might wanna lose the napkin, too."

London lifted the napkin from her lap and dabbed, quite daintily, at each corner of her mouth. "I'll take that under advisement." With a swipe of the screen, she resumed her scan.

Reid looked over at Mug, who sat up and wagged his tail the

moment their eyes met. She knew what he was thinking. A creature of habit, he somehow always sensed when it was the end of her shift, which meant it was time to go home and play fetch in the backyard before dinner. Ambivalent about leaving, she called him over and gave him her leftover crust.

Her reluctance to leave wasn't because of any desire to set a good example by working late. Reid just wanted more cookies.

London paused the video once again. "You're not one to sit idle, are you?"

"Are you kidding? This, right here"—she opened her arms wide and forced a smile—"is my favorite part of the job."

London glanced at the clock and then at Mug. "Why don't the two of you go on home? I still have another few hours in me. I'll finish what I can tonight." She lifted the giant baggie from her briefcase and handed it over. "Here. A deal is a deal."

"The whole bag?" Reid asked, already digging in. "But I thought you said just one," she said around a mouthful of cookie.

"You picked up the pizza and even threw in a compliment about me smelling nice. You're making progress in the manners department, Sylver. That deserves a reward."

Munching her way happily to the elevator, Reid decided the rookie wasn't so bad.

❖

London watched Reid until she disappeared around the corner with Mug in tow. She smiled. This was only the first day, and she was already starting to break through Reid's armor.

She was excited by the prospect of gaining entry into the detective's signature investigative world. She intended to make the best use of her time and soak up everything she could. The only thing that could potentially pose a problem was their chemistry. There was something between them. A spark. A flicker of attraction when they'd touched hands earlier.

London decided she'd have to keep herself in check. Having a sordid affair with a senior detective just wasn't worth the risk. She had more important things to focus on right now. Like her career. That took precedence over everything else.

❖

Reid pulled into her driveway and cut the engine. Her cell rang as she was unbuckling her seat belt. "Sylver," she answered, not bothering to check the caller ID. Probably someone from work. No one else ever called.

"How was your day, Detective Sylver?"

She paused. The caller's voice was unfamiliar. He had a patronizing tone. "Who the hell is this?" she asked.

"You can just call me The Giver."

An unpleasant tingle traversed the length of her spine. "This some kind of joke?"

"The manner by which you solve cases is no laughing matter, Detective Sylver."

"You killed Beatrice," she said, cutting right to the chase.

"So why haven't you caught me yet?"

"I will." Feeling exposed in her driveway, she opened her car door to step outside and survey the area.

"Until now, you've had a perfect record in homicide. I'm here to change all that for you."

"How?" She laughed. "By being too clever to get caught?"

"Liken me to a cat, Detective Sylver. A great hunter who shows his affinity for you by leaving dead mice on your doorstep. With each mouse you receive, you'll inch closer to having your secret revealed. Closer to being truly free for the first time in your life."

There was no way he knew about her ability to talk to the dead. He had to be bluffing. Reid hooked the Bluetooth device over her ear, slipped her cell inside her coat pocket, and unsnapped her holster. She waved Mug to her side and gave him the silent command to heel. As if sensing her tension, he instantly obeyed and went on high alert. "What are you talking about?"

"You're like me, Detective Sylver. You get your information from, shall we say, unconventional sources."

Sure sounded like he knew about her secret. She needed to draw him out more. "I still have no idea what the fuck you're talking about."

"A homicide detective—mind you, one who doesn't much care for the living—solves all her cases by talking to the dead."

Her mind raced. How the caller could've possibly unearthed that fact was beyond her. "Let's meet, face-to-face. I can get you the help you need."

"Admit it," he went on. "You're more comfortable with dead people than you are with the living."

Flustered by the truth of his words, Reid said nothing. She had always felt the most at ease when she was communicating with spirits. How could he possibly have known that?

"I'll let you in on a secret, Detective Sylver. I, too, am more comfortable with the dead. We just enjoy our time with them a little differently."

She hoped that didn't mean what she thought it meant.

"Like two peas in a pod, you and me."

"I beg to differ."

"Speaking of begging, I left you a mouse."

She felt her heart pick up speed.

"Marge wasn't very kind to you today. I informed her she should've had better manners."

How in the world would he know about that? Was Marge's house bugged?

"She sends her apologies, by the way." He cleared his throat. "But I'm sure you, of all people, don't need me to pass that along."

"Where?" she asked through clenched teeth.

"Where what?"

"Where. Is. Marge."

"I expected more from you, Detective Sylver. Frankly, I'm a little disappointed." He sighed. "Where does the cat always leave the mouse?" And with that, the killer hung up.

Reid drew her weapon and flashlight and started for the front porch of her house. But instinct told her the killer wasn't there. He didn't seem the type to risk a physical confrontation. He would survey the game board from a distance, carefully plan his next move, and then execute it with obsessive precision.

Her front porch was uncharacteristically dark. The light was set on a timer. For some reason, it hadn't come on. She directed her flashlight at the porch steps and then slowly upward. There, propped in one of four chairs surrounding a rectangular wooden table, was Marge's body. She told Mug to stay and carefully ascended the stairs to get a closer look.

Marge was wearing the same blue housedress she'd seen her in earlier. Her hands were cupped around a plateful of oatmeal cookies, as if offering them to Reid. Her mouth was fixed in a permanent smile, and her eyes had been removed, just as with Beatrice.

He's right. Marge was suddenly standing beside her, looking down at her own body. *I am sorry, you know.*

"No need to be," Reid assured her. "London shared. Best oatmeal cookies I ever had, by the way."

Marge's gaze darted to the plate of cookies on the table. *He forced me to bake those before he killed me.*

"Did you get a look at him?" she asked, knowing she'd never eat another oatmeal cookie as long as she lived. One of the hazards of the job, unfortunately. Other foods had been permanently scrubbed from her diet in much the same way—scrambled eggs, yogurt, her once-beloved chili cheese fries.

Marge shook her head. *I only heard his voice. He must have hacked the security system in my house. Before I knew it, he was controlling everything: the lights, TV, thermostat, my home phone, cell phone… everything.*

"Why didn't you just walk out the front door?"

I tried that. Marge shrugged. *But I couldn't. I have smart locks on every door. I couldn't get any of them to open.*

"You never saw him?"

Never.

Reid stepped behind Marge's corpse and pointed the flashlight at her back. She'd been stabbed, just like Beatrice. "Walk me through what happened."

Shortly after you and the other detective left, I got a call from my alarm company.

"How long after?"

Marge thought for a moment. *Thirty minutes, maybe?*

That was fast. Too fast for a meticulous killer to plan a murder down to the tiniest detail, as his profile had so far indicated he would. Something wasn't adding up. "What did your alarm company want?"

They asked me to enter my code and disarm the system so they could run a quarterly maintenance check.

"Have they ever done that before?"

No. But I've only had the system a few months. It was a man who called. The voice was the same as the man you were just talking to on the phone.

"You sure about that?"

Marge nodded. *The moment I disarmed the system, everything went haywire. The lights flickered. All the TVs came on. The phone line went out. Then the air conditioner turned on, full-blast. It was like, all of a sudden, my house had a mind of its own. I was terrified and tried to call nine-one-one from my cell phone, but the screen was locked. I kept entering my passcode, but it wouldn't let me in. Next thing I knew, a man's voice came over the TV in the kitchen. He told me not to panic and instructed me to bake those cookies.*

She pointed to the cookies in the middle of the table.

I went to the front door and tried to get out, but the lock wouldn't turn. I realized then that I was locked inside my own house. I went to the window and started to open it to call out for help when his voice came over the living room TV. He told me he would blow up every house on the street—including mine—if I didn't stop. Then he said he would let me go free. The only thing he wanted me to do was bake a dozen oatmeal cookies.

Reid looked down at the plate. There were only six cookies. Had the killer taken the other six with him as an edible souvenir? "What happened next?" she prompted.

I did what he asked and started baking. When the timer went off, I slid my hand into the oven mitt and opened the oven. I was just setting the baking sheet on the stove when I felt sharp pains in my back, over and over again. I fell to the floor. Marge met her gaze and shrugged. *That's all I remember.*

CHAPTER EIGHT

Had the killer previously planned Marge as his next victim, deceptively claiming he'd murdered her as revenge for being rude to Reid? Maybe he'd been monitoring Marge's house, overheard their conversation at the front door, and used that information to his advantage. That's the only theory that made any sense.

If he'd overheard the conversation and improvised, that would mean he'd hacked Marge's security system and devised her murder in thirty minutes. A lot of work in a small amount of time but not impossible. The part that didn't sit right with her was his obvious compulsion to make things perfect. Perfection and obsessive attention to detail took time. This was not a killer who'd want to hurry through a murder. He would savor every gruesome step. Rushing through the murder and subsequent staging would not only increase his chances of making a mistake, it would also compromise his art.

Reid thought back to the comparison he'd made between them. *You're like me, Detective Sylver. You get your information from, shall we say, unconventional sources.* He was obviously a technology wiz. *Unconventional sources* could be referencing his ability to hack his way into someone's life and get their personal information. You could learn everything about a person by listening in on private conversations and watching them when they believed they were alone.

Was that how he'd found out about *her* secret? Was he monitoring her inside her own house? She shook her head. Impossible. True, she had all the gadgets that everyone else seemed to own these days—home security system, laptop, smart TV, iPad, iPhone. But her house had always been strictly off-limits to spirits. She'd never invited anyone inside—not even the cable man who'd insisted she shouldn't splice her own wires to get connected. Her home was her sanctuary. A respite from both the living *and* the dead. It was the only sacred space she had, and she was fiercely protective of it.

That left her car and cell phone. She'd had plenty of chats with the dead inside her car. Her car had an alarm, but that wouldn't be much of a deterrent for this tech-savvy killer. He would've had plenty of opportunity to bug her car while it was parked in her driveway overnight. Her iPhone was a different story, though. She always kept it in close proximity. It was possible he'd hacked it from afar. She'd have computer crimes do a sweep of the car and phone to know for sure.

Her cell rang. She jerked in surprise, holstered her Glock, and checked the caller ID before answering. "How'd you get my number?"

"I'm still at the precinct. You're listed in the database here." London paused. "Are you okay?"

"I'm fine. But I can't say the same for Mrs. Ruger." She told London about the phone call and the dead body on her porch.

"He called me, too," London admitted. "He gave me your address and told me to send a forensics team."

"Did he say anything else?" Reid held her breath, remembering his threat. *With each mouse you receive, you'll inch closer to having your secret revealed. Closer to being truly free for the first time in your life.* Had he shared her secret with London?

"He challenged me to figure out how you solve your cases." She heard London hesitate on the other end. "He said you have a secret weapon."

"Two secret weapons, actually: experience and kick-ass instincts. Did you already notify Forensics?" she asked, changing the subject.

"Not yet. I dispatched nine-one-one to your residence. I'll be there as soon as I can."

"Don't bother. I've got it covered. I'll give you a rundown on everything, first thing tomorrow," she lied. "Go home and get some sleep. We'll start fresh in the morning." She hung up and heard sirens in the distance.

Reid descended the porch steps and waited with Mug. This was too close for comfort. She refused to be the killer's pawn in this crazy cat-and-mouse game. The only way to end the game was to take herself off the game board.

So that was that. She'd put in her papers tomorrow. Looked like it was time for plan B.

❖

Reid stepped inside Boyle's office at four thirty a.m. on the nose. Boyle slid his glasses off and looked up from his desk as Mug settled on his bed in the corner. "You showed up," he said with a look of surprise. "But not in your workout clothes." His eyes darted to the envelope in her hand. "What's that?"

She set the envelope on his desk. "My resignation."

He sighed and gestured to the chair in front of his desk. "Sit."

She crossed her arms and remained standing. "I'm good."

"Either we sit and have this conversation like civilized human beings, or we stand and talk like…"

She waited for him to finish but offered no help because she had no clue what the hell he was trying to say.

"Like less-civilized human beings," he finished.

"Standing makes us less civilized?" she mocked.

"You know what I mean," he replied with a wave of his hand.

"I seriously don't."

"Just sit the hell down, Sylver."

Wanting to get this over with as quickly as possible, she complied.

"I heard what happened last night. This sick bastard got under your skin, huh?"

"Not at all," she lied.

He leaned back in his chair and narrowed his eyes, studying her. "Listen, I get that a lot has happened. What Cap asked you to do was… Well, it'd push anyone over the edge."

"It didn't." She remained stoic.

Ignoring her, Boyle went on. "Then I come in, take over command, assign you a rookie, and a serial killer case drops in your lap. Before you know it, you're in this guy's crosshairs. I don't care if you *are* Superwoman, all that is bound to take a toll."

"You think I'm Superwoman?" she asked with a grin, feeling her guard come down just a little.

"I think you're damn near the toughest cop I ever met," he admitted, his gaze unwavering on hers. "Whatever this is, Sylver, you can talk to me. I'll have your back."

If there was ever a moment in time when she felt like she needed someone, it was now. But it was Cap she wanted, not Boyle. She could only imagine Boyle's reaction if she told him how she'd been solving her cases all these years. Confessing the truth about how she'd ousted him from his throne thirteen years ago would accomplish nothing. He'd never forgive her. For the first time since joining Homicide, she was ashamed. She felt like a cheater.

Reid stood and called Mug to her side. "I'm cooked, Boyle. It's time for me to go."

Boyle reached across his desk for the envelope, turned it over in his hands, and then slid it inside a drawer, still sealed. "I have no knowledge of what's inside the envelope—"

"I just told you. It's my resigna—"

"Per your request, I'll open the letter that you just handed me in two weeks' time."

"No way." She set her hands on her hips. "I'm resigning. Now. Today. Effective immediately."

He stood and set his hands on his hips right back at her. "You had an unexpected death in the family. I'm granting you a two-week bereavement."

"But I don't have any family. Everyone here knows that." Her grandmother had died years ago. There was no one else left.

"What do you call Cap?" he fired back.

Reid said nothing. She felt her eyes well up and looked away.

"Take the two weeks. Get your head on straight, Sylver. Make sure this is really what you want."

Why was Boyle making this harder by being so damn reasonable? She had never wanted to be anything but a homicide detective. Part of her couldn't imagine walking away from this job. It was more than a job. It defined who she was.

Conflicted, she turned and stormed out.

❖

London had just climbed back inside her car when her cell rang. Reid's name appeared on the caller ID. "Speak of the devil," she answered.

"You were just talking about me?" Reid asked.

"Well, no. I was just *thinking* of you. But answering with *think* of the devil just sounded weird." She realized she was babbling and forced herself to focus. "Anyway, I just stopped by your favorite spot and grabbed you some coffee."

"But you don't have my mug."

"Here's a thought. It's just an idea, so bear with me." She paused for effect. "What if you transfer the coffee…into the mug…when I get to the precinct?"

"Not the same."

"How can that not be the same?"

"Won't be as hot."

London rolled her eyes. "Ever heard of a microwave?"

"Microwave and coffee should never be in the same sentence." She frowned. "Why not?"

"Because then the coffee tastes like whatever was heated up before it. Ruins the flavor."

Who knew a woman who drank coffee from a mug that looked like it had survived a drop from a helicopter into the Grand Canyon could be so picky? A simple *thanks for thinking of me* would've been nice. "Why are you calling me?" she asked, mildly annoyed.

"Turned in my papers this morning. Wanted you to hear it from me first."

London felt her heart drop. She was stunned into silence. The killer obviously had something on Reid. Now Reid was jumping ship.

"I'm not sure who Boyle will assign you to—"

"I came to Homicide to learn from *you*, Sylver. Can't you just man up, find this psychopath, and close the case?"

"Did you just tell me to *man* up?"

"I didn't tell you. I asked," London corrected.

"You think I'm retiring because I'm scared?" Reid laughed. "I'm retiring because, unlike you, I've put in my twenty with the department. I'm done."

"And that revelation just happens to come on the heels of a serial killer threatening to reveal your secret?"

"He's bluffing. I don't have any secrets."

"Everyone has secrets."

"Not me. What you see is what you get."

"I don't believe you."

"I don't care if you believe me." Reid sighed. "It is what it is."

"This is it, then? It's the end of the road for us?"

Reid laughed dryly. "You make it sound like we're breaking up. We were partners for one day, Gold. Deal with it."

"Fine. But if you decide to grow a pair, you know where to find me." London hung up, more disappointed than she'd felt in a long, long time.

Reid stared in disbelief at the phone in her hand. The rookie had hung up on her. Told her to grow a pair and actually hung up on her! Who the hell did she think she was, anyway?

Okay, maybe London had a point…but still.

For a fleeting moment, Reid wondered if she *should* grow a pair and confront this thing head-on. March up to the precinct, stand in the middle of the bullpen, and announce to her colleagues that she could talk to the dead. No more hiding. No more pretending she was some prodigious Sherlock Holmes when she clearly wasn't. A part of her longed for the truth to be known. She shook her head. On the heels of that truth would come rejection and ridicule. She couldn't bear to go through that again.

Frustrated, she tossed her cell on the back seat of the car. When it came down to it, she was a coward. Plain and simple. Part of her loathed herself for being the very thing she despised in others. Another part of her realized keeping her ability secret was necessary to accomplish the greater good: getting justice for victims who could no longer speak for themselves. It was a justification she couldn't hide behind anymore because she had effectively resigned this morning. None of it should matter anymore.

But it did.

She was afraid of being exiled from the BPD, the only family she'd ever truly been a part of. If she left now, before the shit hit the fan, at least she'd be leaving with a solid reputation and a career she could be proud of. With any luck, the killer would leave her alone once she wasn't a threat to him anymore. Someone else would have to solve the case. Chances were the FBI would be stepping in soon, anyway. Serial murders fell under their umbrella. Just as well. She couldn't imagine having to work alongside the rookie *and* the FBI, both of whom would be scrutinizing her every move.

She pulled into her driveway and decided to eject the case from her mind completely. It was time to start enjoying her overdue vacation. A road trip with Mug to do some hiking in New Hampshire was just the thing she needed. It would do both of them good.

She threw a bag together with a week's worth of food, clothing, and supplies. Bag in hand, she unlocked the RV and packed everything inside. She'd just finished cranking open all the windows to let in some fresh air when she heard an approaching engine slow and come to a stop in front of her house.

Mug barked in warning at the intruder. She stepped down from the RV as a large man climbed out from a black Suburban. His thick black beard was a stark contrast to his bald head. "Detective Reid Sylver?"

She set her hand over her firearm. Something didn't feel right. "Who wants to know?"

"The governor sent me."

She waited. "And?"

"He'd like a word with you."

"About what?"

"I'm not at liberty to say anything more."

"If the governor wants to talk to me, tell him to make an appointment with my secretary." She turned to climb back inside the RV.

The man bellowed out, "He knows!"

Reid lingered in the RV's doorway. He knew about her arrangement with the captain, or about her secret? "Knows what?" she asked nonchalantly.

"How you've managed to stay at the head of the pack in Homicide for the last thirteen years."

Shit. "By being good at my job?" She laughed.

"By utilizing talents the rest of us don't have."

Talents? That was a new one. Only Cap, her grandmother, and, most recently, the nun at Saint Mary's were privy to her secret, but no one had ever referred to it as a talent. Leave it to a politician to put a positive spin on things. "I resigned this morning," she said, hoping to put a pin in the conversation indefinitely.

"He knows that, too. He doesn't accept your resignation."

What the fuck? "I don't work for the governor."

He reached inside his suit and froze the moment she unsnapped her holster and drew her weapon. "Easy," he said. "I have a cell phone in my pocket. Governor Sullivan is waiting to speak with you."

She refrained from lowering her gun. "I'm not in the mood to talk."

"He says he'll make it worth your while."

She noticed the man's earpiece and realized the governor was probably listening remotely. "Is Governor Sullivan trying to bribe an officer of the law?"

"He says your captain reached out to him."

"From beyond the grave?" she asked, only half joking.

"One phone call." The man held out his cell. "That's all he's asking."

CHAPTER NINE

Something told Reid getting this man off her property would prove challenging if she didn't take the damn call. "Give the phone to my dog." She pointed and told Mug to retrieve.

The man clicked off his earpiece and watched Mug as he trotted over. With a look of revulsion—presumably at Mug's wrinkled, scarred, and near-furless appearance—he held the phone as far away from his body as possible.

Mug gingerly wrapped his teeth around it, trotted back, and deposited it, unscathed, in her hand. "Good boy. Now, *watch*," she commanded, pointing at the governor's goon once again. Mug trotted over and stood exactly halfway between them, facing the man. He bared his teeth and growled in warning.

"What kind of dog *is* that?" the man asked, taking a few steps back.

"A demon dog I summoned up from the depths of hell, so I'd stay put if I were you." With Mug standing guard, Reid could now turn her full attention to the conversation at hand. The governor had clearly gone to a lot of trouble just to get her on the phone. Instinct told her she couldn't afford to be distracted. She pressed the phone to her ear.

"Detective Sylver, this is Governor—"

"Sullivan. I know. Let's move this along." Reid checked her watch, itching to hit the road. "What the fuck do you want?"

"Some patience and time to finish a sentence, for starters," the governor replied, clearly not accustomed to being hurried along.

There was a long pause. Sounded like the governor was waiting for an apology. She didn't offer one.

He cleared his throat. "What can I offer you to make you stay on with the BPD?"

She was surprised by the question and impressed by the governor's ability to cut right to the heart of things. "Nothing."

"Everybody has a price," he countered.

"Not me." She couldn't believe the governor was actually attempting to bribe her. She knew stuff like this happened all the time in politics, but it still came as a shock. She couldn't fathom why her resignation would matter so much to the governor. Did she make his numbers look good? Couldn't be that simple. Something told her this ran deeper. Much deeper. And she had a feeling she wouldn't like what she was about to hear.

"Let me cut to the chase."

"Thought you already did."

"Either you tell me your price—and benefit nicely from our friendly chat—or you refuse and lose your pension."

She tightened her grip on the phone. "You can't do that."

"Indeed, I can," he said with the arrogance of a man accustomed to getting what he wanted. "Especially after you aided and abetted your former captain's suicide. It'd be a pity to see an exemplary career flushed down the toilet because of one reckless mistake."

Helping the captain near the end of his life was one of the hardest things she'd ever done. It wasn't a mistake at all. She took a deep breath to compose herself. It was a good thing the governor wasn't standing in front of her. She'd have clocked him across the face hard enough to break his nose.

Reid thought for a moment. There was no way the captain had gotten into bed with this guy. He never would have betrayed her by sharing her secret, at least not with this prick. "I'll cooperate on one condition," she said finally.

"Name it."

"You answer my questions. Truthfully."

"Easy. Shoot."

"How did you find out?" she asked, intentionally vague and not wanting to tip her hand about anything.

"About what you did for your captain, or about your aptitude for talking to ghosts?"

"Both." But she feared she suddenly knew the answer. He'd had

Cap's office bugged. It was the only answer that made any sense. Which would also explain how he'd learned about her resignation. Every fiber of her being told her Boyle had kept his word and informed no one of her plans to resign.

"Suffice it to say," the governor whispered, "when it comes to worthwhile departmental assets, privacy is a thing of the past."

Her status as a human being and homicide detective had been reduced to *worthwhile departmental asset*? Reid felt her self-esteem growing by the second. "Why does whether I stay or go matter so much? What's in it for you?"

She heard him hesitate on the other end. "The truth," she reminded him. "Or I walk—pension or no pension." She needed him to lay all his cards on the table.

"The Golds are friends of mine. They were big contributors to my campaign, and I owe them a favor."

London's parents? Reid failed to make the connection. What did London have to do with this? The rookie said she hadn't spoken to her parents in over a decade. "They're not even on speaking terms with London."

"They've maintained their distance, yes, but they're still her parents. They want to do everything they can to help her succeed."

"London doesn't need any help." She laughed, remembering how London had dished it out just as hard as Reid had given it. "Trust me, she's perfectly capable of forging her own path." Bulldozing was more like it.

"Nevertheless, they're adamant. They want you to be the one to train her. They know your record for solving cases is unparalleled."

"Did you happen to share with them *how* I solve my cases?" she asked, failing to understand why they'd insist she train London after learning the truth.

"My job is simply to give them what they want. I intend to do just that."

"In other words, you didn't tell them." Reid was relieved they didn't know but frustrated that withholding the truth from them kept her firmly in place as a pawn on the game board.

"Revealing such sensitive information isn't in your best interests, Detective Sylver. I would think you'd be grateful."

"Your sudden concern for my welfare warms my heart." Feeling her anger rise to the surface, she started pacing. "You just figured this was an easy way to pay off your debt to them. Who cares about the truth, right?"

"If you care so much about the truth, why have you withheld it for so long from your colleagues at the BPD?"

It dawned on her that Boyle was the one who'd thrown the rookie in her lap. Could Boyle be working with this prick? She didn't think he was, but she needed to know for sure. "How'd you make it so London landed with me?"

"A quick call to the chief got that ball rolling."

She let out a breath. At least the governor didn't have Boyle under his thumb.

"My offer still stands, Detective. Name your price. I'm feeling particularly generous this morning."

Reid hung up. She'd never taken anything she hadn't earned. She wasn't about to start now.

She relieved Mug of guard duty, tossed the cell to the bearded man, and locked up the RV. Their road trip would have to wait.

❖

Reid called Boyle on her way to the precinct.

He picked up before it even rang. "Two weeks, Sylver," he said without skipping a beat. "That was the deal."

"Boyle, I don't need two—"

But he had already disconnected the call. She glanced at Mug on the seat beside her. "Is this hang up on Reid day or what?" First the killer, then London, and now Boyle. Mug returned her gaze, looking equally baffled. She dialed Boyle again.

"We can do this all day," he announced. "I kind of enjoyed hanging up on you."

"I changed my mind," she blurted before he had the chance to hang up again.

Momentarily silenced on the other end, Boyle cleared his throat. "About what?"

"I can't, in all good conscience, keep calling you *Lieutenant*."

"Does this mean you're coming back?"

"On my way now."

"You can still take the two weeks if you need them."

"I don't. Head's on straight. I just want to close this case, Boyle."

"Good." He sighed. "Heads-up: the FBI's setting up shop as we speak."

She'd expected as much. "Who'd they send this time?"

"Barnard."

"The whistling germaphobe?"

"Yup."

"Damn." Special Agent Barnard was obsessed with cleanliness. He carried a bucket of Lysol wipes wherever he went and sanitized the surface of every single object before he actually touched it. He also whistled. Incessantly. It had taken Reid weeks to scrub her brain of his last song, "You're Welcome" from the movie *Moana.*

And now the song was back with a vengeance. Shit.

Boyle interrupted her thoughts. "Oh, and Sylver?"

"Yeah."

"Call me *Boyle* one more time, and I'll move our morning workouts to three thirty."

"Roger that, Lieutenant."

"In case you were wondering, Gold's at your desk, looking all lost and abandoned."

She felt the first stirrings of guilt. "Really?"

"No. She's kicking ass on this case. Might wanna put the pedal to the metal and get here before she solves it on her own."

❖

Reid stepped off the elevator and headed for her desk, scanning the room as she went. Each desk was now adorned with a Purell hand-sanitizer pump. Barnard's touch, no doubt.

London was sitting in the foldout chair beside Reid's. As she drew closer, she could see that London had covered her desk with a timeline of events and information pertinent to the case. It was organized, detailed, and thorough. The one thing that jumped out was Reid's name, circled in red, with arrows pointing to both victims. Had the rookie also come to the same conclusion: Reid was the killer's main target?

The more she'd thought about it, the more she suspected finding

Beatrice was no mere coincidence. The beginnings of a theory were starting to take shape. But she didn't like her theory. Not one bit.

London glanced up with a look of surprise as Reid approached. "What are you doing here?"

"I grew a pair. Let's go."

"Where?" London asked, reaching for her coat.

"Computer Crimes." She had to find out if her car and cell phone were bugged.

London stood in place. "I've already consulted with them. They're working with victim number two's alarm company to see how the breach occurred."

She stared at London. "You know about the breach?"

"Mrs. Ruger was pretty rattled by her neighbor's murder. When I interviewed her, she said she'd be arming her security system at all times from now on. I heard it activate when she closed the door behind us." London shrugged. "Deductive reasoning suggests either the killer abducted her when she was outside her home—which she wasn't, by the way, because I already checked—or he hacked his way inside somehow. Mrs. Ruger had audio and video cameras installed in every room. I already reviewed the footage—"

"Did you see the killer?" She couldn't help but ask, even though she knew he was too clever for that.

"It recorded everything right up until the killer set foot in her house. Looks like he deleted all audio and video recordings thereafter." London paused and narrowed her eyes. "Wait a minute. How did you find out about the breach?"

Reid didn't have an answer prepared. She shrugged. "Just a hunch." Boyle was right. London was kicking ass.

London gestured to a desk that had been added to the room. "We're working in tandem with the FBI now."

And just like that, Barnard came a-whistling around the corner.

Reid grabbed London by the arm and bolted for the nearest exit.

"What are you doing?" London asked as they entered the stairwell.

"Avoiding."

"Special Agent Barnard is our liaison. He's very capable of—"

"Sending me to an early grave," she whispered. "Murder by way of whistling."

"I think his whistling is beautiful. It gives us some nice background music."

Reid rolled her eyes and sighed. How this rookie would survive in Homicide with a sunshine-and-rainbows attitude was beyond her. "Do you have your phone?" she asked.

London nodded.

"And the keys to the truck?"

"Right here." London fished around inside her coat pocket and held them up. "Why?"

"Shut off your phone. Follow me."

London grimaced at her new pager as they made their way to the undercover parking lot. "I can't believe I let you talk me into trading in my iPhone for *this*."

"You'll get your precious iPhone back when we catch this bastard." Computer Crimes had already determined Reid's cell was compromised. They were checking London's now, too. Part of her was relieved to find out the killer had hacked her phone. At least it put a dent in her theory that he was psychic. A ridiculous theory, she told herself. In all her years on the job, she'd never met one, and—in spite of her own ability—wasn't even sure they existed. There must be more people out there who could do what she did. But she'd never made any effort, whatsoever, to find them. She had no desire to network with people who could talk to the dead. All weirdos, most likely.

She unlocked the door to her Camaro, grabbed Mug's leash and portable water bowl, and tucked the keys behind the visor. Computer Crimes would do a sweep of the car and let her know if a listening or tracking device had been installed. They'd already checked Boyle's truck—it was clean.

London led the way to the truck, and they both stepped to the driver's side. Reid held out her hand. "Keys, please."

"No way. My truck. My keys. I drive."

"This isn't your truck. It's Boyle's. And I'm training *you*. Not the other way around. Trainer always drives."

London crossed her arms, unyielding.

"Besides, I said *please*," she added, in a last-ditch effort to get her way.

London nodded. "True. That *was* a big step for you." She thought for a moment. "Okay, I'll make you an offer. If you can get through one whole day without cursing, these keys are yours."

"Shit. A whole day? Like, twenty-four *hours*?" She couldn't remember the last time she'd gone that long without dropping the F-bomb. Maybe never.

"One whole day. Starting now." London glanced at where her Apple Watch would have been if she hadn't turned it over to Computer Crimes.

At that moment, Reid realized she hadn't heard London swear—not once—since they met. Was this rookie actively trying to tarnish the image of a proper Boston cop? "Have you ever cussed?"

The rookie shook her head. "Never."

"Never ever?"

"Nope."

"So shit, fuck, bitch, and asshole"—she watched as London visibly flinched with each cuss word—"are totally absent from your vocabulary?"

"Totally."

This Goody Two-shoes thing ran way deeper than she'd imagined. London might, in fact, be beyond her help. Reid shook her head. She definitely had her work cut out for her if London had any hope of sticking it out with Homicide. "Tell you what. I'll let you drive for the next six months if you promise to expand your vocabulary to include the words I just listed."

"That's hardly worth compromising my values for. And let's not forget, I'm the one with the keys. I get to make the rules."

Reid was tempted to wrestle them from London's grasp, but something told her the rookie would give her a run for her money.

As if reading her mind, London added, "I grew up with an older brother who practiced his wrestling moves on me. Don't even think about it."

"Fine." Reid walked around to the passenger's side and helped Mug climb into the back seat.

Chapter Ten

London slipped behind the wheel of Boyle's truck as Reid fastened her seat belt. "You only get one chance."

"For what?" Reid asked, her thoughts already on the case.

"These." London held up the keys before starting the ignition. She tapped the dashboard clock. "If you can make it until ten thirty tomorrow morning, I'll happily relinquish the driver's seat."

Reid tried to remember how long it had been since she was a passenger in someone's car. Sixteen, she realized. The day she'd gotten her driver's license. She'd bought a car with money saved from her lawnmowing and snow-shoveling jobs, filed for emancipation, and was living on her own before her seventeenth birthday. The last two years of high school were a sleepless blur. She'd managed to graduate on time while working a full-time job to pay her own bills. She'd never accepted a drop of money from the state. Those two years were, by far, the most challenging of her life. But it had all been worth it. She would've done just about anything to get out from under her grandmother's thumb.

London extended her hand across the empty space between them and waited.

"What the hell?" Reid asked, jolted from memories of the past.

"Shake on it."

"Shake on what?"

"Our no cursing in exchange for keys to the truck deal. And *hell* counts, by the way."

Sighing, Reid slipped her hand around London's. "There. Now drive."

"I will. If you ask nicely."

Reid brought her fingers to her temples. She felt a headache fast approaching. "Would you please be so kind as to provide transportation to my place of residence?" she asked, doing her kick-ass impression of a British accent.

London sat up straighter and answered in the clipped accent of a fellow Brit, "Oh yes. It would be my pleasure, Inspector Sylver."

"You just dropped me down a rank."

"I know, but we were in England. Inspector just sounded better."

Reid turned away to hide her smile as London threw the truck in drive and pulled out of the lot. This rookie was something else.

London was glad to be back in Reid's company. The detective hadn't offered any explanation as to why she'd decided to return, and London didn't press for the details. Something told her Reid's decision had less to do with her desire to solve the case and more to do with some unforeseen outside circumstance.

With Reid a reluctant passenger, she felt more in control behind the wheel of Boyle's truck. No matter what happened with Reid— regardless of whether she was in or out of this investigation—London promised herself she would see this case through to its rightful conclusion.

Even if that meant compromising the detective beside her.

After Marge's murder, one thing had become clear: the killer was focused on Reid like a hungry predator tracking wounded prey. If Reid had a secret that the killer knew about, which appeared to be the case, then perhaps it would be best for everyone if that secret came to light.

❖

London parked across the street from Reid's house, cut the engine, and gave the house a cursory look. "That's your house?" she asked, wide-eyed.

Reid nodded. "Why's that surprising?"

"Based on the appearance of your coffee mug and dog, I expected something a little more"—London shrugged—"dilapidated." She threw a glance over her shoulder at Mug. "No offense there, buddy."

Reid had put a lot of work into her house over the years. With an eye for detail and unreasonable expectations of perfection that, fortunately, didn't stray into other areas of her life, she'd single-handedly renovated both the interior and exterior of the house. The pristine but modest-looking Cape with forest-green siding and white trim sat on an acre of land. The front porch spanned the width of the house, its dark mahogany floor perfectly complementing the entry door. Three small dormers protruded from a charcoal-gray roof, each of them leading to quaint rooms on the second floor—her bedroom, an office, and an exercise room with just enough space to fit the basic equipment she needed to stay fit. Two large twelve-paned windows flooded the main floor with natural light. One belonged to the living room, the other to a formal dining room that she never used. A redbrick chimney climbed along the right side of the house, and a one-car garage was attached to the left.

Having completed the renovations on her own, she felt a kinship with this house that she couldn't imagine sharing with any other dwelling. She loved this house and had every intention of living out the rest of her life here.

London glanced in the driveway. "The new Wonder Class C RV, by Leisure Travel?" She locked eyes on Reid. "Is that *yours*?"

"Whose else would it be?" she answered, hopping down from the truck.

London climbed out and joined her on the sidewalk as they waited for a car to pass. "A courteous human would answer with a simple yes, and then we'd proceed to talk about the fact that you like to—oh, I don't know—go camping, hiking, kayaking, mountain biking—"

"How'd you know I like to do those things?" She set her hands on her hips, suddenly suspicious.

London pointed to the RV. "Dual kayak and bike rack, sticker from the White Mountains—the RV gave me my first clue, albeit subtle, about your affinity for camping."

They walked to Reid's front porch with Mug in tow as London droned on, "Had you chosen the path of a courteous human, our conversation could've progressed to include the fact that I, too, enjoy those particular pastimes, etcetera, etcetera."

"You do?" Reid asked, stopping dead in her tracks, surprised as hell.

London halted beside her. "Why's that so hard to believe?"

"You went to Harvard."

"And?"

"You used the word *etcetera*," Reid said. "Twice."

"It means and so on, and so forth."

"For Christ's sake, I know what it means, London. But who actually uses it in everyday conversation?"

"You addressed me by my first name." London grinned, apparently pleased with herself. "I'm growing on you."

"If you mean like a giant pimple on the tip of my nose before an important public speaking engagement, then yes, you're growing on me." London was right. Reid hated to admit it, but she felt herself starting to warm up to the rookie. "Let's get back to the case." She jogged up her front porch steps and ducked underneath the crime-scene tape.

Reid paced the length of the porch as London joined her.

"I already reviewed the crime-scene photos," London said. "I'm up to speed."

"Good. What stands out to you here?" She was curious if the rookie was adept enough to pick up on the killer's tell, a clue that provided a glimpse into his psyche. So far, no one else had noticed.

London looked around. Her gaze lingered on the wooden table and four chairs. Marge's body was gone, of course, carted away to be examined by the ME. The plate of cookies had also been removed, but the table and chairs remained.

"How long have you lived here?" London asked.

"Thirteen years."

"This set looks new."

Reid nodded but offered no assistance.

London glanced back and forth between Reid, the RV, and the table and chairs. "You're a loner. Not one for entertaining. This table has four chairs when it should have just one—maybe two if you have someone special in your life." She paused. "Is there someone special in your life?"

"You mean a partner?" Reid asked, amused by the rookie's

nosiness. "Not that it's any of your business, but no. Not at the moment."
Who was she kidding? *Not at the moment* spanned her entire life to
date. She wasn't beyond the occasional hookup for sexual release, but
she had never allowed anyone into her world on a permanent—or even
semi-permanent—basis.

Reid knew most people would probably see her refusal to enter
into a relationship as a supersized flaw. But she saw it as a strength. It
kept her head in the game so she could do her job and do it well.

Seemingly satisfied with her answer, London went on, "You'd
never waste your money on something you wouldn't use. You also
wouldn't put a table on your front porch. Doing so would be opening
the door for social engagement with your neighbors. But you never
socialize with your neighbors."

Not if she could help it. Reid waited, careful to keep her poker
face intact.

"The killer transported this set here to stage the crime scene.
Everything had to be perfect. Killing and staging the victim is akin
to displaying his art." London stepped slowly around the table. "He
identifies with you as a loner. The table and chairs illustrate his own
longing to be part of a group. He thinks that's what you want, too. His
motive for killing is to bring the two of you closer." She looked up.
"He's trying to *bond* with you."

Reid nodded, impressed. London's instincts were spot-on.

"Nothing was mentioned in the forensics report about the killer
bringing the table and chairs to your house."

Reid kept her gaze on London but said nothing.

"You didn't tell them the furniture doesn't belong to you. Without
this information, the FBI can't profile the killer."

Reid leaned against the porch railing. "It's *my* case."

"It's *our* case," London corrected her. "The FBI has precedence
here. We're bound by law to share everything we know with them."

Once again, Reid said nothing. She had to let London put the
pieces together herself and, hopefully, come to the right decision.

"You'll be pulled off the case if they learn you're the killer's true
target." London frowned. "You brought me here to share this with me
and ask me to keep quiet about it."

"I didn't intend to share anything with you. Needed to see if you'd
figure it out for yourself."

"This was a test?"

"Sort of," Reid answered honestly.

"And?"

"And your instincts are solid." That was a gross understatement, but she couldn't go throwing compliments around at a time like this—she would look insincere. No detective she knew, herself included, would've been able to piece the killer's profile together so quickly.

London leaned against the wooden railing, opposite the spot occupied by Reid. She shook her head. "I don't know about this. We're supposed to keep the FBI in the loop."

"Do you trust me?" It was a bold question, and it cut right to the core. They hadn't known each other long, barely twenty-four hours. But it was enough time for the rookie to surprise her and impress her more than once. At that moment, she realized she was actually starting to trust London.

Silently, they locked gazes from across the porch. Even from afar, Reid could feel their connection. Part of her wanted to abandon ship and look away. Another, deeper part dared her to hold on for as long as she could bear.

Her gaze unwavering, London finally broke the silence. "Does anyone know?"

"That I'm the reason he's killing?" Reid shook her head. "As far as I know, we're the only two with that informa—"

"Does anyone know about your secret?" London clarified. "Other than the killer, is there anyone else who knows about it?"

Reid thought long and hard before answering. She made a decision, then and there, that she would never lie to London again. "My old captain knew."

"Anyone else?"

She started to shake her head before remembering her visit to Saint Mary's. "The nun knows, too."

"You told Sister Margaret?" London asked, clearly offended.

"She asked me about it, so I told her the truth. Can't lie in church. To a nun."

London raised an eyebrow. "But lying to the rest of us mere mortals is okay?"

Reid shrugged. She kept her gaze steady on London's. "You have my word that I won't lie to *you*."

"Anymore," London added. "Because we both know you already have."

The rookie had a point. "No lying from this moment forward. *And* I'll grant you partnership status for the duration of this investigation." By making this larger-than-life offer, she realized she had just stepped out of her comfort zone.

"Equals?"

Reid nodded.

London counted on her fingers. "Taking on a partner, no lying, and no cursing. That's a tall order for someone who's used to going it alone and doing things her own way." She frowned. "Are you sure you're not biting off more than you can chew?"

The first two she could handle. It was the no cussing that could very well do her in. "I'm good," she said with feigned confidence.

London sighed and looked away, steeped in thought. Long seconds ticked by in silence. She finally stepped over to Reid and leaned against the porch railing beside her.

"Does the killer identify with your secret?"

Reid thought for a moment. "I'm not sure yet if he does or not." She still couldn't rule out the possibility that he was psychic. "I think he identifies more with the fact that I'm a loner *because* of my secret."

"Okay. But if that changes, and we discover that he does identify with your secret, then you'll need to tell me what it is. I can't be an effective partner if you're withholding key information. Agreed?"

Reid nodded, cringing at the thought of revealing her ability. She could only imagine how disappointed London would feel after learning the truth behind her success as a homicide detective. That was a bubble she didn't want to burst.

"Your word, Reid."

Goose bumps broke out on her arms and legs. It had been a very long time since anyone had addressed her by her first name. Too long, she decided. Hearing it from London's lips was strangely appealing. "My word," she said.

"Whatever this secret is, it's yours. I won't pry, but I'm here if you want to talk about it. Can't be all that bad if Sister Margaret invited you to Sunday mass."

"Us," Reid said. "She invited *us*. There's no way in"—she caught herself—"H-E double hockey sticks that I'm going by myself."

"Nice catch. Brunch after? Your treat."

"Deal." Reid reached over, and they shook hands.

"Guess we're on a first-name basis now?"

"I wasn't planning on making it awkward by drawing attention to that fact, but...yeah, that seems to have happened."

"Great. Can I see the inside of your house now?"

Reid stood, called Mug to her side, and jogged down the porch steps. "Nope."

CHAPTER ELEVEN

London ran to catch up with Reid. "Why can't I see the inside of your house?"

"Because I said *no*."

"That explanation won't do. I need more." London paused. "Are you hiding dead bodies inside?"

Shaking her head, Reid kept walking to the truck.

"Do you have a hoarding problem?"

"No."

"Do you own a hundred cats and your house is like a giant litter box?"

"Gross. No."

"Is it saturated with dog feces because Mug isn't housebroken?"

"Of course not."

"Do you have cardboard furniture because you can't afford real furniture?"

Reid stared at her. "Who the he—" She caught herself again. "*Heck* has cardboard furniture?"

"I read about this man in Iowa who couldn't afford real furniture, so he constructed his own out of cardboard. It was quite beautiful. The only problem was, he couldn't use it."

"Because it was made of cardboard?"

"Exactly. But he really was quite an artist. A journalist discovered him, took photos, and featured his story in a local newspaper. This man's collection of cardboard furniture is now on display at the Metropolitan Museum of Art in New York."

Reid stopped and turned to face London. "My house is clean, organized, and furnished. I don't have a hoarding problem or own any cats, and Mug was already housebroken when I got him."

"That leaves countless other possibilities. It'll eat up a lot of our time going through each one. Time that would be better spent on this case, if you don't mind me saying."

Reid sighed. "Fine. If I tell you, will you drop it and move on?"

London nodded.

"No one—not a single human being, other than me—has set foot in my house since I bought it."

"Ever?"

"Never."

"Why not?"

"It's the only private space I have that's all mine. I'd like to keep it that way."

"So you're the opposite of an agoraphobe. Instead of being afraid to leave the house, you're afraid to let anyone inside."

"I'm not afraid," Reid argued. "My house is just...my personal space."

"It's kind of symbolic, though. Don't you think?" London buckled her seat belt and stared at Reid until she buckled hers.

"You referring to the case?"

"No. You. You're afraid to let anyone inside."

"For the last time, London, I'm not afraid. And quit psychoanalyzing me. Let's grab lunch, someplace quiet, and go over the case."

"Great. I'm starving." London slid the key in the ignition and put the truck in Drive. "I know just the place."

London was definitely making headway with Reid. She was sure she had put at least a few small cracks in her armor.

She thought back to their conversation on the porch. Something had changed between them as London profiled the killer. Reid had challenged her, and she'd proven herself. A foundation of trust was starting to take shape. That trust worked both ways.

Learning that Sister Margaret was aware of Reid's secret came as a huge relief. Though still curious as to what the secret was, London was now able to put it on the back burner and focus on other more pressing aspects of the investigation.

She glanced at Reid, sitting silently beside her. She'd made progress for sure, but there was still a long way to go to get Reid to open up and let her in. Maybe it was time to turn the tables, to focus less on getting Reid to share, and volunteer more about herself. Let Reid see who she was. Then Reid could decide just how much she was willing to reveal.

❖

Reid stared at the dock overlooking the bay. "You live on a boat?" This rookie was just full of surprises.

"It's a houseboat," London replied.

"Like I said, you live on a boat."

"A 2006 Gibson 50 Classic. My grandfather gave this to me as my graduation gift." London glanced at Reid and grinned proudly. "Come on. You have to admit, it's pretty cool."

Reid conceded, "Maybe a little."

They climbed over a metal railing and onto the main deck of the boat. "That's the upper deck," London said as she gestured to the space above them. It was enclosed in a clear plastic cover with white zippers running along the seams, presumably to keep the boat protected during the colder months. "We're standing on the main deck," she went on, "and my quarters are slightly below this." London pointed to a small window near their feet.

Reid suddenly found herself more than a little curious about London's personal living space but refused to let on. "Nice. Can we get on with it?" She glanced over her shoulder at Mug. Frozen in place, he scrutinized the narrow gap of water between the dock and boat before gazing up at her uncertainly. "Come on." She patted her thigh. "Hop on over and climb through the railing."

With one last glance at the water, he planted his furless butt on the dock.

"Seriously?" Reid asked. "You're embarrassing me here, Mug."

Not budging, he pierced her with his steady golden gaze.

"If you expect me to come over there and haul your furless a—" She caught herself and threw a glance at London.

"See?" London winked at Mug. "Old dogs *can* learn new tricks." She held up a finger. "Be right back."

Reid turned to Mug. "Did she just call me an old dog?"

Mug chuffed from his place on the dock.

"That's what I thought."

London returned with a two-by-four. She set it on the deck and slid it across the gap to the dock. "There," she said, standing. "Better?"

Mug rose on all fours, pranced across the wooden bridge, and ducked underneath the metal railing to join them on the deck. He gave London's hand a lick before resuming his post at Reid's side.

They followed London to the side of the boat where she unlocked a door and slid it aside. She extended her arm across the doorway to bar Reid's entrance and gestured to Mug. "Gentlemen first," she said with a scowl meant only for Reid.

Okay. Point taken. Maybe stuffing London in the back seat so Mug could ride in the front was a shitty thing to do. She waited for Mug to enter and then stepped inside to have a look around.

A charcoal-gray L-shaped sofa faced a sixty-inch TV. Plush white throw blankets and navy-blue pillows with tiny white sailboats decorated the sofa. Pinewood walls accentuated dark mahogany floors. Large curved windows surrounded them on all four sides. To the right, at the helm of the boat, lay the ship's wheel and console. A short flight of stairs to the left presumably led to the bedroom the rookie had mentioned. The living space was organized and meticulously kept. No knickknacks. Everything in plain view had a purpose. Although compact, there was ample space for someone to live there comfortably—enough space even for two.

London lifted a remote from a bracket on the wall and switched on the TV. Preset to a music channel, soothing jazz sounded through speakers that were built into the walls. "This is obviously the main cabin," she said. "And down there"—she gestured to the left—"are the galley, head, and forward berth. There's a small office, another head, and a second berth to bow over there." She gestured to the right.

"Who's giving birth to a head?" Reid asked.

"Sleeping quarters on a boat are called a berth. The head is the bathroom." London walked toward the rear of the boat. "I'll be right back. Make yourself comfortable at the dinette. I'll make us some lunch in a minute."

"Meet me at the *dinette* for tea at high noon," Reid said under her breath in a snobbish tone.

"I heard that," London called out from the other room. "The dining area is called the dinette on a boat."

"Why can't you just be normal and call it a table?"

"If you're going to be a frequent visitor, you should really brush up on your boat lingo."

With Mug at her heels, Reid descended the short staircase, stood in place, and looked around the kitchen. The *galley*, she corrected herself. Granite countertops, dark mahogany cabinets, stainless-steel refrigerator and microwave. There was even a miniature dishwasher. "Who said I want to come back?" she asked, taking a seat at the table.

"Figured this could be our new hangout since you're being so weird about your house." London emerged with a fuzzy blue blanket draped over one arm and a ceramic dog bowl in hand. After filling the bowl with water from the kitchen sink, she set the bowl and blanket on the floor for Mug. He watched her with interest as she withdrew a box of dog biscuits from a nearby cabinet. "Would you like a treat?"

Amused by London's hospitality, Reid watched as Mug graciously accepted a large biscuit, lay down on the blanket after much circling, and munched away contentedly. She glanced around, curious as to why London had dog biscuits on hand. Clearly, there was no four-legged companion in residence.

"I have a friend with a dog who stays here sometimes," London said, watching her.

Was the rookie seeing someone? Reid suddenly felt uncomfortable in London's private space.

"We've been best friends since junior high," London explained, grabbing two waters from the fridge. "He lives in Vermont and comes to the city once a month on business. He always brings Buckley. Hence, the treats." She tossed the bottle of water to Reid. "Do you like Brie?" she asked.

Reid nodded, feeling a sense of relief wash over her. Maybe London wasn't seeing anyone. But why should she care?

London slid out a griddle from a hidden compartment in the wall. With a skill and grace that Reid found mesmerizing, she whipped up two Brie paninis in minutes. She added some fresh-cut apple slices to their plates and carried them to the table. "I always brainstorm best with food in my stomach."

Reid just stared at her plate. She couldn't remember the last time someone had cooked for her.

"I'll admit I was tempted, but I promise I didn't spit in it. *This* time." London set a napkin in her lap and took a bite of the panini.

She realized she was still staring at her plate like a moron. Mug lapped up the crumbs from his dog biscuit and pierced her with curious eyes, looking back and forth between her and the untouched panini. Hearing the phantom taunts of her colleagues from afar, she followed London's lead and plopped a napkin in her lap.

The panini was delicious. It tasted even better because London had made it.

"I think it's fair to assume the killer has been stalking you," London said, downing the last bite of her sandwich with a long drink.

"Agreed." Reid was loath to admit it, but she had already come to the same conclusion. "Except he's not our traditional stalker. He doesn't get off on following me or watching me." If someone had been tailing her, she would've noticed.

"He gets off on listening." London nodded. "An audio stalker. He uses technology to eavesdrop on his victims."

"And technology is everywhere. He likes the idea of making me feel like no place is safe."

They both eyeballed London's laptop on the counter. "It's turned off," London assured her. "But it's probably best to be paranoid at a time like this." She carried her laptop into the bedroom, shut the door, and took a seat at the table across from Reid. "Run me through your phone call with the killer."

Reid did, editing any reference the killer had made to her ability to communicate with the dead.

"He actually said you're more comfortable with dead people?" London paused and met her gaze. "Is that true?"

"Maybe. In case you haven't noticed, I'm not much of a people person."

"But how would *he* have known that?"

Reid shrugged. "Haven't figured that out yet."

"And he said he enjoys his time with the dead differently?"

She nodded, remembering his words. *I'll let you in on a secret, Detective Sylver. I, too, am more comfortable with the dead. We just enjoy our time with them a little differently.*

"I hate that my brain even went there, but what if he's a mortician or an undertaker, and he, you know…"

"Has sex with dead bodies?" Reid finished. "Yeah. I wondered the same." There was a long silence as she struggled to figure out exactly how this all came together.

"I'm trying my hardest not to ask this question, but there's no way around it."

Jolted from her thoughts, Reid looked up.

"Do you have any sexual fetishes"—London sighed—"involving the dead?"

"Seriously?"

"It just occurred to me—maybe *that's* your secret. Is that why you don't allow anyone inside your house?"

"Because I'm busy doing the wild thing with dead people?" Reid asked, dumbfounded.

"Maybe you're into zombie pornography, and you have photos of naked dead people all over your house." London leaned forward on the table. "If that's the case, now's the time to come clean," she said in all seriousness.

"I hope you're joking. But if you're not, the answer is no. That's beyond gross." She put her hands on the table. "My secret has nothing to do with a sexual fetish of any kind. Let's focus here. Less speculation about me. More on the killer."

"And therein lies the problem. In his mind, the two of you are intertwined. Learning as much as I can about you will shed more light on him."

Reid found herself dancing precariously close to revealing her secret. Although tempted, she just couldn't bring herself to do it. There had to be another way to figure out who this bastard was.

The beeping pager hijacked her attention. She glanced down as the ME's number flashed across the pager's window. This was unusual. With a deep breath to steady her nerves, she dug the borrowed cell—an old flip-style phone—from her pocket and started dialing.

"Hey, where'd you get that?" London asked. "I thought we had to ditch our phones."

"We did. Todd from Computer Crimes slipped it to me on the down-low."

London frowned. "He didn't give me one."

"You didn't ask."

"Neither did you. I was there with you the whole time."

"I didn't have to ask. Todd and I have been working together a long time." She shrugged. "He read my mind."

London crossed her arms, looking offended. "How long is this going to last?"

"How long's what going to last?"

"This whole shut the rookie out of the boys' club thing."

"There is no boys' club. And, if there was, I wouldn't be in it." Reid raised an eyebrow, wondering if it had momentarily escaped London's attention that she was, in fact, a woman.

"Whatever. You know what I mean."

"Well, if it makes you feel any better, I grabbed one for you, too." She reached into her other pocket and dug out an identical flip phone.

"Why didn't you just say that in the first place?"

"Why didn't you just call this a table?"

London caught the cell as Reid slid it across the table. "You really are impossible."

"Now, if you don't mind, I should give Fred a call back."

"Fred?"

"The ME. He just paged me."

"Us."

"Huh?"

"He called us. We're working this case together now, remember?"

"Right. Please accept my apologies, O wise and experienced partner."

"All is forgiven," London said perkily.

Shaking her head, Reid punched in Fred's number and put it on speaker. "It's Sylver."

"And Gold," London chimed in.

Reid sighed. One of them had to change her name.

CHAPTER TWELVE

Curious as to what the ME had to say, Reid cleared her throat. "What's up, Fred?"

"Haven't finished the autopsy on the second vic yet but wanted to give you a heads-up on something peculiar."

Whatever it was, it had to be more than just peculiar. She could think of only two other times Fred had called her in the last thirteen years—neither of which had been work related. He'd simply called to beg her to pitch for his team in the annual softball tournament hosted by the BPD.

"Both bodies are devoid of blood and internal organs."

"Come again?" Reid said.

He cleared his throat. "Both've been drained of fluids. Internal organs were removed."

"What the—How?"

"Killer made a Y-incision. Ribs and collarbones were cut and the organs removed."

"Everything?"

"Everything."

"What about the brain?"

"Gone. Scalp was peeled forward, a section of the skull was sawed out, and the brain subsequently removed."

Reid remembered a time when these details kept her appetite at bay for days. Now they were just a part of the job. Like a pediatrician who, over time, developed immunity to slimy-nosed patients, she'd built a tolerance over the years for all the juicy wonders of a dead human body. She'd also attended enough autopsies to realize the killer seemed to know exactly what he was doing. "Hesitation marks?"

"Not a one," Fred replied. "Also, the body was embalmed. Results haven't come back yet, but the substance appears consistent with standard embalming fluid."

She and London locked eyes. Looked like their theory about the killer being a mortician or undertaker was right on the mark.

London stood from the table and carried their dishes to the sink.

"One more thing you should know." Fred cleared his throat again. "Killer penetrated both victims vaginally."

Reid leaned forward. "Before or after he killed them?"

"Definitely postmortem. Semen was present in both bodies. That's the only fluid he left behind."

"Sick sonofabi—"

London chucked her half-empty water bottle across the room. It smacked Reid in the forehead, halting her midsentence.

"Anything else?" Reid asked, considering whether or not she should retaliate. With something heavier.

Fred was quiet for a moment. "Fundraiser's this weekend. If you're looking for a new team, I'll make a spot for you."

"Thanks, Fred. But Boyle already got to me. I'm playing for him now."

"Damn."

London turned from the sink. "Playing what?"

"Softball," they both said in unison.

"Ooh." London hurried over and sat back down. "Can I play, too?"

Fred hesitated. "You any good?"

"Pitched all through high school and college. Broke a few records," London boasted.

Unsurprised, Reid massaged the growing lump on her forehead.

"Then welcome to the Toe Tags. First practice is Wednesday. I'll send the team info in an email—"

Reid pressed a button and ended the call. "Oops. Finger slipped."

"You're just jealous because I'm in the boys' club now."

"Jealous of you playing for *Fred*?" Reid laughed. "Did you happen to catch the name of your new team?"

"The Toe Tags. I think it's funny."

"Suit yourself. My team name is way cooler."

London stared at her, suddenly quiet. "Well? Are you going to tell me what it is?"

"Packin' Heat," she said proudly.

London rolled her eyes. "Lame with a capital *L*. You're going down."

Reid felt her smile falter. "You're not allowed to trash-talk. You haven't even met your team yet."

"They could be the worst team in the tournament." London shrugged. "Wouldn't matter."

"You're *that* good?" She frowned. "No one's that good."

London flashed a knowing smile. The rookie's confidence was unnerving. "Guess you'll find out when we send you home packin', with a big fat zero on the scoreboard."

She mentally reviewed the team roster, one by one. Boyle had landed all the best players. London—and her distastefully named team—didn't stand a chance. She almost felt bad for the rookie. "Care to place a small wager?"

London didn't flinch. "You took the words right out of my mouth. What do you have in mind?"

"We win, I get to cuss whenever I want and still drive Boyle's truck."

"If we win, you invite me over to your house for pizza and a movie. I pick the movie."

"You're on." Reid reached across the table to seal the deal. Like taking candy from a baby. "So, what do you know about necrophilia?" she asked, her mind returning to the case.

"That it's gross beyond comprehension. Aside from that, not much. You?"

She thought for a moment. "I think it falls in line with our profile of the killer so far."

London nodded. "He likes to play it safe. He utilizes whatever technology is available to stalk, monitor, and interact with his victims from a distance. What better way is there to keep a safe distance than having sex with a corpse?"

Reid was confident they were on the same page now. "Why would he want to have sex with someone who was dead?"

London wrinkled her nose in disgust. "He doesn't want to be seen."

"And why would he go to such lengths to keep himself hidden?"

"We only hide what we're ashamed of. He's afraid of being judged."

Reid suddenly knew what she and the killer had in common, why the killer had targeted *her*.

"You just figured something out. I can see it on your face," London said, scooting forward. "What is it?"

She had never told a soul about the physical abuse she'd endured as a child at the hands of her grandmother. How could she speak of it here? Now? With a woman she barely knew?

Obviously intuiting that something had changed, London reached across the table and set her hand over the top of Reid's arm. "Talk to me, Reid. Whatever it is, I promise it won't leave this room."

❖

London watched as Reid struggled to reclaim her poker face. The vulnerability that she'd been sensing from the beginning resurfaced, like a mysterious sea creature rising briefly to the surface for air. It was clear to her now that Reid was not only aware of this vulnerability but worked hard keep to it below the radar.

Whatever it was, it had something to do with this case. For that reason—and that reason, alone—London decided to push Reid just a little bit harder.

❖

Reid took a deep breath and met London's unwavering brown gaze. "I've never told anyone before. I have no idea how he would've found out." She let the silence breathe to further punctuate the moment. "I've been attracted to corpses my whole life. That's why I'm in homicide. I thought about becoming a mortician, but being alone with all those dead bodies every day would be too tempting. I've never had sex with one, but I've come close. It's hard. I fight the urges every day." She looked at the floor and sagged her shoulders, feigning defeat. Somehow—she had no idea *how*—she managed to keep a straight face.

"Oh. My. God." Without warning, London threw her arms in the air. "Me, *too!*" she shouted excitedly. "I've had a thing for dead people since I was a kid! I can't tell you how good it feels to get that off my chest."

Even with her Academy Award–worthy performance, London hadn't fallen for it. Reid shook her head. This rookie was smart *and* funny.

"Try again." London sighed. "The truth, this time."

If she wanted to solve this case and lock the killer behind bars before he hurt anyone else, it was time to put her cards on the table. Not all of them. But some. She chose her words carefully. "My parents died in a car accident when I was four. My grandmother raised me. She wasn't really a kid person. Knocked me around some." Reid knew that was an understatement. From the time she'd set foot in her grandmother's house, she remembered knowing her grandmother didn't want her there. The woman was thorny, impatient, and unkind. Tension in the house mounted when Reid was repeatedly caught talking to her dead parents. At age five, she finally confessed to her grandmother that she could see and talk to ghosts. That's when the abuse started.

Beatings, long stretches without food or water. She shuddered at the memory of being locked inside that damn metal dog crate in her grandmother's pitch-black basement where all she heard was the relentless scratching and scurrying of nearby rodents. An avid smoker, her grandmother's favorite form of punishment was burning her with a lighter or, better yet, with the butt of a cigarette. Reid's back and stomach were covered with scars—too many to count.

London remained quiet for long seconds, studying her. Reid shifted uncomfortably. She couldn't bring herself to say anything more, so she had to give London the time she needed to read between the lines.

"She physically abused you."

Reid nodded.

"How bad?"

"Bad."

"Where is she now?"

"Dead. Thankfully." Reid realized, too late, how that sounded. "I didn't kill her."

"I wouldn't lose any sleep over it if you did."

There was a long silence between them.

London finally leaned back and sighed heavily. "If I was your friend—which I'm not, by the way, because my friends don't make me ride in the back seat behind the dog, ditch me at the precinct and speed away, or lock me in a car with childproof locks—I'd probably say something like, I'm sorry you went through that. You didn't deserve it. No kid does. And if you ever want to talk about it, I'm here."

"Then it's a good thing we're not friends." Reid let out an audible sigh of relief. "Because my friends don't get all sappy like that."

"Everyone needs at least one."

"Sappy friend?" Reid asked, amused.

London nodded. "Someone who knows your darkest secrets and still has your back."

Reid knew it was her turn now to read between the lines. In no uncertain terms, London was committing to their partnership. This clever rookie was also offering Reid her loyalty, friendship…and maybe something more. There was definitely something between them. She was sure of it now. A spark of electricity. A connection. The moment felt surreal. For the first time in her life, she didn't want to run as far and as fast as she could. "Do sappy friends ask for a secret in return?" She cleared her throat. "To, you know, balance out the scales of their friendship?"

"They don't have to. Such secrets are usually shared on a voluntary basis when the moment is right." London stood from the table, stepped to the fridge, and grabbed what looked to be an entire cheesecake and a plastic container full of syrupy strawberries. Without bothering to ask Reid if she wanted some, she grabbed two small plates from the cabinet and served them each a slice with a generous helping of strawberries. She returned to the table, her expression serious and difficult to read.

Reid waited for London to sit down before she took a bite. She'd have to run a few extra miles tomorrow to make up for all these calories. Totally worth it. "Wow." She closed her eyes to savor the richness. "Did you make this?"

London nodded. "I found the recipe online." She set a napkin in her lap. "You have scars, don't you?"

Reid looked up from her plate but didn't answer. She felt her wall of thorns and barbed wire shoot up around her in an instant.

"I have a theory about the killer," London said gently. "That's why I'm asking. I need to know."

Having lost her appetite, she set down her fork. "I have scars," she confirmed, her walls anchored and fortified.

London pushed her plate aside, cheesecake untouched. "From what?"

Reid shrugged. "Cigarettes…lighters…small torches."

"Burns." London glanced across the kitchen at Mug, no doubt putting two and two together, now comprehending why Reid had adopted him. "Where are the scars located on your body?"

"Back and stomach, mostly."

"Where you can cover them up with clothes, so they're not readily visible."

Reid simply nodded. She had never felt so exposed and vulnerable in her life. Surprised to find herself on the verge of tears, profound grief and shame welled up from some long-forgotten place. She wasn't normally a crier, though she'd certainly been doing her fair share of that lately, since the captain's death.

The instinct to run or fight suddenly kicked in. With razor-sharp focus, Reid snapped to full attention. It probably wouldn't end well if she punched London in the face, so all that left was fleeing the scene, which she happened to be particularly good at. Feeling the cabin walls close in around her, Reid stood abruptly from the table. Mug was at her side in seconds.

"Wait," London said, rising from the table alongside her. She reached out to set a hand on Reid's arm.

Reid sent her a look of warning. It took every ounce of willpower not to jerk away. Mug stepped closer and growled at London.

Chapter Thirteen

"Don't you see?" London peered into Reid's eyes, ignoring the menacing teeth that were now bared in her direction. "The *killer* can't cover his scars. He doesn't want to be seen because he's disfigured in some way."

Reid let out a breath. Mention of the killer brought her back to the present, reigniting her need to solve this case. The storming seas within her instantly calmed. "He was physically abused—maybe even sexually abused—by an older woman. That's why he's having sex with them postmortem."

London added, "A grandmother, aunt, neighbor, babysitter. It could've been anyone."

"But how'd he find out my grandmother abused me?" Reid asked.

London thought for a moment. "Is it in your medical file?"

She shook her head.

"But isn't that something your PCP would've made a special note about at some point?"

"I've had the same doctor since I was sixteen. I never told her what my grandmother did."

"Right, but I'm sure she noticed the scars and asked you about them."

"She did," Reid confirmed.

"And?"

"I told her I had an accident with boiling water when I was a kid."

London's mouth fell open. "And she never questioned you about it?"

"I wove a very convincing tale."

London was quiet for a moment as she thought. "Did you ever file a report or tell the police about what she did?"

"No." By the time the courts granted her emancipation, all she'd wanted to do was move on with her life and never look back.

"Did you tell a friend, girlfriend, school counselor, priest—anyone?"

She shook her head.

"How about a support group?"

Reid gave herself a dope slap, instantly regretting it as the lump on her forehead made its presence felt. "How could I forget about my support group? Going there is the highlight of my week because I *love* to talk about myself and share the painful memories of my past."

London stared at her for long seconds. "Is that a *no* on the support group?"

"Smart, tough, *and* discerning. I see now why you were promoted to detective."

"You just called me smart and tough," London said with a grin.

"What I said wasn't meant as a compliment." Reid shook her head. "Might as well add resilient. You're apparently immune to my insults."

"Come on, you must have told *someone*." London glanced at Mug. "What about him?"

Mug had already returned to the blanket. He lifted his head at the mention of his name.

"He plays things close to the vest," Reid joked. "He would never go spilling my secrets around town."

London was suddenly serious. "Think about it, Reid. Have you ever told him what your grandmother did to you?" she pressed. "Have you ever told him about the burns?"

She thought back to the endless hours she'd spent at the hospital with Mug, whispering words of encouragement as he went through the excruciating process of healing from second- and third-degree burns. That was the only time she'd ever spoken of her past. She'd told Mug about her own burns—even showed him the scars on her back and stomach. "I told him. But that was a long time ago," she said, thinking back. "Six years." London listened closely as she shared Mug's story.

"Could someone have overheard you in the hospital?"

She shook her head. "Mug had a private room. I made sure the room was empty before I spilled my guts."

"And you're positive that's the only time you've talked aloud about what your grandmother did to you?"

"Other than today, that's it," she confirmed. It struck her then that Mug, the only living being she'd chosen to confide in, had quickly become her best friend and most-trusted confidant. She suddenly found herself wondering if the same would happen with London. Was it already happening?

"The killer must have been listening somehow."

"We know he's adept at eavesdropping, so it's definitely possible. But why'd he wait six years to start this killing spree?"

London shrugged. "Maybe something happened to set him off."

The notification of her grandmother's death flashed through her mind. She recalled her own conflicted feelings that had simmered for months like a slow cooking Crock-Pot—relief that her grandmother was finally gone, grief at losing the only family she had left, and anger over the abuse. "Maybe she died," Reid said finally. "Maybe the woman who abused him died. That could be what set him off."

"First thing we should do is visit Angell Animal Medical Center. We need to get a list of everyone who worked there six years ago."

Reid nodded, grateful that London was working the case with her. This breakthrough wouldn't have happened without her.

"Now that we're partners—and well on our way to becoming sappy friends—do you have the sudden urge to invite me over for pizza and a mov—?"

"No." Reid stood, grabbed a biscuit from the box of treats on the counter, and tossed it to Mug. His powerful jaws made an audible *clack* as he caught it in midair. She glanced at her watch: 2:38 p.m. "Let's head to the hospital." If all went well, they'd have the killer in custody before dinner.

Behind the wheel of Boyle's truck once again, London was still sifting through the pieces of what Reid had shared with her. Learning she had been physically abused as a child was disturbing. But finding out about the scars, who gave them to her, and how they got there was disturbing on a level beyond her comprehension. She did her best to stay focused on the case, but her mind kept returning to Reid. She wanted to ask more questions, to delve deeper into what happened, when it started, how long it went on, and when it finally stopped, but it was really none of her business. She recalled the moment in their conversation when Reid had been ready to bolt. Her heart went out to the detective.

London realized she couldn't relate to Reid's experience—not even remotely. Her own grandmother had been her best friend growing up. In all the years she'd known her, Nana never even said an unkind word in her presence. She couldn't imagine what going through something like what Reid had would do to a person. No wonder Reid was a loner. It all made so much sense now.

Reid clearly carried that shame with her everywhere she went. London imagined it was like hauling a leaden boulder in a backpack on a mountainous trek, day after day, and never arriving at your destination. The boulder's size and weight made it impossible for Reid to carry anything else.

Still, even after today's revelation, London sensed there was something more that Reid wasn't sharing. Something deeper. Her only plan at this point was to be patient and show Reid that she could be trusted.

❖

London got them to Angell in under thirty minutes. No small feat, Reid noted, impressed. London kicked ass on the road.

They walked into the lobby, flashed their badges, and asked to speak with the person in charge of personnel. Moments later, they were shaking hands with the human resources director, George Mustaro, inside his office.

He brought up a long list of employees on his computer. Each name was linked to a personnel file and photo ID. "Do you want access to the employees at both locations? We have a second office in Waltham."

"We'll start with this one first," Reid said, studying the screen over his shoulder.

"Want me to print out all these files?" he asked, swiveling around in his chair to peer up at her over his bifocals.

She shook her head. "It'll be faster if you lend us your office and computer. We can eliminate each employee, one by one."

He frowned. His thick graying mustache twitched like a nervous rodent on his face. "How long do you need?"

Reid had always hated mustaches. She cleared her throat, trying hard to keep her eyes on his, but her gaze kept returning to the massive strip of hair above his lip. Did he even have an upper lip? She couldn't tell. "Hard to say how long it'll—"

"About two minutes," London interrupted. "We'll be out of your hair in no time."

Had London just made a pun about his ghastly mustache?

"Then have at it." He grabbed his mug off the desk and left.

"I was half convinced that thing was about to leap off his face and start populating the planet with a whole new species," London snarked.

"You and me both," Reid said, laughing. She leaned over to have a closer look at the computer screen, set her hand on the mouse, and scrolled down the list of names. "Two minutes, huh?" As she continued scrolling, she cast a glance at London. "Shall I add speed-reader to your growing list of qualifications?"

London pulled out a memory stick from her pocket. "We'll download everything and take it back to the precinct for a closer look."

Reid released the computer mouse and stood. "You just carry that around with you wherever you go?"

"You'll never catch me without the five basics." London reached inside her pocket and opened her hand to reveal a tiny spritzer of hand sanitizer, a pink tube of ChapStick, the smallest travel-size toothbrush Reid had ever seen, and a pack of gum.

"Spearmint or peppermint?" Reid asked, narrowing her eyes.

"Polar Ice." London tossed her the pack of gum.

By the time she'd peeled the foil wrapper from the stick of gum, started chewing, and realized it was her new favorite flavor, London was finished.

Reid second-guessed her decision to focus solely on employees from the Boston office. "Maybe we should upload the list from Waltham while we're—"

"Download. Not upload." London pocketed the memory stick with a satisfied smirk. "Already done."

She scratched her head. "Why am I here again?"

"Because you're the best homicide detective around."

"Clearly." Reid raised an eyebrow. "Evidenced by my savvy tech skills. The idea to *download* all relevant data to a memory stick was exactly what I would've done. I was just waiting to see if you'd think of it first."

"Flash drive," London said.

"Huh?"

"People don't really call it a memory stick anymore."

"My point exactly. I'm not even sure why Boyle saddled you with me as your babysitter." She remembered feeling resentful over having to train the rookie. Scratching her chin, she began to wonder if it was really the other way around. Was Boyle thinking she'd lost her investigative finesse after the captain's death? Because London was clearly more than capable of running an investigation on her own.

"Anyone can learn the tech side of things." London stepped closer and held Reid captive in her brown-eyed gaze. "It's your instincts that no one except you can teach me."

Without warning, the moment grew intimate. Reid couldn't pull her gaze from London's. She felt the heat radiating from London's body and heard her steady breathing. She smelled the subtly intoxicating aroma of London's perfume, like tiger lilies dipped in vanilla. An electric current of attraction sizzled in the narrow gap between them.

How could she go from feeling annoyed by London's mere presence to feeling attracted to her in the span of a few days? Attracted, she realized, just scraped the surface of what she was feeling. There was something deeper here.

Still holding London's gaze, her mind raced. She never mixed business with pleasure. All of her encounters were one-night stands. Nothing more. That was another thing she had in common with the killer. True, one-night stands were a million miles from having sex with a corpse. But emotionally, they both accomplished the same thing: keeping everyone at arm's length.

From the moment she freed herself from her grandmother's reign, she'd adhered to the same doctrine with unrelenting rigidity—never let anyone inside. The only exception to that rule was Mug.

"There could be another trigger for the killer," she said, breaking their eye contact and taking a step back to reclaim her personal space.

"Other than the death of the old woman who abused him?" London perched on the edge of the desk.

She nodded, still mulling over her theory. "He was in a relationship and got dumped." The more she thought about it, the more it fit. That's why he'd waited six years before circling back to Reid. He'd been watching her—no doubt about that—and probably for a while. Maybe he'd even kept tabs on her since learning of her past, six years ago. If he'd been watching her and eavesdropping on her life for the past six years, he'd know she led a mostly solitary existence. It would have eventually become clear to him that she kept everyone at a distance. If he'd been in a relationship when she clearly avoided them, he'd feel superior to her. He'd start to believe he had emerged from the abuse unscathed.

If he was dumped, which she now felt certain he was, he'd experience conflicting feelings of camaraderie and resentment toward her. On the one hand, he'd feel like she was beside him, walking the same path, a twin soul on the planet who truly understood him. On the other, he'd be enraged at the thought of joining her as an outcast to society. Nothing but damaged goods.

When it came down to it, Reid knew that was how she felt about herself. She, too, was damaged goods.

In a state of delusion, he might even believe she had intentionally pulled him down with her. Misery loved company.

She finished sharing her theory aloud, then stopped pacing and set her hands on her hips. "He's dangerous. He has nothing to lose anymore."

London nodded in agreement, her eyes sharp and focused. "Are you able to do that with all your cases?"

"Do what?" Reid asked, looking up.

"Get inside the killer's head like that?"

She thought about it and shrugged. "I guess so. Why?"

"That's what makes you the best. *That's* your secret sauce." London grinned. "It also happens to be what I came here to learn."

"Then learn away." She waved a hand in the air dismissively. "Let's head back to the precinct and see what's on that memory stick."

"Flash drive," London corrected her.

"Whatever."

Chapter Fourteen

Back at the precinct, they printed out all eighty-six personnel files for closer scrutiny.

London glanced up from the computer screen as Reid walked in with the stack of paper. "No one in these files is scarred or disfigured, that I can see," she said. "Then again, we can only see their faces in these photos."

Reid had flipped through the stack and noticed the same. "If your theory is right, and the killer is outwardly scarred or disfigured in some way, then that leaves other exposed body parts to consider."

"Head, neck, hands, and—depending on the time of year—arms and legs."

"It's cold outside now, but he still remained hidden from both—"

"We don't know that," London interrupted.

Reid sighed. Another slip. "Just go with me on this for a minute." She set the stack of personnel files on the desk. "Suppose, just for argument's sake, that he did keep himself hidden from both vics, not wanting to reveal himself until they were both dead. If that's the case, then we're talking head, neck, or hands because his arms and legs would be covered up this time of year."

London reached for the phone on Reid's desk. "I'll call Angell and see if George remembers anyone who fits that description."

Reid started sorting the personnel files by gender while London made the call. She gathered all female employees and set them aside. Unless the killer was transgender—which nothing had so far indicated— the women could be ruled out for now. One by one, she studied each man's photo without regard to age, race, or ethnicity. She didn't care about statistics. Numerous studies were available to law enforcement on the probable age, ethnicity, and background of serial killers. That's what the FBI was here for. Right now, she was evaluating the faces before her from the gut. The gut of a homicide detective who'd seen just about everything.

Beatrice appeared beside her, looking down at the papers in her hands. *Is he in there?* she asked.

Having a spirit instantly materialize beside her used to scare the shit out of her. But she hardly reacted at all anymore. She wasn't sure if she'd trained her body not to react, or if she was so used to it by now that she simply didn't flinch. Either way, it worked to her advantage. She wouldn't have lasted long in the BPD as a jumpy cop.

"Probably," she whispered. "Anyone look familiar?"

I already told you I didn't see him, dear.

Right. If London wasn't sitting so close, she would have pursued this line of questioning and asked Beatrice if she'd seen any of these men *before* she was murdered.

He's going to kill again, Beatrice said. *That's why I'm here. To warn you.*

She locked eyes with Beatrice. It took every ounce of willpower not to ask for more information. She couldn't—not in the middle of the precinct.

Then, just like that, Beatrice was gone.

She looked down at the file in her hands. Gilbert McGovern. His photo sent chills down her arms and legs. Caucasian. Thick dark eyebrows, gray eyes, prominent cheekbones, long nose. This was a straight-on headshot, so his receding chin wasn't visible. But she remembered him. Why hadn't she thought of him before now? "Hang up," she told London.

"I'm on hold, waiting to speak to—"

She leaned over and pressed the switch hook on the phone's cradle. "Don't waste your time. I found him."

"The killer?" London asked, wide-eyed. She set the phone down. "How?"

Reid handed her the paper and pointed at the photo. "That's him." As soon as the words were out of her mouth, they didn't sit right with her. The man she remembered was quiet, hardworking, sheepish, and nonconfrontational. Not the killer's profile at all. But everything else fit. Maybe he had two opposing personalities, like Dr. Jekyll and Mr. Hyde.

"You recognize him?"

"I forgot about him until just now. He worked at Angell as a janitor while Mug was there. He always wore a black beanie hat, the same one he's wearing in that photo, pulled down over his ears. He was bending over to get his bucket one day when a dog jumped on him and pushed his hat up a little—far enough so I could see that the top of one of his ears was missing. It was jagged," Reid said, remembering. "Like someone had cut it off a piece at a time."

He must have worked the night shift because that's when Reid would visit. The hospital lights were always dimmed for the animals in consideration of the late hour. The thing with his ear had happened so quickly. She remembered questioning if she'd even seen the injury at all. Her mind had been so consumed with Mug's injuries and suffering that a part of her had wondered if she'd just imagined it. Eventually, she'd brushed it off to dim lighting, weird shadows, and the gruesome imagination of an overworked homicide detective.

"That's awful." London studied the photo. "If he hadn't brutally murdered two old ladies, I'd feel bad for him."

"There was something else, too," Reid said, thinking back. "No matter what he was doing, he always wore latex gloves. Even saw him eating a sandwich once, and he was still wearing those damn gloves."

London glanced up. "You think his hands are scarred."

Reid nodded. "I'd bet anything they are. He's ashamed of them. Keeps them covered up, along with his ears. That has to be our guy."

London was quiet for a moment, a look of contemplation on her face. "Why didn't you think of him before now?"

The question wasn't accusatory, Reid realized. London seemed genuinely curious. She shrugged. "With everything that was going on with Mug at the time, I was pretty distracted. This guy kept his head down and went quietly about his work. Never even made eye contact with me. That has to be him, but he doesn't fit the profile. He never even crossed my mind as a suspect."

When they ran his record, it came back clean.

"Fred said the killer knew what he was doing when he removed the organs from both vics." London leaned back in her chair. "Does it bother you that he works as a janitor in an animal hospital?"

It didn't sit right with her either. They were missing something. "With you on that," she admitted. "I expected he'd be working in a profession related somehow to corpses. Human corpses," she added.

London threw a glance at Gilbert McGovern's file. "He's full-time at Angell and still there, according to this. Maybe he has a second job somewhere that falls more in line with our profile."

Reid checked her watch. It was closing in on six p.m.

Picking up on the cue, London asked, "Want me to call and see if he's on tonight?"

She shook her head. "Let's make a surprise visit. Don't want to tip anyone off and scare him away. Last thing we need is for this guy to be in the wind."

❖

Reid and London decided not to break for dinner. They did, however, hit the McDonald's drive-through to grab some chicken strips for Mug. His favorite.

Reid pulled into Angell's parking lot and cut the engine. Since the plan was to haul this guy in for questioning, they'd left Boyle's truck at the precinct and took a squad car, instead. It felt good to be behind the wheel again.

London turned in her seat to face Reid. "How do you want to play this?"

"We'll take him in and interrogate him until he gives us something. Easy-peasy."

"Can we play good cop/bad cop?" London asked with a hopeful expression. "I get to be the mean one."

"No way. I have mean written all over me. You have…"

"What?" London pressed.

"The smart, responsible, good-cop vibe going on." She doubted London could play the bad cop if her life depended on it. Bad cops used foul language, for one. In all fairness, though, Reid didn't think she could play the good cop. It wasn't a role suited to her natural God-given talents. She'd worked hard over the course of her career to develop a certain reputation when it came to interrogating a suspect. Cap regularly called her an above-average badass in the interrogation room.

"Fine." London sighed, obviously more than a little disappointed. "Do you want me to come with you, or should I stay here in case he tries to bolt?"

She smiled. London was still thinking like a beat cop and not a homicide detective. "You go where I go, partner. If he runs, we give chase. Together."

Reid stepped out from the squad car and opened the rear door for Mug. Sprawled across the back seat, he lifted his head but made no motion to join her. He'd had a long day, and this was his designated naptime. "You coming or what?"

He set his head back down, never taking his gaze from her face.

"Fine. Sleep on the job, but I expect you to be well rested by the time we get back. You'll be riding with the suspect back to the precinct, so you'll need to look as ugly and ferocious as possible." She closed the door gently but didn't bother locking the car. If anyone was dumb enough to try to hotwire a police vehicle, Mug would be there to set them straight.

They walked into the hospital lobby and waited for the receptionist to finish a phone call. With a straight face, Reid asked for Mr. Mustachio.

The receptionist frowned. "We don't have anyone here by that name."

London stepped forward and elbowed Reid—hard—in the ribs. "We'd like to see the human resources director, please."

"Oh. You mean Mr. *Mustaro*." Reid's jab at the HR director's larger-than-life mustache had obviously failed to find a landing zone. "He's usually gone for the day by now," she said, "but I know he was here late for a meeting." She spun her chair around and asked a woman behind her to man the desk. "Follow me. Let's see if we can find him."

He was packing up for the day when Reid and London stepped inside his office. London closed the door softly behind them.

Standing behind his desk with a black trench coat draped neatly over one arm, he clicked his briefcase shut and looked up. "I thought you two left," he said, surprised.

Reid nodded. "We did. But we found someone of interest in your files."

"Really?" He frowned. "Who?"

"Gilbert McGovern."

"Gil?" He set his hands on his hips, his frown deepening. "To say I'm shocked is an understatement. Gil is the *last* person I would suspect of any wrongdoing."

"Why's that?" Reid asked, scanning his body language for signs of deception.

"Started working here when he was seventeen. Been here for nine years. Never missed a single day. Follows the rules, works hard…"

Reid watched as he looked off into the distance and chewed his lower lip. "What is it?" she pressed. Clearly, he wasn't sharing what was on his mind.

He hesitated. "All the years I've known him, Gil's never looked me in the eye. He's painfully shy and so quiet. Answers in one-word sentences. Keeps his head down, literally, like he's afraid to stand up tall. Frankly, I've always assumed someone got hold of him and"—he shrugged—"broke him a long time ago."

"People who are broken often lash out." London stepped closer to the desk. "Have you ever seen him lash out at an animal or a coworker?"

He shook his head. "Never. Quite the opposite, actually. I've caught him on camera numerous times when he thinks no one's around, touching the animals gently, reassuring them they'll be okay. Intellectually, he's slow. But he's trustworthy and at ease with the animals. It's people he's afraid of. I guess I just find it hard to believe that such a gentle soul could do anything like what you described."

Reid exchanged a glance with London. Gil was looking less like a suspect and more like a victim. But London was right. How often had Reid seen examples of victims-turned-murderers in her career? Too many times to count. Still, the man Mr. Mustaro described was a far cry from the killer they were hunting. Gil wasn't fitting the profile.

"Is he working tonight?" London asked.

Nodding, he sat down at his desk, switched on his computer, and brought up the video feeds for each room. "There." He pointed to the upper right corner of his computer screen. "Gil's cleaning the dog runs now. That's where you'll find him."

Reid and London followed Mr. Mustaro through a maze of hospital corridors. He stopped outside a set of green doors marked *Kennels*. "This is it," he said, sighing heavily. "Really hope it isn't him." He reached into his pocket, withdrew a business card, and passed it to Reid. "I've already spoken with our attorney. Hospital protocol dictates that

Mr. McGovern be suspended pending the results of your investigation. Please keep me apprised." With that, he turned and retraced his steps down the corridor, leaving them alone to do their job.

They peered through the door's small square window and watched in silence as Gil sprayed down each kennel with a hose. "Think he'll run?" London asked.

"Doubt it," Reid said. "But we might get a bath if we're not careful."

"Probably a good idea to shut off the water before we take him into custody."

"Agreed."

They both craned their necks to follow the hose to its source.

"I see it. There," London said, pointing. "Beside that first kennel, under the window."

"Good. You cut the water. I'll go get our guy."

"Why do I have to cut the water?"

"You spotted it first, so it's yours."

London narrowed her eyes.

"Fine." Reid sighed. "I'll cut the water. You go live the dream and apprehend our suspect."

"Thank you."

"Don't mention it."

They pushed through the double doors and headed toward their respective posts. But there was a small hiccup. London called out to Gil and held up her badge *before* Reid reached the water spigot.

Panicking, Gil dropped the hose and held his hands up in surrender. Reid watched as the hose bucked wildly in the air like a feral mustang, spraying London from every possible direction. The rookie's hair and clothes were drenched in seconds. To her credit, though, she didn't flinch. She remained focused on reading Gil his rights and securing his handcuffs.

Barely able to contain her own laughter, and in no particular hurry, Reid leaned over and finally shut off the water.

London led the handcuffed suspect to where Reid was standing. A steady trickle of water ran down her forehead and dripped from her nose. "If I didn't know any better, I'd say you had that planned all along."

"You were the one who insisted on making the arrest." She

shrugged. "Who was I to stand in your way?" Out of pity, she grabbed a towel from a nearby rack and traded places with London.

One of the vets on staff gave London a fresh pair of scrubs to wear for the ride back to the precinct. They led Gil out the side door and through the parking lot to the squad car.

As Reid set eyes on the car, she realized something wasn't right. The driver's side rear door was slightly ajar, but she was sure she'd closed it.

CHAPTER FIFTEEN

L eaving London with Gil, Reid jogged the rest of the way to the car and threw open the front and rear doors. Mug was gone. Raw panic gripped her like strong hands around her throat.

"Put him in the car," she said as London approached with Gil.

London set her hand atop Gil's head, guided him into the back seat, and shut the door. "Where's Mug?" she asked, her gaze drifting over the surrounding lot.

"He took him."

"Who?"

"Same sick fuck who killed our two vics." Reid kicked herself for leaving Mug alone in the car. How could she have been so stupid? If anything happened to him—if he was hurt in any way—not only would she never forgive herself, Reid knew she'd never be the same.

London resumed her scan of the parking lot and glanced up. "Security camera," she said, pointing to a nearby camera that was fastened to a light pole. "Stay with Gil. I'll be right back." She sprinted to the hospital.

Intent on finding Mug, London ran as fast as she could to the hospital's main entrance. Angell Medical Center was where Mug and Reid had started their friendship. She wasn't about to let this be where it ended. Mug obviously meant everything to Reid. Neither of them deserved this.

London stepped in front of the woman at the reception desk. "Who runs your security cameras?" she asked, her tone urgent.

The receptionist glanced up with a look of alarm. "We do." She pointed to the computer monitor on her right. "We can see the parking lot from here and watch who's coming in."

A ray of hope. "Do recordings get saved?"

The receptionist nodded. "For twenty-four hours. Then the system deletes it automatically."

"I need access to the last thirty minutes. Bring it up on the monitor, please." London stepped behind the waist-high swinging doors that separated the front office from the waiting room. She lifted her shirt to reveal the badge that was clipped to the waistband of her borrowed scrubs. "*Now*," she added when the receptionist made no move to comply.

Trembling, Reid squeezed her eyes shut and imagined herself with a surgeon's scalpel. She envisioned excising the fear from her body like a malignant tumor—just like she used to do when she was a kid.

Tumor resected, she opened her eyes and took a deep breath. The pager in her pocket beeped noisily. She withdrew the pager and looked as groups of numbers flashed across the screen. *06...716...437...*

It wasn't even a complete phone number. How the hell was she supposed to call this idiot back?

The pager continued to beep, spewing the same sequence of numbers, as if someone was repeatedly sending them every few seconds.

None of the numbers looked familiar. She looked more closely: 716 reversed was 617. That one, she knew, was a Massachusetts area code. It suddenly occurred to her that these numbers could be a message. She flashed back to a time in elementary school when she'd discovered she could spell *boob* on a calculator. She flipped the pager upside down and studied it, searching for a hidden meaning. Like one of those optical illusions that took a while to actually see—and, once seen, couldn't be unseen—the message swam up from the depths of her subconscious like a giant, hungry leviathan: *Let...gil...go...*

It was the killer. The same man, she knew, who now had Mug.

Were they working together, Reid wondered? A serial killing duo, one dominant, one submissive? It was certainly possible.

Her mind returned to Mug. She instantly understood why the killer had taken him—he wanted to make a trade. Release Gil, and Mug would be returned.

She was willing to do just about anything to make sure Mug was unharmed. Having monitored her from afar, the killer obviously knew how much Mug meant to her. He effectively had her by the balls now, and he knew it.

The flip phone in her pocket vibrated against her leg. Caller ID unknown. "Sylver," she answered.

"I have something here that belongs to you."

"He's not an object. He's a dog. *My* dog." She felt her temper dig in and take hold. "And if you lay a hand on him, so help me God, I'll kill you in the most inhumane, excruciating way possible."

"Promises, promises," he said, his tone revealing a smile that came through loud and clear over the phone's speaker. "You have something that belongs to me. I want it returned."

The killer was demonstrating possessive tendencies—a clear indication that he was the alpha in the relationship. Perhaps her earlier theory was correct: Gilbert was his partner in crime. "Are you referring to the *human being* who's sitting in my squad car right now?"

"You're going to release him in exactly five minutes and offer him a heartfelt apology. Then you'll find Mr. Mustachio—humorous play on the name, by the way—and inform him that you and your partner made a big mistake, and Gil's free to return to his duties."

The sonofabitch had been eavesdropping from the moment she and London set foot in the hospital. "Or what?" she asked. She had to know precisely what was on the line.

"I'll set your friend here ablaze with some gasoline and a match. I'll take a video of him burning alive and send it to every screen you come within ten feet of for the rest of your life. You'll never be able to erase the images and sounds of your best friend during his final torturous moments."

"You win." She didn't hesitate. Nothing was worth that price. She'd never leave Mug in the lurch like that. She'd rather die.

"Oh, and one more thing," he added. "After you make things right for Gil, you should have a heart-to-heart with London and tell her your secret."

"She already knows."

"Not about your grandmother. I realize that must've been difficult to share but, let's face it, not nearly as difficult as your other secret."

She was quiet for long seconds as she pondered his words. He was obviously referring to her ability to communicate with spirits. Was he merely suggesting she share her secret, or was he making it part of the trade? With Mug's life on the line, she couldn't afford to take any chances and assume anything. "Are you making Mug's release conditional on me telling London that I can talk to the dead?"

"Make sure your phone is turned on so I can listen in, please."

Reid couldn't wait to get her hands on this sonofabitch. "And if I do all that, you'll release Mug unharmed?"

She heard a click and realized he'd already hung up.

London jogged over to her from the front entrance. "I reviewed the security footage. He hacked into their system. Deleted everything."

The killer was likely listening to their conversation right now. Probably also watching them via the video camera mounted on the streetlight above. It suddenly felt like he was everywhere. Reid was acutely aware of her words now. She had to play this carefully.

"I'm going to open this door, unlock our *former* suspect's cuffs, and release him—but not before I issue an apology on behalf of the BPD for the terrible mistake we've made." She considered winking to clue London in but thought better of it. She didn't want to do anything to risk angering the killer.

"*Former* suspect?" London asked, looking totally confused.

"That's what I said. Some pertinent information has come to light. I'll fill you in later."

London opened her mouth but stopped short and narrowed her eyes. "Are we also issuing an apology to Gilbert's place of employment? We should probably let them know he's free to return to work."

Reid nodded. This smart rookie was following her lead, just as she'd hoped.

They released Gil and accompanied him back inside the lobby of the hospital. Reid stopped Mr. Mustaro on his way out the door and arranged it so that Gil could return to work immediately.

"Back to the precinct?" London asked from the passenger's seat as Reid slipped behind the wheel of their squad car.

"Not yet. There's something I need to tell you first." She made a point of opening her flip phone and setting it on the dash.

"What's up?" London asked, her eyes on the phone.

"You want to know how I solve every case?"

London studied her, quiet. "Okay, I'll bite," she said finally. "How?"

"I talk to the dead."

"You mean, like, talking out loud and cluing them in on the case? I know lots of people who do that. I still talk to my nana every night before bed. I'm sure people would think I'm crazy, but I tell her all about my day and—"

"Stop. What I do isn't the same as that." Reid fixed her eyes on the dark shadows outside. She couldn't stand to see the look of disappointment on London's face when her confession actually sank in. "I've been able to communicate with spirits since I was a kid."

"Tell me you're joking."

"I'm not. That's how I've solved all my cases. In case you haven't heard, I've solved every case that's crossed my desk for the last thirteen years."

"I heard."

"Well, haven't you ever wondered how?"

"You're testing me again, right?" London asked, shaking her head. "I thought we'd moved past all this."

She leaned back against the headrest. Best just to get it over with. Like the beginning of a mild headache, she felt a slight tug inside her head as she envisioned a door inside her mind. She knew, without even having to open it, that London's grandmother was already waiting on the other side. She was filled with joy at the opportunity to chat with her granddaughter after sixteen long years.

Reid opened the door and invited Beverly to join them.

London's grandmother popped into the back seat of their squad car with an audible *whoosh*. Reid resisted the urge to turn and look at her—she didn't have to. She felt the woman's presence as strongly as she would a live wire. The air always sizzled a bit when a spirit was close.

Please tell her I'm here, that I'm sitting right behind her. Tell her

I have my hand on her shoulder. And if she closes her eyes and remains very still, she'll be able to feel it.

"Your nana passed away?"

"Not recently," London admitted. "It happened when I was—"

"Twelve. She fell down the basement stairs and broke her neck." London sat up.

She felt the rookie's gaze boring holes in her head, but she didn't return the eye contact. She couldn't look at London right now.

"Did you read that in my file somewhere?"

"Why would that be in your file?"

"How else would you know?"

"How do you think?" She couldn't resist the pull of London's gaze. They locked eyes.

"I don't believe you. That's not possible." This time, it was London who looked away. "How could you poke fun at something so hurtful? You've crossed a line, Reid."

"It was right before Christmas," Reid went on, ignoring London's skepticism. "She'd decorated the tree that year by herself because her husband—your grandfather—had died the year before. She was carrying a large red storage container with a green lid up the basement steps. It was full of Christmas decorations. She was getting the house ready for your visit. She wanted to surprise you."

London remained perfectly still and quiet.

"Your nana called you Hug Bug. She was your best friend." Reid hesitated, afraid to share too much. "She says she still is." Finished, she took a deep breath, her thoughts skipping back and forth between London and Mug. She prayed this damn confession would bring Mug home alive. She also found herself hoping she hadn't lost London's friendship in the process.

"No one knew she called me Hug Bug. Not even my mom." London finally met her gaze. "Is she here? Now?"

Reid nodded, glancing over her shoulder at the woman behind them.

Tell her I was there the day she pulled that woman over for speeding and let her off with a warning because she reminded her of me.

Reid told her.

London's mouth fell open. "No one knows about that!"

Tell her I was there for all of her graduations, all the big events in her life. I was there for the small ones, too. I've never left her. Tell her I'm always here, by her side.

London started crying as Reid finished relaying the message.

And I'm so sorry her parents abandoned her when she needed them most. Tell her I would have been there for her. I would have believed her.

Sensing London was on emotional overload, Reid considered reaching over to hold her hand but thought better of it. The sappy friend thing was London's department, not hers. "Those were the big messages she wanted to convey."

London nodded, wiping her cheeks with the back of her sleeve.

"By the way, your grandmother is *way* nicer than mine."

London laughed, in spite of the dark humor. "You said your grandmother and your old captain knew about this. Other than the killer, am I the only one alive who knows about your gift?"

Funny. Reid shook her head and smiled. Cap used to call it that, too. Some gift. It wreaked havoc in her life daily and plugged her into a separate reality from everyone around her. Getting just a glimpse of friendship with London made her realize that she was a loner out of necessity—not out of some deep-rooted desire to be a one-woman army fighting to get justice for the dead, as she'd conned herself into believing. She looked up. "Just you, the killer, Sister Margaret, and the governor."

"Governor Sullivan?" London asked.

Reid nodded. This was her cue to turn off the cell phone. London slipped hers from a pocket and did the same. Whatever the killer had heard, she hoped it was enough to satisfy him and stay true to holding up his end of the deal. But she couldn't let herself forget that they were dealing with a sadistic serial killer—a predator with no conscience, no empathy for living things, and no moral compass. She said a silent prayer that Mug would be okay.

Chapter Sixteen

Reid took a deep breath and cleared Mug from her mind. It was important to keep her head in the game. She didn't know how much the killer knew about her phone call with the governor and his threat to take her pension if she left the BPD. But she couldn't risk giving him more information than he already had.

As she shared the details of her first phone call with the killer and her subsequent conversation with Boyle about her plans to retire, London set a hand on her arm. "Hang on. You were planning to retire because the killer threatened to reveal you can communicate with spirits?"

"He didn't threaten to do that, exactly. It was implied."

"Even worse!" London threw her hands up in exasperation. "I can't believe you'd actually consider throwing away your career because of an *implied* threat the killer made to reveal something that makes you look even more amazing."

"More amazing?" She stared at London, wondering if the rookie was truly missing the obvious or just pretending to. "What the hell are you talking about? I'm a fraud."

"I don't think that." London stared back at her with a look of disbelief. "Who in their right mind would think that?"

"How could you *not* think that?" She was suddenly pissed off with London for dismissing reality as it was slapping her in the face. Seeing things through rose-colored glasses did no one any good. "I've been solving cases pretending to be a homicide detective when all I am is a cheat."

"Did you plant or otherwise fabricate evidence to help you build your cases?"

She shook her head. "Of course not. The evidence in every case I ever worked is legit." That's where the captain had come into play. He'd reviewed all of her investigations with a fine-tooth comb and helped manufacture a logical trail to account for how she found the evidence.

"Then you're not pretending to be anything," London countered. "You *are* a homicide detective. A homicide detective who also happens to communicate with spirits, which just makes you way better at your job than the rest of us. I, for one, think that's commendable. Judging from your success rate with the BPD—and what you just told me about my nana—you could've just as easily chosen a different path in life and cashed in on your gifts. Yet here you are. Not seeking fame or fortune. You've kept your gift a secret all these years, which was no easy task, I'm sure. You're using your gift to find murderers and bring them to justice."

"I don't get it." Reid shook her head, unconvinced. "How can you have any respect for me as a homicide detective after what I just told you?"

"I don't have *less* respect for you. I have *more*. Now I feel like I know who you really are, at your core."

"Shit, London. Is the glass ever half empty with you?" She was fully aware she'd just lost the no-cussing challenge but too wound up to give a rat's ass.

"You just forfeited the keys to Boyle's truck."

She sighed. "Fuck." She'd probably never get another chance to drive Boyle's truck.

"Given the circumstances, I can probably overlook one little slip."

"Might want to hold off on forgiving me for my transgressions, at least until you hear what I have to say next." She hadn't even gotten to the part about the governor and wasn't sure how London would take it. Reid turned the heater down and met London's gaze in the dark. "Boyle refused my resignation. Instead, he pushed a mandatory two-week vacation on me. I went home, fully intending to resubmit my resignation once the two weeks had passed, but then the governor called me. He threatened to rescind my pension if I didn't keep working for the department."

"He can't do that," London shouted. "That's blackmail."

The rookie hit the nail on the head. The governor had, indeed, blackmailed her. She decided to come clean and tell London about her part in helping the captain end his own life.

"Did you pull the trigger?" London asked.

"Of course not." Was that even a serious question?

"Were you present in the room when he pulled the trigger?"

"No." She never would have agreed to that, and the captain never would have asked.

"All you're guilty of is allowing a terminally ill man to end his life on his own terms."

"Precisely. I knew about it and did nothing to stop him."

"But what if you did?"

"But I didn't."

"But what if you did?"

"How can I say I did if I didn't?"

"All I'm saying is there's plausible deniability there. That's all." Besides, in order to run with this, the governor would have to reveal he's illegally wiretapping his own police department. That wouldn't go over well with all our brothers in blue. He has nothing. You should've called his bluff."

Reid raised an eyebrow. "If I'd called his bluff, I wouldn't be here working the case with you right now."

"Good point. Glad you didn't call his bluff."

Reid pondered how to reveal the rest of what she knew about London's parents. Brief and to the point had always worked best for her.

"There's something you should know about the governor," London said, beating her to the punch. "He's my godfather."

The governor had failed to mention that. "Shit. No way."

"Strike two." London frowned. "One more, and those keys are mine indefinitely."

"Knee jerk. My bad." For once, she wasn't sure how to proceed with London. Was this rookie in the governor's pocket, too?

"I've known him my whole life, but I never really liked him. Money, power, prestige—that's all he cares about."

Reid swore she saw the wheels as they turned furiously inside London's head.

"Oh. My. God." London regarded her, wide-eyed. "Did he force you to train me?"

"Sort of. Your parents asked him to make sure you were assigned to me for your training."

"My parents?" London's forehead creased in confusion. "They haven't talked to me in ten years. How'd they even know I made detective?"

"He said they've been keeping tabs on you. They wanted to help."

"I don't need their help." London narrowed her eyes. "Never did."

"Truer words were never spoken."

"I've never once accepted a favor to get ahead on the job," London said defensively.

Reid put her hands up in surrender. "I told him you were quite capable of clearing your own path in life. Pretty sure you came out of the womb with a tiny machete in your hands."

The tension finally broken, London threw her head back and laughed.

Reid had to admit, it felt good to lay everything on the table so they could sift through the pieces together. Better than good, actually. For the first time in her life, she felt like she had someone beside her who truly knew her. Which was crazy, she realized, because they'd met just days ago. "Anyway, now you know everything I do."

"Everything?"

"All my skeletons are out." Reid sighed, feeling cleansed for the first time in a long time. Maybe for the first time ever.

"Good." London nodded, seemingly satisfied. "Now it's my turn to share a secret with you."

London's mind was still reeling from the fact that Reid could actually communicate with spirits. She never in a million years would have guessed *that* was Reid's big secret. She hadn't even realized such a thing was possible. Being able to hear a message from her nana was the most beautiful gift she'd ever received.

Reid had demonstrated unfathomable courage by sharing the secret behind her success as a homicide detective. It was time for London to show her the same courtesy and trust.

She took a deep breath. Part of her could hardly believe what she was about to divulge. She'd never told a soul, aside from her parents. After they disowned her and froze her out of the family, she promised herself she'd take this secret to her grave.

❖

Reid listened intently as London opened the closet to reveal her own skeletons.

"I was eighteen. I'd just graduated from high school and was heading to Harvard in the fall. Bill Sullivan threw a huge end-of-summer party at his mansion every year. My parents and I had been attending his parties as far back as I can remember. We always stayed overnight in his guestrooms." London hesitated. "I remember the party. I remember Bill handing me a Shirley Temple at the end of the night. We talked for a while about Harvard, and I remember suddenly not feeling well. Headache, nausea, confusion. He acted concerned and walked me to my room. I remember nothing after that until I woke up the next morning."

"Someone spiked your drink," Reid said. "Sounds like Rohypnol."

"That's what I thought, too." London nodded. "I woke up naked. It was obvious someone'd had their way with me. Even so, I doubted myself, questioned my recollection of events, and eventually brushed the whole thing off and made myself forget. Until eight weeks later when I discovered I was pregnant."

Reid was stunned. She sat in rapt attention.

"When the pregnancy test came back positive, I could hardly believe it. I'd already come out to my friends during my junior year but just hadn't gotten around to telling my parents yet. I'd never had a boyfriend or had sex with a man—at least, not consensually. I kept telling myself it wasn't Bill. He was my godfather. He'd known me since I was a baby. I finally told my parents. I told them everything I remembered, well, except my suspicions about Bill, but they didn't believe me. They said I was making it up to avoid taking accountability for my own irresponsible behavior."

"Have they met you?" Reid interjected, furious.

"My parents must have said something to Bill because he met me on campus one day. He said he believed me—that something had happened without my consent. But he swore up and down he would never do such a thing because I was like a daughter to him. He vowed to find out who did it and encouraged me to consider getting an abortion. He even offered to pay for it. I was still trying to decide what to do when I had a miscarriage. Bill was so solicitous, so obviously relieved. And I was even more certain then that he'd assaulted me, so I confronted him."

Reid found herself irrationally hoping London would say she'd told her parents the whole truth about Bill. In an ideal world, they would've hired someone to beat his ass and then prosecuted him to the fullest extent of the law. But she knew, without a doubt, it hadn't happened that way. Because Bill Sullivan was currently serving as the elected governor of Massachusetts.

"Bill lurked around my life for a few weeks after. One day he met me outside a friend's house and threatened to ruin my father if I dared to go public with my story. He said he had evidence that my father had committed tax fraud and would serve prison time if that evidence came to light. He said I should tell my parents I'd made the whole thing up about getting drugged." London shrugged. "So that's what I did."

"And they disowned you?" Reid asked, incredulous.

"Not exactly. I also told them I'd had an abortion and was a lesbian. They raised me as a strict Catholic, and I'd basically committed every damnable sin in one fell swoop: sex before marriage, lying to my parents, abortion, and homosexuality. Who could really blame them?"

"Me," Reid stated matter-of-factly. "They're your parents. They should've known you better than that."

"At the time, I knew my coming out would be too much for them to handle, which is what I wanted. I needed to distance myself from them so I could live the life I wanted. Essentially, I'd killed two birds with one stone. Bill and my parents were both out of my life."

"Did you like your parents?"

"Of course. I loved them. Still do."

"Well, then, I think the more fitting expression is, you threw out the baby with the bathwater. You got rid of Bill—a great decision, by the way—along with your parents."

"I know. I still miss them."

"Have you told anyone else about this?"

"No." London shook her head. "You're the first and only. After you shared your two biggies, I figured it was time for me to share mine."

They locked gazes in the darkened car. The moment was intense. It reminded Reid of a childhood friendship she'd once had. They'd pricked their fingertips to draw blood and then pressed them together to seal their friendship. Something told her she and London had just done the same. She put the car in Drive. "Care to accompany me to the governor's mansion to bestow a proper ass-whuppin' that's long overdue?"

London grinned. "I would *love* to say yes, but our time would be better spent elsewhere."

Reid couldn't imagine another way she'd rather spend her time right now. Not only would it teach the governor a lesson, but it would also give her the chance to let off some steam.

"Let's head back to the precinct," London said, already buckling her seat belt. "We have a shot at finding Mug if we can figure out the connection between Gil and the killer."

London was right. She owed it to Mug to do everything in her power to find him and bring him back home. They'd been sitting in the car for over an hour. There was still no sign of her best friend. Part of her was afraid to leave the spot where he was stolen. What if the killer planned to return Mug to this very same place later on tonight, and then arrived to find her gone? Would that piss him off even more? Send him over the edge?

Reid realized she wasn't thinking rationally. By allowing her action—or inaction—to be dictated by fear, she was playing right into the killer's hands. It was foolish to believe anything she did or didn't do at this point would affect Mug's outcome. The killer had already made up his mind. Nothing she did now would change that.

CHAPTER SEVENTEEN

Reid stepped into the elevator with London and pressed the button for the fourth floor. It felt strange not having Mug by her side. Like an extension of her own body, he'd diligently assumed his post on her left for years. There was a deep and indescribable void without him that caught her off guard. She swallowed the lump at the back of her throat.

London reached out and gave her hand a reassuring squeeze. "We'll find him."

She met London's gaze and squeezed back. "We better."

When they stepped off the elevator, the floor was dark and quiet. A lone janitor was shuffling down the line of desks in the center of the room, emptying small wastebaskets into a large yellow trash can on wheels. Everyone had already gone home for the night.

Reid walked over to her desk and flipped on the computer. First thing she intended to do was run Gil's name through the Department of Children and Families. If he'd been abused as she suspected, the abuse had, quite possibly, occurred when he was in the system. Maybe that's where Gil and the killer had met. She turned to London. "What if they're not killing as a team?"

"And killing separately?" London shook her head. "Doesn't seem likely—not with Gil's fragile psychology."

"No, I mean…what if the killer isn't showing possessive tendencies at all?" She perched on the edge of her desk to face London. "What if he's trying to protect Gil?"

"Like an older brother," London finished, following her train of thought.

Reid picked up the printout of Gil's record. There was no one listed for next of kin. He'd been placed in foster care at eight years old. "Wouldn't necessarily have to be blood related."

"Maybe they met when they were kids, and the killer thinks of him as a brother."

"Could be they were in the foster system together. Both abused. Both helpless to do anything about it. One gave up and turned submissive. One turned—"

"Into a vicious serial killer," London finished. "I think you're on to something."

"We," Reid corrected her. "*We're* on to something."

They turned in unison at the sound of a cell phone ringing across the room. The janitor slipped a phone from his coveralls, answered, and threw a questioning glance in their direction. He ambled over. "You Detective Sylver?"

Reid nodded, her hand moving to the gun on her hip. She'd seen this particular janitor here for years. But suddenly, everyone was suspect. The realization that the killer had probably been stalking her—watching her and listening in on her private conversations for God knew how long—hit her and hit her hard. The world would never feel quite the same again. She felt fear and anger doing battle inside her, both vying for alpha status. But she'd be damned if she let them take over when so much was on the line.

The janitor took a step back, carefully set the phone on the edge of her desk, and held his hands up defensively. "No clue who it is, but he's asking for you."

Reid picked up the phone and hit *Speaker*. Her heart raced as she thought about Mug. "Sylver," she answered in as calm a voice as she could muster.

"This is getting old," the killer said. "To stay in touch and communicate effectively, we need phones."

"Me not having a phone doesn't seem to be an obstacle for you," she said, massaging his fragile ego to make him feel superior.

"You're right. It's not. I could track you anywhere. It's just more of an annoying inconvenience. To be perfectly frank, it's siphoning my time from other activities that I find more enjoyable."

"Such as?" She knew from experience that small talk not only served to put a perp at ease, but it could also reveal information that might prove helpful later on.

"You must know about my preferred activities by now. I'm sure the ME has filled you in on the details."

This seemed like an invitation to talk about his necrophilia, but she'd have to handle him with kid gloves. With Mug still in his possession, she couldn't afford to say anything remotely offensive. He clearly wanted as much power over her as possible. If she had any hope of catching this sonofabitch, it was important she let him have that power. People who were intoxicated with power, like those drunk on alcohol, inevitably let their guard down and were more prone to making mistakes.

"He did," she said, careful to keep her tone neutral. "He said you rid both bodies of all organs and fluids before depositing your own."

Looking rather pale, the janitor backed away and sat in a nearby chair.

"Depositing my own?" the killer asked mockingly. "How poetic. You should be the one taking that creative writing class, not O'Leary."

She clenched her jaw. So he'd been listening in on her conversations at the precinct, too. How many cases were now compromised as a result? "What term would you prefer me to use?"

"Detective Sylver, I *freed* both bodies of all their organs and fluids and then *christened* them with a gift from my own body."

An interesting choice of words to be contemplated later. "Why them?" she asked, curious to hear his answer.

"Why not?"

"You know what I like about talking to dead people?"

"What?" he asked, taking the bait.

"They don't judge me. They don't ask questions about my life or pry into anything personal. There's always a safe distance there because I'm the one in control. They're the ones coming to me for help, and that's the way I like it." She thought for a moment, the brief silence heavy with anticipation. "Were you trying to help them?"

"They were looking for redemption, so I gave it to them."

"Redemption for what?"

"*But I say unto you, that whosoever looketh on a man to lust after him hath committed adultery with him already in her heart.*"

London grabbed a piece of paper, scribbled something, and held it up for Reid.

Matthew 5:28. But he changed woman to man.

Nodding, Reid remembered the Gospel of Matthew perfectly. She recited the next verse from memory. *"And if thy right eye offend thee, pluck it out, and cast it from thee: for it is profitable for thee that one of thy members should perish, and not that thy whole body should be cast into hell."*

"I'm impressed. You know your Scripture."

Good. She'd earned his respect. This was as good a time as any to ask for something. "What should I call you?"

"I already told you. You can call me The Giver."

"No. Too weird for me." She sighed. "If we'll be chatting on a regular basis, I need a name. Your real name."

He was silent for so long that she wondered if she'd pushed too hard. "Matthew," he whispered.

Her knee-jerk reaction was not to believe him. Having just referenced Matthew in the Bible, he'd probably just grabbed the first name that occurred to him. But she remained quiet and gave herself a beat or two to let the name settle. Something told her he was telling the truth. "Matthew's a nice name." She was flying by the seat of her pants now. "You can drop *Detective Sylver*. Just call me Reid."

"You haven't even asked about your stupid dog."

"Figured you'd bring it up when you were ready," she said nonchalantly. Her back bristled at the word *stupid*. Mug was anything but.

"It's damn ugly, Reid."

"I know. That's why it's mine." Objectifying Mug felt like a betrayal, but she knew it was important to follow the killer's lead. Humanizing Mug would mean she cared about him, effectively canceling the rapport she'd just built with Matthew. He was a psychopath, through and through—incapable of experiencing empathy, compassion, or even the most basic of human emotions. He was obviously intelligent and most likely aware of this abnormality in his own psychology. Dangling her feelings in his face when he didn't have any would only highlight his inadequacies and anger him. She was also making the point that she'd taken Mug in because he was an outcast. A reject. Just like he was. If she could accept something as ugly as Mug, maybe the killer would believe she could accept him, too.

"Why didn't you just put it out of its misery when you had the chance?"

"You should know by now I don't do something just because other people think I should." She waited for a beat before going on, letting her words sink in, letting Matthew relate. "I'd never throw something away because people think it's ugly. Something so ugly is beautiful in its own way. Like a rare piece of art. It'd be a shame to throw it away just because it's different."

He breathed into the phone.

Reid knew this was the make-or-break moment for Mug. The killer was now contemplating Mug's fate.

"Go home, Reid," he said.

She heard a click, and then he was gone. With a quick look at London, she set her finger over her lips. She tossed the phone back to the janitor and grabbed a notepad from her desk drawer. *Heading home,* she wrote as London looked on. *Have a feeling he's returning Mug.*

London grabbed a pen off a nearby desk and wrote a reply. *I'm coming with you.*

Reid shook her head. *Go home. Sleep. But be careful. Eyes and ears open. Meet at my place, 7 a.m. Start fresh tomorrow.*

London looked skeptical. *What if he comes after you?*

He won't.

London frowned, apparently unconvinced.

Check in at 3.

How? No phones.

Email, Reid proposed.

London thought about it for a moment and nodded. *Coming over if I don't hear from you.*

The last thing she needed was a beautiful late-night visitor to her home. That would only distract her from the case. *Careful going home,* Reid warned her. Instincts told her London was more at risk of becoming the killer's next target than she was. She didn't think he wanted *her* dead, but she sensed he was conflicted. It was clear he wanted to exert power over her and make her suffer. At the same time, he also wanted her to relate to and accept him. He wouldn't harm her—at least not until he figured out exactly what it was he wanted from her.

You, too, London wrote back. *Hope Mug comes home safe.* She set the pen down and stepped closer, wrapping her arms around Reid.

Taken aback by the unexpected gesture, Reid froze.

London whispered in her ear, "I promise you won't spontaneously combust if you hug me back."

"I might…if you squeeze me any harder," she whispered back, choosing, against her better judgment, to return the tight embrace. She couldn't remember the last time someone had actually hugged her.

"Sorry." London finally released her, straightened Reid's sweatshirt like a mother hen, and searched her face. "I'm just an email away if you need me, partner," she whispered.

"Me, too," Reid whispered back. Trying not to smile, she grabbed her coat and took the stairs two at a time. Felt good to have a partner. It was too early to tell for sure, but maybe the captain wasn't the only one in her corner.

London didn't last long at the precinct. She decided to head home, shower, and hit the sack. Sleep would help her mind tie up the loose ends of this case. Lying in bed, she couldn't help but think about Reid, all alone at home. Without Mug. She could only imagine what Reid was going through right now—probably wracked with guilt and beating herself up for leaving Mug in the car. After thirty minutes of tossing and turning, with sleep nowhere in sight, she decided to take a trip to Reid's house to check on her.

She'd bet anything the detective hadn't eaten since lunch. She'd pick up a pizza on the way.

Joey answered on the first ring. "Hey, sis."

"You still at the restaurant?"

"Yeah." He yawned. "Just closing up."

"Can you make me a pizza?"

"Seriously? Now?" he asked, making no effort to mask his annoyance.

"Now," she replied, unapologetic. "I'm calling in my favor."

He sighed. "You waited all this time to cash in your favor for a *pizza*?"

Joey had owed her one since his junior year in high school when he shattered a vase that had been in the Gold family for twelve generations. He was already on shaky ground with their parents for letting his grades slip, so she'd taken the hit for him. "This will make us even."

"Seems like a waste of a favor, if you ask me."

"It's not." Reid was worth this small sacrifice. "Better be *really* yummy."

"Extra yummy, coming right up."

CHAPTER EIGHTEEN

Reid arrived home to a dark house. It was the first time in six years that she walked in without Mug chomping noisily on a tennis ball beside her. The silence was definitely unwelcome. Getting a taste of what having a partner would feel like and losing her dog all in one day made her feel—it took her a few moments to identify the feeling—*lonely*. It was a totally foreign emotion. She realized then how lucky she was to have made it through forty years without ever having felt this.

Because it really sucked.

So, this is where you live.

She spun around to see the captain standing in her living room. He was wearing the same baby-blue button-down shirt and gray slacks as when she'd last seen him. She never communicated with spirits inside her house, but she was more than happy to make an exception for Cap. "It's about time," she said, grinning. "What the hell took you so long?"

There were a lot of hoops to jump through with the Big Guy upstairs in order to pay you a visit.

"Really?" She'd never asked a spirit anything whatsoever about the other side. She always figured she'd find out for herself, sooner or later. This time, though, she was unable to vanquish her curiosity. "God's really a man?"

No, no, Cap said, frowning. *That's the Bigger Guy upstairs. Haven't met him yet. Or her. Have no idea on the gender…or if there even is one. I'm talking about my guardian angel. Tall guy, angry face, huge wings. Hey, did you know everyone has a guardian angel? Mine was pretty pissed that I, you know, took my own life. Thanks for the heads-up on that, by the way. A lot of help you were*, he said with a scowl.

Right. She'd forgotten about that part. Reid knew there was no hell to speak of, but she'd neglected to consider how suicide would affect Cap's welcoming committee on the other side.

His lecture was longer than all Ma's lectures combined. Cap set his hands on his hips, shaking his finger at her. *Life is a gift. Every life has a purpose. All suffering has meaning. It's not our place to decide when to call it quits. Blah, blah, blah.*

"Pretty important stuff. Hope you paid attention."

I did. But enough about me. It's you I'm worried about, kid.

"How much do you know?" she asked, grateful to have someone to talk to in her too-quiet house.

I know there's a killer on the loose, and he has Mug. That's about it, I'm afraid. They have this rule over here about free will. We're not allowed to interfere. Supposed to let humans make their own choices, let things unfold naturally. If we see someone making a mistake, even if it's a big one, we can't interfere. I had to swear to it. That's the only way they'd let me come see you.

Reid found herself wondering who *they* were but decided it wasn't important. "Do you know who the killer is," she asked, "and where I can find him?"

No. I only know he's dangerous. I'm allowed to give you a warning to be careful. Oh, and maybe consider leaning on your partner a little. I like her, he said with a wink. He turned, as if hearing someone's voice on the other side. *Probably shouldn't have said that last part.* He took a few steps back and gave her a salute. *Gotta run. See you soon, kid.*

Just like every other spirit she'd met, he vanished on the spot. The air around her felt suddenly devoid of energy. Once again, Reid was alone.

Exhausted from the day's events, she hopped in the shower for a quick rinse and then headed to the living room to start a fire. Her house was well insulated—she'd done it herself when she'd stripped it to the studs for renovation—but she always kept the thermostat low when she was at work and hadn't bothered turning it up tonight. What was the point? She was just going to sleep anyway.

She stacked three logs in the fireplace, wedged several crumpled-up pages from *The Boston Globe* beneath the logs, and then set everything ablaze. Curled up with a blanket on the couch, she stared into the flames for long minutes. She couldn't stand the thought of sleeping in her bed without Mug there beside her.

She tossed and turned on the couch, convinced sleep was forever beyond her reach until Mug returned. Even with the crackling fire, the house was just too damn quiet. She finally sat up, turned on the TV, and channel surfed.

Her stomach growled. She hadn't eaten since lunch. At this time of night, she'd usually have a bowl of popcorn in her lap with Mug beside her. Sharing their favorite late-night snack, they'd watch old reruns of *NYPD Blue*. But she couldn't even bring herself to make the popcorn, let alone eat it. Not without her best bud.

She felt her adrenaline kick in and switched off the TV, suddenly angry with herself for putting Mug in harm's way. Not knowing if he was okay was driving her nuts. How would she live with herself if something happened to him?

Deciding a brisk stroll around the neighborhood would do her good, she stood from the couch. The doorbell rang, and she froze. Could this be the killer returning Mug? No one ever came to her door. She checked her watch: 11:02 p.m.

She crept silently across the living room in her bare feet. Careful not to touch the door for fear of making a creak, she peered through the peephole.

London smiled and waved.

Maybe, if she was quiet, London would give up and go away. All she had to do was wait her out.

"I know you're looking through the peephole, Reid."

Reid held her breath, determined to ride this out in stealthy silence. The trick here was to remain quiet and make London believe she was dead.

"If you don't open this door in thirty seconds, I'll break a window and climb in to make sure you're okay. And this time, I'll really do it."

She sighed, half intrigued at the prospect of having company and half annoyed at the unexpected visit. "You again?" she called out through the door.

"Me again," London replied with a thumbs-up.

Reid made no motion to open the door. She simply continued to stare through the peephole.

"I realize your social skills are a little rusty," London said, "but the next step in being a courteous human is to open the door and invite me inside."

"Sure, I'll invite you in…on the eve of Saint Never's Day," she shot back. "We already went over this. No visitors."

London rolled her eyes. "Is Mug back?"

"No."

"I figured you'd have a hard time sleeping tonight without him," London said sincerely.

"And you decided the solution to that was to linger on my doorstep like a stalker?"

"Not exactly. Though I am feeling kind of stalkerish at the moment, which is being compounded by your refusal to open the door like a normal person." London held up a large white pizza box. "I bear gifts. Let me in, and I'll share."

Reid crossed her arms, her stubbornness overriding her growling stomach. "Not hungry."

"I can hear your stomach from here." London lowered the pizza and frowned. "Have you eaten anything since lunch?"

"Where the hell did you find a pizza place open this time of night?"

"I have connections," was all London offered. "Since you're hungry and not going to sleep anytime soon, how about pizza and a movie?" She held up *A Dog's Purpose* in front of the peephole.

"A sappy movie about a dog who dies over and over again? You suck at this supportive partner thing."

"Correction: it's about a dog who's reincarnated and eventually reunited with his owner."

"Great. Thanks for spoiling the movie. Now I definitely don't want to see it."

"Will you just open the door, Reid? I'm freezing my buns off out here."

She paused, wondering if she'd heard London right. "Your what?"

"My buttocks, derriere, booty, caboose—whatever you want to call it—is freezing as we speak."

She shook her head. "You mean, your *ass*?"

"Sure." London shrugged. "I've heard it called that, too."

Reid set her hands on her hips. "I'm not opening this door unless you say it."

"Say what?"

"Ass."

"You know I don't curse, Reid."

"Then my door stays closed."

"Fine." London stepped closer to the peephole. "You know what's now numb from impending hypothermia? My *ass*. Happy?"

"Damn." Reid sighed. "I didn't think you'd say it."

"Come on. Just open the door. This beer's getting heavy."

"Beer? You didn't say anything about beer."

"Samuel Adams, Octoberfest." London held the case aloft. "That's the one you like, right?"

"Some detective you are." She reached out to unlock the door. "Could've saved us both a lot of time if you'd just led with that."

Reid led London to the kitchen in her bare feet and grabbed the bottle opener from a drawer. She cracked open two bottles, then handed one to London.

"Thanks." London took a sip and turned in a full circle. "This kitchen is beautiful. Will you give me a tour of the rest of the house?"

"Nope." Reid wasn't in the mood to be hospitable. She was hungry and tired, and her dog was missing.

"How about pizza and a movie first, then a tour?" London removed her coat and draped it over a nearby barstool. Her blond hair was wet, presumably from a recent shower. She was wearing dark gray sweats and a matching Harvard sweatshirt.

Reid took a long drink from her bottle and narrowed her eyes. "Why do you want to see my house so bad?"

"Plates?" London asked.

She pointed to a cabinet near the fridge.

"Do you want the truth, which might sound kind of creepy on the heels of this impromptu visit, or do you want the less creepy, more socially acceptable answer?"

Reid smiled, amused. "I'm a homicide detective who talks to the dead. Obviously, I'm going with creepy."

London set two blue dinner plates on the counter, lifted the pizza box lid, and served each of them a slice. "Napkins?"

Reid pointed toward the sink. "Paper towels."

London tore off two paper towels and folded them neatly in half. She tucked one under each plate, then handed Reid hers. "I'd like to learn more about you."

She laughed, "Like you don't know enough now?" London was already privy to the two wrecking-ball secrets in her life. What the hell else did she expect to find?

The rookie shrugged. "I want to know more."

"Why?" she pressed.

"Creepy alert, dead ahead." London cast her chestnut-brown gaze on Reid, suddenly serious. "I've had a crush on you for years."

Reid stared at her, waiting for the punch line. "Years? You can't be serious."

"Dead. I warned you it was creepy." London took a bite of her pizza and daintily wiped at the corners of her mouth. "I figure, if I learn more about you, maybe I won't like you as much."

Reid belched. "There. How's that?"

London stared at her.

"I can fart, too, if that'll help."

London shook her head and laughed. "Wish it was that simple. So far, nothing has thrown me off course. You're smart, sexy, brutally honest. What you see is what you get with you. You're not afraid of what other people think—"

"Oh, I'm plenty afraid," Reid corrected her. "I'm just better than most at covering it up and making it seem like I don't give a shit." How could this crazy-beautiful rookie have a crush on *her*? The moment felt surreal. She chugged the rest of her beer and set the empty bottle on the counter. Butterflies took flight in her stomach. "This is turning into one of those sappy friend moments, isn't it?"

"Only yourself to blame. You chose creepy."

"I don't do relationships, London. I do one-night stands. And I never, *ever* return their calls the next day like I promised."

"I know that, too. Word gets around. Do you have anything else that'll make you less palatable?"

Reid stared at the floor in contemplation. "I play the cello," she admitted, looking up.

"I said *less* palatable. Not more."

"Naked," she added. "Except for the socks."

London raised an eyebrow.

"I'm kidding. Playing the cello is weird enough. Just thought that might make the con list."

London set her beer down and stepped in front of Reid with the bold confidence of a seductress. "Tell me you don't feel this."

Reid would be lying if she said she didn't.

It was no use. London couldn't keep her crush under wraps any longer. Who was she kidding? This was way more than a crush. A glutton for punishment, she'd been steadily falling for Reid since the moment she set eyes on her five years ago. Could you really love someone from afar, without even knowing them? Of course not, she told herself. But getting to know Reid had only made her feelings stronger. As irrational as it was, she knew she was falling in love.

CHAPTER NINETEEN

L ondon was standing so close that Reid could feel her body heat and smell her perfume. She studied London's lips and wondered what it would feel like to kiss her. "You're gorgeous, smart, witty, resilient, and about the only cop I can think of who's tough enough to put up with me."

London inched closer, pressing her hips against Reid's and trapping her against the granite countertop.

She grabbed London's shoulders, spun her around so they'd traded places in the blink of an eye, and held her firmly in place against the counter. She needed this rookie to understand what was at stake. "If we go here, London, you *will* get hurt. I know me. You don't. For Christ's sake, my longest relationship is with a dog."

"Just because you've never been in a relationship doesn't mean you can't have one."

"I know my limits. If you're looking for a one-night stand, I'm totally game. It'll be amazing because our chemistry is off the charts. I'd love nothing more than to distract myself right now with sex. But beyond that, there's nothing here for you."

"You make it sound like you have no choice in the matter."

"I don't." Realizing her grip was too firm, she released London's shoulders. "I'm damaged goods, London. You should stay away from me. A six-month partnership with occasional sappy friend moments is one thing. Venturing anywhere beyond that is just stupid. You'd be like Moses, wandering around the desert for forty years. Except you'd be wandering out there *way* longer." She paused, trying to decide how best to drive her point home. "Wandering around the desert all by yourself. No food. No water. No sunscreen—"

London held up a hand to stop her. "I get the analogy." She stepped closer and searched Reid's face. "Is that really what you believe?"

"It's not a belief. It's fact." She took a step back, trying to put some physical distance between them. "I don't trust anyone. Never have. Never will. Listen to what I'm saying, London. You won't be able to fix me. Don't even bother trying." She turned and cracked open another beer.

"I wasn't planning to. You're already fixing yourself."

"What the hell planet are you on?"

London crossed her arms. "Have you ever turned down a one-night stand before?"

"With a woman as beautiful as you? No, never." She let her eyes travel the length of London's body, shaking her head as she questioned her own sanity. Even in sweats, London was sexy as hell. "And it's not easy, believe me."

"My point exactly."

Reid took a long drink and waited for London to explain what the hell she was talking about. But the rookie just stared at her as if she already knew. "Points are best made when they're comprehended by the party they're intended for. Care to clue me in?"

"Let me put it this way. Not to be crude, but do you want to have sex with me?"

"Of course, that's a no-brainer. Look at you. Who wouldn't?"

"Then why are you holding back?"

"How bad is your memory?" Reid sighed. "I just told you."

"And I remember every word. Just do me a favor and answer the question. But this time, give me an abbreviated answer. CliffsNotes, if you will." London uncrossed her arms and stepped in front of Reid, closing the distance between them once more. She set her hands on Reid's hips and pulled her so close that their noses were practically touching.

Reid didn't resist.

"Why are you holding back?" London whispered.

She felt her mind shift gears. Feelings of anger gave way to raw, carnal cravings. And there was something else there, too. Something she hadn't felt before and couldn't immediately identify.

Longing.

She found herself wanting to be something more than who she was…for London. "I'm afraid," she admitted.

"Of what?"

"Hurting you." She could feel London's breath on her neck. Her perfume was more intoxicating than the beer. "And losing the only sappy friend I've ever had."

"See?" London grinned. "You're fixing yourself."

"How does me feeling afraid mean I'm fixing myself?"

"You said you've never trusted anyone. After what you told me about your past—about growing up with your grandmother—you have all the reason in the world not to trust anyone. Yet here we are." London paused, her eye contact steady, strong, and alluring.

It felt to Reid like London was seeing her for who she truly was, and she wasn't put off in the least.

"You're feeling scared because you've taken a risk," London went on. "The risk of caring. The risk of trusting that someone will care about you."

Reid couldn't hold herself back any longer. She pressed her lips against London's for a sweet, slow kiss. She'd kissed countless women in her life, but this kiss felt different. There was anticipation, respect, uncertainty, partnership. Kissing London, she decided, was both hot and intimidating in a way she'd never before experienced.

Her mind and body reeling, she set her hands over London's jawline to draw her closer and patiently waited for an invitation inside. She didn't have to wait long. London opened her mouth and invited her in.

She slipped her tongue inside London's mouth and was rewarded with a throaty gasp of pleasure. London tasted like Sam Adams. From this point forward, Reid knew she'd associate her favorite beer with her favorite kiss.

London suddenly pulled back. "Wait a minute," she said, breathless. "Before we go any further, do you have any video cameras in the house?"

"Way ahead of you," Reid said, just as winded. She pointed to the tangle of wires on the dining room table. "I already disabled everything. Laptop is powered down and buried under some blankets in a closet upstairs."

"In that case, I've always wanted to have a one-night stand on a blanket in front of the fire." London smiled seductively, took her by the hand, and led her toward the living room.

"Hold up." She paused, her feet anchored in place. "I thought the whole point of this conversation is that we're *not* doing the one-night-stand thing." Suddenly confused, disappointed, and hurt, she found herself in foreign territory. She was usually the one calling the shots when it got to this point. Here she was about to have sex with this incredible partner turned friend turned lover, and for the first time ever, she wasn't certain how to proceed.

London winked seductively and kept walking backward, pulling Reid along by her hand.

"Ah, I see what you did there. Reverse psychology. You dangled the carrot in the air and then pretended to take it away."

"Did it work?" London asked, running her hands underneath Reid's shirt, along her back, and over her bare stomach.

London's touch made her brain go fuzzy along the edges. "Actually, yes. It did. I don't want just a one-night stand with you."

London grabbed the plush queen-size blanket off the couch and set it on the floor in front of the fire. Reid watched, mesmerized by the grace and confidence with which London moved. This was a take-charge, no-nonsense woman who knew what she wanted. She'd never been with a woman quite like this before and found herself uncharacteristically nervous. She was used to being the one in charge—being in control of how much, how far, and when everything happened in bed. Something told her that was all about to change with this rookie.

She decided she needed to stop thinking of London as *the rookie*. They were beyond that now.

"How old are you, by the way?" she asked as London returned to pick up where she'd left off.

London hesitated. "Why?"

"I'm robbing the cradle here, aren't I?"

"I'm turning twenty-nine next month. Just think of me as an old soul."

"There's a twelve-year age difference?" Reid stepped back and set her hands on her hips. "No way."

"Yes way. But I don't care about that."

"You will when I'm old and wrinkled, and you're still looking like a brand-new baby chick."

London threw her head back and laughed. "Get over here, and quit being so nervous. If I didn't know any better, I'd think this was your first time."

In a way, Reid realized, it was.

London lifted her Harvard sweatshirt above her head, quickly shed her black lace bra, and stepped over to do the same for Reid.

Reid set her hands over the tops of London's to stop her. "My scars—they're bad." She'd never felt self-conscious about them before, but tonight was different. More was at stake.

Without a word, London drew off Reid's T-shirt and sports bra and tossed them aside. Meeting Reid's gaze the whole time, she ran her fingers slowly down Reid's back, around her hips, and over her stomach. "Can you feel me touching you?" London asked.

Reid nodded.

"Do your scars hurt?"

"No. Never."

"Is there anyplace you don't want me to touch?" London asked, pulling their bodies together, skin to skin, breast to breast.

Reid shook her head. Nothing, she decided, would be off-limits to this incredible woman.

"You're beautiful and sexy and amazing," London whispered. "Your scars are just part of that package." She stepped back, lowered herself to the blanket, and patted the floor beside her.

Reid didn't need to think about what she wanted to do next. Joining London on the blanket, she felt the warmth of the fire at her back. In one swift movement, she slipped London's panties off and positioned herself so that London was beneath her, thighs parted. She dove into her mouth with a fury, feeling London's wetness as she lay over her.

London writhed against her. Reid teased her way down London's body with her tongue until she found the sweet, succulent center of her core, where she made herself right at home.

❖

London lay awake, rehashing the night as she snuggled against Reid. The steady rise and fall of Reid's chest assured her she was fast asleep.

She'd been intimate with women before—she'd even had a few short-but-sweet relationships—but none of her experiences to date compared to this. Reid's skill in bed was unparalleled. But why should that surprise her? Everything else about the detective was legendary.

Knowing Reid thought of herself as damaged goods was hard to take in. Reid had so much to offer. How could she not see that? Her grandmother had obviously done a number on her. The scars that were left behind on Reid's body were severe. But they didn't detract from Reid's beauty. They were part of her.

❖

Reid's cell rang. She sat up in bed and cast a glance at the alarm clock, suddenly wide awake: 5:46 a.m. She never left her ringer on. It was always set to vibrate. She reached over and plucked the phone from the nightstand. Wait a minute. This looked like her phone, but she'd left hers with Todd in Computer Crimes. What the hell? She glanced at the caller ID: Boyle. "Sylver," she answered.

"Either I have Mug here with me, or he has a twin who's just as obsessed with those yellow bouncy things."

She swung her feet over the side of the bed. "Is he okay?"

"He's fine. Can't say the same for the governor, though."

"Dead?"

"As a dried-up worm on the concrete. And I don't use worm lightly. Turns out, he was one. I have a few other choice words to describe our late governor, but I'll spare you. Killer left a note, along with one hell of a crime scene. Head over here as soon as you can. Bring Gold with you. I need her to see this, too. Oh, and if I were you, I wouldn't eat breakfast." He gave her the governor's address and hung up the phone.

Reid turned on the bed to face London, but London was already throwing her sweatshirt over her head. "Another victim?" she asked, astute as ever.

She nodded, unsure of where to start. "Mug's okay. Boyle has him."

London sighed, visibly relieved. "Then let's go get him."

She stood from the bed, slipped into her T-shirt and boxers. "Something else you should know," she said, stepping over to London. "Bill Sullivan's dead."

London's eyes grew wide.

"Don't look at *me*. I'd love to take credit, but I can't."

London sat on the edge of the bed. "Oh my God. The killer must've heard what I told you about Bill last night in the car. But how?" She looked up as Reid sat down beside her. "We'd already shut off the phones."

Reid shook her head. "The sonofabitch must've planted a bug in the squad car when he took Mug." She didn't know how London would feel about Bill's murder. Sure, he was a swine and obviously got what was coming to him. But London had known him her whole life. He was, after all, her godfather. Reid knew, firsthand, that abusive relationships could be complicated. Even after everything her grandmother did, there had been moments as a child when she still loved her grandmother. Fiercely. "You okay?"

"I think so. Just shocked. I mean, I spent a lot of time around Bill when I was growing up. He was like a part of our family, which made what he did even more reprehensible. But I saw through him at a young age. He always seemed fake to me, you know?"

Reid nodded.

"So I kind of just…" London trailed off as she stared at the floor in thought. "I kept my distance, kept my guard up, never really invested myself in caring about him." She met Reid's gaze, her eyes haunted. "Sounds awful, doesn't it?"

"Sounds like a discerning kid who'd make a great cop someday," she said honestly.

They held eye contact for long seconds in silence. Reid had never shared this kind of moment with someone before.

"My parents—I can't imagine what they're going through right now. Bill was their best friend. There's a part of me that feels relieved he's dead," London admitted through tears.

Stunned, she realized London was thinking about her parents' loss—the same parents who'd abandoned her when she needed them most. She reached out, pulled London to her chest, and kissed her on the forehead. She had no words of comfort to offer, just the embrace.

"Hey"—London slid the cell phone from Reid's grasp and sat up—"where'd this come from?"

"He was here last night. He left it on the nightstand for me while we were sleeping." She had considered shutting it off after the phone call from Boyle, but what was the point? The killer was obviously adept at surveillance. She could take extreme precautions and drive herself crazy thinking about all the ways he could be monitoring them. But something told her it wouldn't make a bit of difference.

CHAPTER TWENTY

Reid watched as London shot up from the bed to check her gun belt on the chair. "Still loaded," she said. "He could've killed us while we were sleeping."

"He could've." She nodded. "But he didn't."

London stared at her like she'd completely lost her mind. "Why aren't you freaking out right now and searching the house?"

"Because he's long gone. And freaking out won't do us any good. He feeds on fear. He wants to make us afraid so we alter our normal behavior. He wants us to think he's all powerful, unstoppable. But he's not."

"Do you think he saw us last night?" London bit her lip uncertainly.

"I don't know. But if he did, it doesn't take away from how amazing it was." She stepped over to London and kissed her. It felt good to kiss the woman she'd made love to the night before—better than making a hasty departure in the wee hours as her one-night lover slept. She slipped her tongue inside London's mouth, flashing back to the groans of ecstasy that her tongue had elicited the night before. "I won't let him ruin what we shared last night."

London smiled against her lips. "Agreed."

Through sheer force of will, Reid released London and set her mind on the case. "From now on, we stop taking measures to keep him from monitoring us. Seems like wasted energy anyway. By giving up our phones, computers, security systems—hell, even our cars—we're sacrificing valuable resources that we could be using to our advantage." She set her hands on her hips. "So if he wants to watch us hunt him down and put him behind bars, we should let him."

Despite the fact that a psychopathic serial killer had just been inside her home, Reid felt calm and in control. Part of the reason for that, she knew, was because Mug had been safely returned and was now in Boyle's capable hands. She suspected the other reason had to do with something she'd never thought possible: she was falling in love.

❖

Showered and changed, Reid and London drove together in Boyle's truck to the governor's mansion.

"Massachusetts is one of only three states that's never had an official governor's mansion," London explained. "That is, until Bill came along. He donated his just before the election and bragged quite a bit about it on the news. I swear his sole motivations in life were money, power, and being the center of attention."

London pulled up to the black wrought iron gates and flashed her badge to the uniformed officer. He unlocked the gate and held one side open as they drove in and parked in the circular driveway behind several patrol cars.

A brick federal colonial with stately white pillars sat in the middle of the long circular driveway. London unbuckled her seat belt, eyeing the mansion with palpable dread. "Haven't been here in a while."

Reid turned to face London in her seat. "I can take it from here if you want. Tell Boyle you had an emergency."

London bit her lip, and Reid could tell she was considering the offer.

"Don't do that," London finally said, thumping her hands on the steering wheel.

"Do what?"

"Be extra super-duper nice just because we slept together."

"You want me to go back to trying to ditch you?"

"I'd take that over being babied."

"Fair enough." Reid nodded. "For the record, though, I was still trying to ditch you. This time, I was just being nice about it."

The tension broken, London laughed.

They sat in the truck for long seconds, staring at the mansion in silence. London took a deep breath and looked over at Reid. "Let's do this. And you don't have to keep checking in with me to make sure I'm okay. I'll talk about it later with you if I need to."

"Copy that," she said, impressed with London's directness. She liked that London put everything on the table. No guessing games with this one.

The front door of the mansion opened. Boyle stepped out, cupped his hands around his mouth, and shouted, "What the hell's taking you two so long?" Mug was there beside him.

Reid frowned, wondering what would possess Boyle to allow Mug inside a crime scene. It wasn't like him to be so careless. She threw open the truck door and stepped out as Mug trotted over. White booties were fastened to each of his paws with duct tape. Boyle's handiwork, no doubt. She knelt down and hugged him tightly.

Mug appeared unharmed, but she'd already made up her mind to take him to the vet for a thorough exam. She'd be sure never to let him out of her sight until the killer was caught.

"Where'd you find him?" she asked Boyle as they approached.

"Inside. Neighbors heard a dog barking. They knew the governor didn't have a dog, so they called us. Patrol officers entered to do a wellness check and found the governor's body. Here, you'll want these." He handed each of them a pair of white booties and latex gloves. "I should warn you, it isn't pretty. All my years in homicide, I've never seen anything so gruesome." He threw a glance at London. "Brace yourself."

She and Boyle had witnessed unspeakable atrocities over the course of their careers, so she knew it must be bad.

"This way," he said. "Don't know how Mug managed to stay out of the blood, but he didn't have a drop on him anywhere that I could find."

Early on, Reid had trained Mug to sidestep puddles. Which hadn't been difficult because he wasn't a big fan of water. She guessed now that he'd simply avoided the blood, out of habit.

"Didn't want him at the crime scene," Boyle went on, "but I wasn't about to put him in my car. Not after what happened." Reid had notified Boyle of Mug's abduction the night before. It was the right thing to do. Boyle was just as invested in Mug as she was.

He led them through the foyer and up a granite split-marble

staircase with massive pillars on each side. On a normal day, under normal circumstances, the mansion's decadence would be of interest to her—an architectural marvel to behold. But Reid refused to let herself be corrupted by the grandiosity of her surroundings. She took everything in with the cool, detached eyes of a cop, reminding herself that she was in the devil's lair.

"From what I can tell, Governor Sullivan was tortured in his office and then dragged through the house, piece by piece, to his final resting place in an upstairs guest bedroom."

Smears of blood snaked along the marble stairs. She and London were careful not to step on them.

Boyle stood beside a closed door and paused with his hand on the ornate golden doorknob. "Don't say I didn't warn you." He took a deep breath and opened the door.

The governor's naked, blood-soaked body lay in the middle of a king-size bed. His wrists and ankles were tied to the headboard and footboard with expensive-looking silk ties. All of his fingers were missing—sawed off with some type of serrated blade. One-inch stumps with bony ridges and jagged flaps of skin were all that remained. Hollow eye sockets stared off into the great beyond. His nose and ears were gone. Penis and testicles were also notably absent.

This murder was remarkably different from the other two. The first two victims had been killed with meticulous precision. The governor, on the other hand, appeared to be the victim of pure unadulterated rage. If Reid didn't know better, she'd think these murders were totally unrelated.

Out of the corner of her eye, Reid noticed that Boyle seemed to be paying particular attention to London's reaction as they all stepped inside.

London put an arm over her mouth as she stepped away, turned, and threw up in the corner.

"I'll tell Forensics not to bag that as evidence," Boyle said nonchalantly as she returned to them. He handed her a small bottle of water and a stick of sugarless gum. "No need to be embarrassed. Barely made it to the toilet myself. Everyone who's set foot in here so far has lost their shit. Pardon the expression." He withdrew a second bottle of water from his coat pocket and offered it to Reid.

"I'm good, thanks," she said, declining the water.

He shook his head. "Not even this, huh?"

She was the only detective in their squad who'd never thrown up at a crime scene. "Close, but no dice," she said, patting her stomach. But even she felt a little queasy.

"We found every body part, except the genitals."

Reid pulled on her latex gloves and stepped over to the body. "Look no farther." She set her fingers over the governor's top and bottom teeth and, with substantial effort, pried his jaw apart. "Testicles are in here. Penis is lodged in his windpipe."

"Didn't think to look there." Boyle cleared his throat and looked away. "And I'm not sure I could've, even if I had thought of it."

"You said you found all the other body parts," Reid said. "Where?"

"In the den, where it looks like all this started." He led them back downstairs and through an expansive kitchen before pausing at a closed door once again. "Our governor had more dirt in his closet than he knew what to do with. I am not, by any means, condoning this bloodbath. Let's just say, I won't be losing any sleep over it."

Reid, London, and Boyle stepped inside the den. Straight from the pages of a Sherlock Holmes mystery, dark walnut surrounded them from floor to ceiling. Built-in bookshelves teeming with hardcover texts comprised two walls. Brown leather armchairs with matching ottomans sat atop a Persian rug and faced a massive stone fireplace.

This was probably where the governor spent much of his time and obviously where he was tortured. A faded eighteenth-century French tapestry had been moved aside to reveal a hidden panel in the wall. The panel lay open, exposing a large walk-in closet with empty shelves.

Reid stepped over for a closer look.

London followed at her heels. "Why would he have a hidden closet with nothing inside?"

A metal stepladder was folded up and lying on its side in the far corner of the closet. Reid slid it out, pried it open, and ascended the narrow steps. There, on the highest shelf, hidden from plain view, was a leather-bound journal. Her stomach somersaulted. She had an inkling about what was inside. For London's sake, she hoped she was wrong.

"How'd you know that was up there?" London whispered as Reid climbed back down.

"Deductive reasoning," she answered defensively. She knew what London was thinking, but no one had paid her a visit from the Great Beyond to help her this time.

"Okay." London shook her head and sighed. "Whatever you say."

She pointed to the stepladder. "Why would he hide a stepladder in a secret closet unless he needed to reach something high?"

London nodded. "Good point," she conceded. "That explains why you're the trainer, and I'm the trainee."

Even after the short time they'd worked together, she realized it wasn't like London to miss something so obvious. London was understandably distracted.

London peered over her shoulder as she flipped through the journal's pages. It was less like a journal and more like the scrapbook of a proud parent. Dozens of photos with handwritten captions filled its pages, chronicling a young girl's childhood from infancy through adolescence. The captions started out innocent enough, detailing memorable moments and milestones reached. But the caption that was written alongside a photo of the girl at her sweet-sixteen gala revealed the governor's not-so-innocent cravings.

The young girl in the journal was London.

Unable to hold herself back, Reid flipped forward to the final entry. It detailed the night he'd had his way with London when she was eighteen.

London stared at the journal in Reid's hands but said nothing. She looked like she was in shock.

"There are others," Boyle called out from across the room.

She closed the journal and scanned the empty shelves around her. "Where?"

"He kept files on all of his quote-unquote"—with a look of disgust, he made air quotes—"*conquests* in his computer."

Boyle's complete lack of surprise about the discovery of this journal was suspect. He also made no move to join them to see what was inside, which could mean only one thing: he'd already found it.

London stepped forward. "You *know*."

Boyle nodded.

❖

London closed her eyes and took a deep breath in an effort to ground herself. She was determined not to cry in front of her lieutenant. How could her own godfather have done this? She felt betrayed, humiliated, and angry all in one breath. In that moment, she hated Bill more than ever. For violating her trust. For violating her body. For standing between her and her parents for the last ten years. He'd stolen so much from her already. Now *this*.

On the heels of her anger came guilt. She glanced at Bill's computer. There were others? Had she thought for a second that he was preying on other women, she would have confronted this thing head-on. But at eighteen, she'd been inexperienced, naive, and embarrassed. She'd made the mistake of thinking it was somehow her fault. Deep down, for all these years, she'd believed she'd done or said something to encourage him. She shook her head, chastising herself. She should have known better.

Reid watched as Boyle crossed his arms and spoke to London sternly. "I need to know—one cop to another—did you kill him?"

She stepped to London's side, feeling suddenly protective. "She couldn't have killed him, Lieutenant. Gold was with me last night. We were working the case at my house and ended up crashing there. I have the leftover pizza and empty beer bottles to prove it."

London looked from Reid to Boyle. "The killer must've overheard me telling Sylver about…about what happened. But it was a long time ago, Lieutenant."

"Ten years," Reid added in London's defense.

Seemingly satisfied with London's alibi, Boyle uncrossed his arms.

"You said the governor kept files on his victims in his computer?" Reid asked.

Boyle nodded.

"Does he have one on Gold?"

Without a word, Boyle strode over to the governor's grand, ornately carved mahogany desk in the corner of the room. He leaned over, made a few clicks with the mouse, and straightened. "Not anymore."

London let out an audible breath.

"What should we do with the journal?" Reid asked, holding it up. Boyle didn't blink. "What journal?"

Reid slipped the book inside her coat pocket, grateful to Boyle on London's behalf. Cap would have done the same. Maybe her new lieutenant wasn't such a far cry from the captain, after all.

"I read the ME's report on the other two vics," Boyle went on. "Organized, meticulous, but *this*"—he gestured around the room— "this is pure rage. Totally outside his MO, if he even has one. Because now, I'm not so sure."

"He has one," Reid said. Of that she was certain. "This was just his knee-jerk reaction to a sexual predator."

"Are you saying even psychopathic killers have standards?"

"I'm saying he lost his shit on this guy after he heard what he did to London. I think our killer was physically and sexually abused as a kid by an older woman. That's why he sexually violated the first two vics postmortem."

Boyle shook his head. "Poor bastard."

Reid was anxious to find out from the ME if the killer had also sexually assaulted the governor. That would yield even more insight into his psychological profile.

Boyle pointed to the center of the desk. "He left a note for you, Sylver."

CHAPTER TWENTY-ONE

R eid and London stepped over to the governor's desk. The note was written in blood. Reid couldn't help but wonder if the killer had forced the governor to write it as he lay dying.

One less cockroach afoot. Consider this my engagement gift to you and your new partner.

It appeared the killer was aware of her involvement with London. Knowing Reid was now embarking on a relationship when his had just ended—and had, more than likely, ended against his wishes—was just too big a pill for him to swallow. No longer superior to Reid in the relationship department, he'd feel the sting of rejection even more deeply. That feeling of rejection no doubt contributed to his loss of control, inciting his violent attack on the governor.

Reid was fairly certain the governor had been tortured, that he'd been dismembered while still alive, but she wouldn't know for sure until the ME determined official cause of death. Judging from the amount of blood scattered throughout the den, it appeared as though he'd exsanguinated, and over a prolonged period of time, from the looks of it.

"What's your next step?" Boyle asked. "How can I help?"

Boyle was obviously just as anxious to get this killer off the streets. She checked her watch: 7:19 a.m. "We'll pay a visit to my good friend Wanda, over at the—"

"Department of Children and Families?" Boyle finished, snorting in disbelief. "Good luck with that. Mrs. Alinski will be *thrilled* to see you. Make sure you're wearing your vest."

Reid had brought Wanda four apple pies last year to share with the rest of her office staff. She'd been attempting to butter her up in an effort to get some quick—and rather sensitive—information for a case she was working. She'd mistakenly claimed that she made the pies herself. Problem was, she hadn't. An ex-con she'd helped put behind bars had gifted them to her after his release from prison. He'd dropped by the precinct to thank her, claiming he was a reformed man. Turned out the pies—all four of them—had been laced with a rather potent laxative. Reid had singlehandedly wiped out the entire DCF office in one fell swoop.

"Not a problem. I'm sure she's forgotten all about it by now." Since DCF didn't open their doors for another ninety minutes or so, that left her some time to swing by the vet and get Mug checked out.

Boyle cleared his throat. "How about I keep Mug with me for the day? I can drop by Angell on my way back to the station, get him looked at, and make sure he's good to go," he suggested, as if reading her mind.

Boyle kicked ass at co-parenting. Reid nodded as she stroked Mug's back and shoulders. She trusted Boyle. Mug would be safe with him. "Just do me a favor—take him to a different vet. There's someone we're looking into at Angell who might be connected to the killer," she explained. "And don't take your eyes off Mug. He's with you every second."

Boyle pointed to his overstuffed pockets. "Dog biscuits in this one. Extra tennis balls over here."

She leaned over and kissed Mug between the eyes. "You're staying with Boyle today. I'll see you later."

As she and London turned to leave, Boyle called out behind them, "Don't think I didn't notice you never showed for our workout this morning. I cut you some slack for today, but I plan to be a real dick about it next time."

"Promises, promises." She flipped him the bird and rounded the corner.

"That's going in your file, Sylver!" he shouted.

Back at Boyle's truck, London tossed her the keys. "You drive," she said.

They climbed inside and buckled their seat belts in silence. Though tempted, Reid said nothing, remembering London's request not to be babied. She reminded herself that London would talk about everything when she was ready.

"We have to find who did this to him."

Reid reached over to hold London's hand. "We will."

"Bill did terrible things, but he didn't deserve that. No one deserves that."

Reid said nothing. She wasn't sure she agreed. "Here, this is yours." She slid the journal from her pocket and handed it to London.

London set it in her lap and sighed. "Okay, lay it on me."

Reid pulled out of the governor's driveway and glanced at London, confused. "What am I laying on you?"

"On a scale of one to ten, how much does Mrs. Alinski hate your guts?"

Reid didn't hesitate. "Like…a one. Definitely a one. Barely even a one."

London rolled her eyes. "Let's stop by the precinct so we can pick up our vests."

❖

They walked through the front doors of the DCF office promptly at 8:45 a.m. Reid shifted uncomfortably in her vest. "Can't believe you talked me into wearing this thing. Killer isn't coming after us with bullets. That's not his MO."

"This isn't for him," London whispered as they checked in with security, got their visitor stickers, and strode with purpose to the elevator. "It's to give us some extra protection against Mrs. Alinski and the rest of her office. Considering everything they have to deal with, DCF workers are on edge enough as it is. Giving them pies filled with laxatives probably sent a few *over* the edge. No doubt, they'll want to grab your gun and shoot you on sight."

"You can't be serious. It's been a year. I'm sure they've forgotten all about it by now." She felt suddenly nervous. Her hands grew clammy. "Besides, I didn't do it on purpose."

"You said you were sorry, though. Right?"

"Well, no. Not exactly, but—"

"You never called to apologize? Explain what happened?"

"Cap advised me not to. Said he'd handle it."

London sighed. "I'm not sure why we even bothered coming here. No one is going to help us."

"Can't you just save the day, and do that thing you did with the nun?"

"Sister Margaret?"

"Yeah. Her."

"What thing are you referring to?"

"You know, that bonding thing you did."

"You mean when I was courteous, honest, and respectful?"

"Yeah. You're good at that stuff."

"This might come as a surprise to you, but lots of people make those behaviors part of their everyday routine. It's called basic human decency."

"How come I feel like there's a lecture coming on? Are you really mad about those pies?"

The elevator doors parted. "I just think you owe Mrs. Alinski an apology."

"It'd be insincere, so what's the point?"

"Sometimes, it doesn't matter if you mean it," London said, stepping off the elevator. "Just saying it and putting it out there for the other person does a world of good. Haven't you ever heard of karma?"

"Whatever. She probably won't even remember who I am." Reid led the way to Wanda's office. DCF workers were darting about with files, coffee mugs, and overstuffed briefcases. Thankfully, no one paid her any mind as she and London traversed the jungle of the overworked and underpaid.

She knocked on Wanda's open door and hesitated in the doorway. Wanda was just hanging her overcoat on the hook behind her desk. A plump woman with short gray hair and rose-colored glasses, she'd been on the job longer than Reid had been a cop.

"Mrs. Alinski"—Reid held up her badge—"a word, please?"

She turned and pierced Reid with a gaze that said she wasn't happy about the interruption. She crossed her arms, giving Reid a once-over. "Put on a few pounds, did we?"

"It's the vest." She pointed at London. "My partner made me wear it. She's convinced you're holding a grudge from the unfortunate misunderstanding we had last year."

"I have no idea what you're talking about."

Reid turned to London. "See? I told you."

"Better be quick." Wanda stepped over to her desk and sat down. "There are about fifty people in line ahead of you."

"Really?" Reid pretended to look around the office. "Well, they must be pretty small because I don't see them anywhere," she said, hoping to lighten the tense mood.

Shaking her head, London stepped forward, her hand outstretched. "I'm Detective Gold. We know you're busy. Hope not to take up too much of your time."

Wanda didn't bother to stand as she reached back. Her eyes quickly sized London up. "What zone?" she asked. "Green, yellow, orange, or red?"

"I beg your pardon?" London replied.

"Trivial, pressing, critical, or life-threatening? Each worker's time is in such high demand around here that we must allocate our time with the utmost care. All meetings, phone calls, and conversations are tiered according to their level of importance. If it's not in the red, then you'll have to take a seat and wait." She pointed to the sitting area immediately outside her office door.

London didn't skip a beat. "This is way beyond red."

"There's no such thing as way beyond red."

"Then you should add it. Because we're in the blinking fluorescent-green three-people-have-already-died-with-more-to-come zone, if we don't get information from you."

"That's not a recognized zone in this office. Sorry, I can't help you."

London looked dumbfounded. "But—"

"I'm kidding," Wanda retorted without even breaking a smile. "I'll reschedule my nine o'clock call." She picked up her cell phone and sent a quick text. "There. Done."

"Wanda?" A worker Reid didn't recognize rapped lightly on the door and poked his head inside. "You said we could use your office for our meeting at nine."

"Of course." Wanda grabbed her cell as she stood from the desk. "Follow me," she said, already on the move. "We can continue this discussion in another room."

She led them down the hallway to a door at the very end, scanning the keycard at her hip to unlock the door electronically. "We call this our Smash and Bash room. Workers in this office see things no human should see. As a result, we experience all the intense feelings that go along with that, including anger. Rather than stuffing it down, I encourage all workers to come in here and let loose at least once a week. We keep a sign-up sheet outside. No one's usually here at this hour. But the day is still young."

Reid looked around. The room was large with four distinct stations. Each had its own punching bag and—What was *that*? She stepped over for a closer look. There, staring back at her, was a life-size cardboard cutout of her. It was riddled with holes. "What the hell is this?"

"Is there a problem, Detective Sylver?"

"That's me!"

"No." Wanda shook her head. "You must be mistaken."

"It sure the hell is. Look!" She stood alongside the cutout of herself and assumed the same pose.

Wanda stepped over and frowned. "It does bear an uncanny resemblance."

"Uncanny resemblance my ass. That's me!" She glanced at the punching bag on her right and realized a paper cutout of her head was pinned to the top.

"There are several cutouts from which to choose." Wanda pointed to a bin alongside the punching bag. "But yours is definitely the most popular. Turns out beating you to a pulp or aiming slingshots at you is very therapeutic."

"You admit it, then." She set her hands on her hips and turned to London. "Is that even legal?"

"I admit nothing," Mrs. Alinski stated. "Only that I had to do *something* to keep my staff from seeking revenge on the officer responsible for their near-death experience."

"That was an accident! How was I supposed to know those pies were loaded with laxatives?"

"Full disclosure would have been nice. Something along the lines of, *Hi there, Mrs. Alinski. An ex-con just got sprung from the joint and gave me these lovely apple pies.* Right then and there, I would've told you to shove them where the sun doesn't shine." She crossed her arms and addressed London. "Instead, she lied and told me she baked them herself."

"No *way*," London said, looking horrified.

"Way."

London gave Reid the evil eye. "You should be ashamed of yourself."

"You can't be on her side," Reid said. "You're my partner."

"And she never said sorry," Wanda went on, still fuming. "No note. No phone call. Nothing."

"Karma," London said, raising an eyebrow in Reid's direction.

"Fine. Maybe I should've called or sent flowers or some—"

"You think?" Wanda gave her the most intimidating stare down she'd ever received, nuns included. Shaking her head in apparent disgust, she turned to London once again. "You two are partners?"

London nodded. "Unfortunately."

"Hey, I heard that." Was this the same woman who'd made passionate love to her the night before? What the hell was happening here?

"Then I imagine you'll benefit from a pass at the punching bag."

"Don't mind if I do." London slipped out of her coat and draped it over a nearby chair.

Wanda bent down and plucked Reid's likeness from the bin. "Full-body cutout or just the head?" she asked, holding each one up.

"Ooh. Definitely full body." London allowed Wanda to slide boxing gloves over her hands, then turned to Reid. "Can you please take my firearm?"

"You want me to hold your gun while you beat me up?"

London nodded happily.

Sighing, she lifted London's sweater, unsnapped the leather holster, and withdrew the Glock. "I'm sure there are cutouts of other cops in that bin, too. Aren't there?" she asked, hearing the note of desperation in her own voice.

"Nope," Wanda replied, lips pursed. "Just you."

Reid humbly took a seat. She watched, mesmerized and a little unsettled as London landed powerful blows and quick jabs, one after another, to the paper cutout of her. Could having to ride in the car behind Mug cause this type of residual anger?

After several minutes, London stopped, a little out of breath and grinning like an idiot. "Wow. That felt great."

Wanda stepped over to help London remove the gloves. "What do you need?" she asked, apparently pleased with the rookie's boxing skills.

"Can you look someone up in your system? He was in foster care for a while. We're looking specifically for the names of any individuals who might've overlapped with him in one of his foster homes."

"How many years ago?"

London looked to Reid.

Reid mentally subtracted Gil's age at the time he entered foster care—eight—from his current age—twenty-four. "About sixteen years ago," she answered.

"We kept everything on paper back then. All those files are in the basement." Wanda shook her head and sighed. "Come on. I'll take you there myself."

Chapter Twenty-two

Poor Reid. She was such a good sport, looking on helpless as London beat up her paper replica. London had done so, of course, solely for Wanda's benefit. Wanda was holding a grudge—a *big* grudge—and rightfully so. The only way they were going to get Wanda's help was if London threw Reid under the bus. Once they had what they needed, she had every intention of picking Reid up, dusting off the tire treads, and making it up to her later in the best way she knew how…with her tongue.

Flashes of their night together kept surfacing in her mind as she dug through old files in the basement. She caught Reid's eye and winked.

"I saw that," Wanda announced from across the room.

"Something in my eye," London said, squinting.

"Don't think I fell for your scam. Nope. Not for one minute. I just wanted to see how far you were willing to go to get my help."

"Good," Reid whispered to London. "Now, maybe *your* face will be added to the pile."

❖

Three hours and countless file boxes later, Reid and London were bidding Wanda farewell outside her office door.

"Wait right here," Wanda said, ducking inside to grab something from her desk drawer. She returned and held out a white keycard to London. "This unlocks the door to the Smash and Bash. Office hours are eight forty-five to four forty-five, Monday through Friday." She winked. "I know you two are getting along fine right now, but she's a troublemaker"—she pointed at Reid—"so I'm guessing that'll change in the future. When it does, feel free to drop by and beat her up."

London accepted the keycard with a grin. "Thanks."

"Don't I get one, too?" Reid asked, holding out her hand. "I'll bring my own paper cutouts. In fact, I already have someone in mind. I'll give you a hint—gray hair, glasses, and really good at holding a grudge."

Without bothering to answer, Wanda stepped inside her office, flipped Reid the bird, and slammed the door.

"She doesn't want to, but she likes me. I can tell." Reid glanced at the white keycard in London's hand as they walked to the elevator. "You're not really going to use that, are you?"

"Actually, I was planning on selling it to the highest bidder. I'm guessing there's a high demand for putting holes in your face with a slingshot."

"Funny."

London slipped her hand inside Reid's as soon as the elevator doors closed. "Thanks for being such a good sport. I had to make Mrs. Alinski believe I didn't like you so she'd help us get what we needed."

And now, thanks to London's charming ways, they had a list of names to run through—boys around Gil's age who'd come in contact with him during his years in the foster care system.

"Well, you were pretty convincing in there," Reid admitted, a little hurt.

London withdrew her hand, stepped in front of her, and gently pushed her against the elevator wall. "I'm sorry for beating up the paper you," she whispered. "I'll make it up to the real you later. I promise." She slipped her tongue inside Reid's mouth in a fury of passion, taking Reid back to her own cries of pleasure from the night before.

"Apology accepted," Reid whispered back, out of breath and feeling tingly in places she couldn't think about now as they made their way to Boyle's truck.

"Notice how the apology worked its magic?" London raised an eyebrow. "Just something to think about."

"Not so much the apology that did it as the kiss. And I am *not* apologizing to Mrs. Alinski."

"Then maybe you should kiss her."

❖

Back at the precinct, Reid and London stepped off the elevator.

"Still alive, I see," Boyle called out from his office. He stood, walked around his desk, and leaned against the doorframe. "Did you like the Smash and Bash?"

"You knew about that?" Reid asked, incredulous.

"Cap's idea," he replied.

"Unbelievable. Cap promised me he'd take care of it and smooth things over."

"And take care of it he did." He held up a paper cutout of her face. "Found a whole box of these when I was cleaning out his office."

"Hey, Lieutenant." Marino stood from his desk. "Can I get one of those? I'm heading over to the shooting range later."

"In that case, you'll want the whole-body cutout." Boyle threw a thumb over his shoulder. "In my office. Second box to the right."

Mug trotted over to greet her. Apparently eager to test out his new stash, he'd managed to fit two tennis balls in his mouth—one in each cheek.

She turned as the elevator doors parted behind her. An attractive, well-dressed couple in their sixties stepped out, holding hands. There was an air of familiarity about them—like Reid had seen them somewhere before. The man scanned the room and set his eyes on her.

She gave Mug one final pat on the back and straightened. "Can I help you?"

"Detective Sylver?" he asked, releasing the woman's hand as he stepped forward.

"Who wants to know?"

"Mom? Dad?" London came up beside her. "What are you doing here?"

Neither of them acknowledged London—not with their eyes, body language, or words. Instead, they kept their attention fixed on Reid. "We need to speak with you," Mr. Gold said. "Urgently."

Reid cast a quick glance at London, who stood frozen in place. She could hardly believe they weren't greeting their own daughter after not seeing her in ten years. Definite candidates for parents of the year. Feeling herself getting hot under the collar, she pointed down the corridor and turned to Marino, who was now holding her full-body cutout and watching them with interest. "Detective Marino will escort you to somewhere we can talk. I'll come find you in a minute."

Marino sidled up alongside her, obviously sensing the tension. "You want me to put them in an interrogation room?" he whispered, looking bewildered.

She nodded. "Room four." The dirtiest of the lot. A wino had recently treated it as his own personal urinal.

Without another word, he introduced himself and led London's parents away, her paper replica streaming behind him.

Reid felt her heart thumping wildly against her rib cage. She turned to London, flushed with anger over the Golds' insulting behavior toward their daughter. No one treated a member of the BPD like that, especially not in their own house. "Where is it?" she asked, trying in vain to take her anger down a notch.

London looked at her, confused. "Why?"

"I need it."

London gazed down the corridor as her parents disappeared around the corner. "Reid…"

"Do you trust me?"

London hesitated. Her eyes welled up as she reached inside her coat pocket. "I do," she said, handing Reid the leather-bound journal.

London's heart skipped a beat when she saw her parents. But they wouldn't even acknowledge her, let alone look at her. How dare they show up *here*, of all places, and embarrass her in front of her colleagues?

Her anger was quickly replaced by a hurt so deep, so soul-shattering that, for an instant, she actually felt her own grief as it manifested itself in her throat, chest, and stomach. Determined not to let them see her cry, she held strong to the anger and stood her ground, silent as she watched Reid interact with the strangers before her.

Reid was composed, but just barely. She knew Reid well enough now to realize she had a plan. As Marino led her parents away to an interrogation room, Reid turned to her and asked for the unthinkable. She wanted the journal. The truest test of trust presented itself, fully, like a dog rolling over to expose its vulnerable belly.

With her heart in her throat, she relinquished the journal and then headed to the interrogation viewing room for a front row seat.

❖

Reid stepped inside interrogation room four and closed the door behind her. She made sure her cell was on and hoped the killer was tuned in, listening.

The Golds were standing in front of the two-way mirror, hand in hand. A united front, apparently. They'd opted not to sit at the scarred metal table in the center of the room. The pungent stench of old urine made Reid's eyes water. "What can I do for you fine upstanding parents?"

"Excuse me." Mr. Gold tightened his grip around his wife's hand. "You're not taking a tone of sarcasm with *us*, I hope. Especially not after we just lost our dearest friend."

Reid shook her head, silent. Were these people for real?

Mr. Gold looked from his wife to Reid. "They told us downstairs that you're the detective handling Governor Sullivan's case. He was viciously attacked and murdered last night."

"I'm well aware of that." Try as she might, she just couldn't wipe the smirk off her face. "Karma's a bitch."

"We came here to talk to you and offer our help. Perhaps it would be best for everyone if a different detective was assigned to the case. Someone who actually gives a darn," Mr. Gold said sternly.

"No need. I'm on it." She tossed the leather-bound journal on the table. It landed with a hard slap.

"What's that?" Mr. Gold asked.

"This was found inside a hidden closet inside the governor's den."

Mr. Gold narrowed his eyes. "And?"

"And it's exactly what it looks like. A journal."

"Why are you bringing this to us?" Mrs. Gold asked, her forehead creased in confusion.

"Because he wrote about the sexual assault he perpetrated ten years ago," she answered, barely containing her anger now. "On your daughter."

Mrs. Gold started to shake. "Did London kill him? Is she the one who did that to Bill?"

"Shit." Reid looked from one to the other. "You two really have no idea who your daughter is, do you?"

They stared at her blankly, obviously not comprehending the message.

"London had nothing whatsoever to do with his murder. In fact, even though he raped her—"

Mr. Gold visibly cringed at the word.

"Yeah, that's right," Reid went on. "Even though your dearest friend raped your daughter, she still wants to get justice for him. *That's* the kind of person your daughter is. And she's a damn good detective, too—one of the best I've ever seen. There's no need for you to sneak around behind her back, trying to give her a leg up in the BPD. She's managing just fine on her own." Without another word, Reid turned and stormed out, leaving the door open behind her.

She grabbed her mug from her desk and headed for the coffee maker. London was nowhere in sight, but there was no need to go looking for her. Reid knew exactly where she was.

With two cups of coffee in hand, she made her way to the viewing area of interrogation room four. London was standing there, alone in the dark, looking in from the other side of the two-way mirror. Reid let her eyes adjust before handing her a disposable cup of coffee. "We need to get you a proper travel mug," she said, holding hers up as an example. "Best thirty bucks I ever spent."

"They took it," London said, staring at the now empty table in the center of the room. "Do you think they'll read it?"

"I do." She sipped the bitter coffee, her anger at the Golds like glowing embers in a fire. "They need to see for themselves how wrong they were. That's the only way any of you can move forward."

They stood there together, shoulder to shoulder, looking in at the empty room and drinking coffee in silence.

"I'm a good detective, huh?"

Reid shrugged. "You're okay."

"I'm one of the best you've ever seen."

"No idea what you're talking about."

❖

Reid grabbed a notepad from her desk, motioned for London to follow her, and strode to Boyle's office.

Boyle was standing over the dual-compartment stainless steel trash bin he'd gotten for Mug. "Watch your step," he said over his shoulder. Dozens of tennis balls littered the office floor, each one chewed just a little. He stepped on both pedals and gestured to the now empty bins. "I might have to put a timer on this thing," he said, frowning at Mug on his dog bed in the corner.

"They're his potato chips," Reid observed. "One's never enough." She set her phone on the desk and began writing. *Killer probably listening.* She held up the notepad, pointed to her phone, and set her finger over her lips.

Boyle and London nodded.

High chance Golds will be his next target.

London's eyes grew wide.

That's how we'll catch him. Wait for him to strike.

London grabbed the pen from her. *NOT using my parents as bait!*

Boyle walked around his desk, slid a drawer open, and withdrew his own notepad. *When?* he wrote, trusting her instincts and skipping right to the chase, rather than asking why Reid believed the killer would target the Golds.

Today? Tonight? Soon.

He put the pen to his lips, thinking. *Marino, Boggs, Garcia, O'Leary, and I will sit on their house. We'll keep them safe. My word.* He looked to London, waiting for her stamp of approval.

Sylver and I go, too.

Reid set her pen to the paper. *Too risky. Killer might spot us. This is our chance to get him.*

Stay close to residence, Boyle wrote. *But not too close. I'll keep you posted every step. When he shows, I'll sit on him until you get there. Your collar.*

Nodding, London finally conceded. They all locked eyes.

Boyle put his hand in the middle of their circle, palm down. "Team name?"

London didn't hesitate. "Team Miranda."

When Boyle and Reid just stared at her, she said, "Miranda rights. Get it?"

Reid exchanged a glance with Boyle. "Sad," they said in stereo.

"I was thinking more along the lines of Pulverizing Predators," Boyle said.

"Or Demonic Destroyers," Reid added.

"Terrifying Terminators," Boyle went on.

"Dangerous Deathstompers," Reid said. She could do this all day.

She and Boyle waited, awkwardly holding hands as London stared at the floor in thought. "I've got it," she said, finally looking up.

"Took her long enough," Boyle whispered. "Better be good."

"Wait a minute." London craned her neck, peering through the office door. "We need the others in here to make it official." She hurried out of the office.

CHAPTER TWENTY-THREE

"Do we just wait here, holding hands until she comes back?" Boyle asked.

Reid shrugged. "I guess so."

They stood in silence.

She rubbed the tops of Boyle's knuckles. "Your hands are very soft."

"Cetaphil lotion." Boyle reached over with his free hand and pulled a green-and-white plastic jar out of his desk drawer. "Keeps my hands moisturized. But it's unscented, so I don't smell like a girl."

She nodded, impressed.

London finally returned with Marino, Boggs, Garcia, and O'Leary in tow. "Hands in, everyone."

"What for?" Garcia asked suspiciously.

Reid rolled her eyes. "Team cheer."

"Cool." O'Leary nodded exuberantly.

"Is this a new thing you're starting, Lieutenant?" Boggs asked. "Because it's kinda weird."

Marino interjected, "What's our team name?"

"Gold was just about to announce that if you'd all shut up for a minute," Reid said impatiently. Her arm was getting tired.

One by one, they piled their hands over hers and Boyle's. All eyes turned to London.

"Ready?" the rookie asked.

They all nodded.

"Our new team name is...The Good Guys," she announced excitedly.

They all frowned, quiet as a silent fart.

"It lacks the intimidating quality that we value in a kick-ass team name," Boyle said finally. "But it's not bad."

"Actually, I kind of like it," O'Leary admitted.

"Hell, we *are* the good guys," Marino bellowed.

"Everyone except you," Garcia joked.

"Okay, then." Boyle counted out, "One, two—"

"Wait a minute," O'Leary said. "Are we saying *Go, Good Guys* or *Go, The Good Guys*?"

"Are you shittin' me, O'Leary?" Boggs asked. "Didn't you ever play Little League when you were a kid?"

"No," O'Leary answered honestly. "No one ever wanted me on their team."

They all discreetly exchanged glances.

"This is my first team cheer." O'Leary shrugged. "I want to get it right."

"Well, that's just—"

"Sad," London interjected.

"I was going to say pathetic," Garcia said, "but let's go with sad."

"Remind me to give you a hug later, man," Marino joked.

"*Go, Good Guys* just sounds better." Boyle winked at O'Leary. "On three. One, two, three…"

"Go, Good Guys!" they cheered in unison, lifting their hands in the air and grinning like idiots.

Reid, London, and the rest of the Good Guys left their phones at the precinct, stopped by Computer Crimes to grab some surveillance equipment, and headed off in unmarked cars. They weren't taking any chances with the killer's hacking and tracking skills.

Mug looked on from the back seat as Reid selected a spot on the map on the outskirts of the Golds' neighborhood. They'd park and lie in wait, getting periodic updates from the rest of the team. Reid glanced at the clock on the dash: 3:12 p.m. Depending on when the killer decided to strike—nighttime, most likely—they could have a long wait ahead.

She hoped he wouldn't grow suspicious about their whereabouts and postpone his murderous plans. She doubted he possessed the self-control to hold back, even if he wanted to. Instinct told her his rage was approaching a climax, which could only be expressed through extreme violence. He needed to take his anger out on someone. Assuming the Golds were suitable substitutes for his own childhood caretakers, she felt confident he'd go after them with a fury.

Everything was riding on her instincts—they'd never let her down in the past. She glanced at London. She just hoped her instincts weren't being clouded by the woman beside her.

London was in the driver's seat today. Despite the ten-year fallout with her parents, Reid could sense London was more than a little nervous about their safety. The rookie needed to be behind the wheel and in control if the shit hit the fan.

London broke the heavy silence. "We don't even know what the killer looks like."

"He'll be the one wearing a mask and wielding a pointy weapon."

London braked at a red light. "Do you think Bill Sullivan saw his face?"

Reid said nothing. She knew where London was going with this.

"Because I was thinking, it might be a good idea if you—"

She headed London off at the pass. "No."

"You didn't even let me finish."

"I already know what you're thinking."

"You read minds, too?" London focused her eyes on the road as the light turned green. "That must come in handy."

"I can't do what you're asking. It'd be too hard."

London nodded. "But could you? I mean, if you wanted to?"

She'd talked to plenty of homicide victims over the years—gang members, Mafia, murderers, rapists. She realized leading an exemplary lifestyle wasn't a prerequisite for spiritual communication. "He'd probably come if I opened the door," she admitted, reminding herself of the promise she'd made to London never to lie to her again.

"All I'm saying is if he has important information about the killer, now's the time to find out. My parents' lives are on the line here, Reid."

She shook her head. "That was a low blow."

"I know, but it's true. We're using my parents as bait right now. I'll blow even lower to keep them from getting hurt."

Reid stared at London from the passenger's seat. "Did you just offer me a blow job?"

"I guess I did, didn't I?" London laughed at her own expense. "That was a poor choice of words."

She understood why London wanted to use every tool available to them. If things went sideways and the Golds ended up hurt—or worse, dead—the rookie detective could look back and find comfort in the fact that she'd left no stone unturned. London was their loyal daughter and protector to the end.

"If I open that door, Bill will be here in the car with us. You okay with that?"

London nodded. "Creeps me out a little, but I'll manage. Just make sure he sits in the back so Mug can keep an eye on him."

All she had to do was envision Bill Sullivan's face and open the door inside her mind. She angled the rearview mirror and caught his reflection in an instant. He was now sitting in the back seat beside Mug. It always surprised her that Mug didn't startle at the sudden appearance of a spirit. He reacted no differently than if a light was switched on to illuminate a dark room. It was almost as if he knew spirits were just harmless manifestations of energy. Mug chuffed under his breath to let her know they had company.

Didn't expect to be invited back so soon, especially by you, Bill admitted.

Reid didn't bother turning in her seat to address him. She could hear him perfectly inside her mind. "I need to know if you saw the killer's face."

I saw him. Got an up-close-and-personal view.

"Can you show me?" An image of a young man hovered in her mind, his expression contorted by rage. The left side of his face was badly scarred with the distinct imprint of an iron—the pointed end resting just above his cheekbone. This scar was made even more prominent by the absence of eyebrows and hair on his head. He probably shaved as a precaution against leaving any trace evidence behind. She couldn't tell if he had any other scars because the rest of his body was hidden beneath stark white coveralls—much like the Tyvek suit she wore upon entering a crime scene. Like an artist's apron, the coveralls were spattered with bright red blood. In an instant *whoosh* of information, she knew Bill's last moments had been excruciating.

A fitting end to the life I led, he said sadly, his regret palpable.

"Anything else you can tell me or show me that would help us find who killed you?"

He kept calling me Harold. Told me I had no right to touch him like that.

Looked like her theory about the killer was right on the mark. He'd been physically and sexually abused—but not by a woman, as his first two victims suggested. Perhaps Harold's wife was aware of the abuse and did nothing to stop it. That would explain the killer's anger toward older women. It would also explain why he'd removed their eyes. See no evil. The puzzle was beginning to come together now.

Can you please tell London how sorry I am?

"No." She turned in her seat to look directly into the eyes of Bill Sullivan's spirit. "How dare you try and make amends after all this time?"

"It's okay, Reid." London reached out to touch her arm. "Let him speak his piece."

"Too late. He's gone," she lied, silently kicking herself for breaking her promise to London. She told London about Harold and the scar in the shape of an iron.

"Either he and Gil shared the same foster parents, or his were no better than Gil's." London shook her head. "How do people get away with that kind of abuse? Especially when there are marks in places where everyone can see?"

"You'd be surprised," she said, remembering the adults in her life who'd turned a blind eye when she was a kid.

London reached out for her hand, entwining their fingers. "Your grandmother abused you because she didn't like that you communicated with spirits."

Reid nodded. "The beatings started after I told her I could still see and talk to my parents."

London gave her hand a squeeze. "I know nothing about talking with the dead, but can't you just summon your grandmother's spirit, like you just did with Bill, and talk to her about your history together? I bet she regrets what she did to you and wants a chance to apologize."

Almost immediately after Reid's grandmother had passed, she'd felt the old woman knocking on the door inside her mind, pleading for contact. Reid had flat-out refused to let her in, telling herself that particular door was cemented shut. Forever. But it didn't keep her grandmother from trying. Even now, she felt the old woman's unmistakable presence. Lying in wait like a patient and very hungry lioness.

Reid shook her head. "Sorry isn't in her vocabulary."

"But what if dying changed her?" London asked. "I believe everyone changes the moment they set foot on the other side, regardless of the choices they made while they were living. I've always imagined that being here in this life is like taking a test, a test you never got the chance to study for. You take the test blind and get most of the answers wrong. But as soon as you cross over—*bam!*—you get all the answers at, like, warp speed, and you're no longer left guessing."

London's theory pretty accurately depicted the changes spirits seemed to undergo on the other side. At least that was her take after having communicated with them for so long. Whenever a spirit provided her with information on a case, other bits and pieces inevitably crept in. She'd labeled these miscellaneous stowaways as unintentionals. Images, words, sounds—sometimes entire strings of perfectly preserved memories that played inside her mind like previews to a movie— often accompanied the answers to her investigative questions. These unintentionals readily conveyed a spirit's gratitude and love for those they left behind, along with regret, loss, lessons learned, and heartfelt apologies. Spirits never imparted these messages directly to Reid. They simply drifted out like swirling tendrils of fog as each spirit stepped through the doorway in her mind.

"I'm sure your grandmother is very sorry for what she did to you," London went on. "I was raised Catholic, but I don't believe in hell. God wouldn't throw us away like trash and cast us into hell to suffer for all eternity because we made some stupid mistakes, not even for the big mistakes. Not the God I know." She shrugged. "Talking to her could bring you some closure, Reid. Maybe, just maybe, it would allow you to heal and find some peace while you're still here in *this* life."

On the heels of London's words, Reid found herself reconsidering her decision to keep the door sealed shut. Food for thought. "He asked me to tell you how sorry he was," she admitted. "And the bastard never left." She threw a thumb over her shoulder. "He's still there."

London didn't flinch. "Tell him I forgive him."

"Just like that? After everything he did to you? Your parents haven't talked to you for ten years because of him," she said, shaking her head.

"My parents need to take accountability for their own choices in life. And Bill needs to take accountability for his." London glanced over with a sad smile. "Sounds to me like he just did."

She deserved so much better from me, Bill said.

When the air grew still, Reid turned to check the back seat. Mug was alone.

London took a deep, cleansing breath. Closure. After all these years, she'd finally gotten the closure she needed with Bill. And she had Reid to thank for that.

She wished the same for Reid. She was obviously carrying so much hurt, anger, resentment, and shame over the abuse she'd suffered at the hands of her grandmother. If only Reid would use her gift to help herself, it would feel like the weight of the world had been lifted— much like what London was feeling right now. She decided then that, no matter what, she would continue poking and prodding until Reid agreed to have one last chat with her grandmother.

At the very least, Reid deserved to know what it would feel like to remove that leaden boulder and trek the rest of the way up the mountain with an empty backpack.

Chapter Twenty-four

They parked on a side street about a mile from the Gold residence. Reid withdrew the laptop from the case at her feet and turned it on, wirelessly connecting the phone and earbuds they were using for the stakeout.

She inserted the tiny earbud and handed London hers. "Team Alpha and Omega here," she said aloud.

O'Leary's voice sounded over the earbud, "What I'd like to know is, who's alpha?"

"Mug," they replied in unison.

"Been working together less than a month, and already they're finishing each other's sentences," O'Leary said. "Reminds me of us, Boggs."

O'Leary and Boggs were opposite in every conceivable way, right down to the color of their skin. But they were the best of friends. Where one went, the other was sure to follow.

"Only difference is, I don't like you, O'Leary."

"I'm not that crazy about Sylver, either," London admitted. She punched Reid playfully on the arm.

"Everyone in position?" Boyle asked.

"Here," came Marino's reply.

"Yo," Garcia said.

"The eagle has landed," O'Leary called out. "I repeat, the eagle has landed."

"Suspect's in your line of sight?" Boyle asked.

"No. Mr. and Mrs. Gold just got back from grocery shopping. I've just always wanted to say, *The eagle has landed*."

"Everyone knows the eagle in this case would be the killer, dummy," Marino griped.

"Eyes and ears open, team," Boyle reminded them. "All joking aside, the sonofabitch we're after is one clever...um..."

"Sonofabitch?" Garcia finished for him.

"Thanks, Garcia. I was having a brain fart there."

Hours passed with no sign of the killer. The day grew dark. Reid reached in the back seat and rubbed Mug's neck. "Hey, Lieutenant. Thanks for Mug's new collar, by the way."

Boyle didn't answer right away. "I didn't get him a collar."

Reid froze. The collar could have come from only one other place. She suddenly felt very conspicuous in their unmarked car.

"You thinking what I'm thinking?" Boyle asked.

"Same page." She was already unbuckling Mug's collar to confirm her suspicions. A small device had been stitched into the fabric. Probably a GPS tracker or an audio/video surveillance device...or both. Damn. So much for the element of surprise. "We've been compromised."

"Listen up, team," Boyle commanded. "Suspect knows we're here. Proceed with caution. I repeat, proceed with caution."

Reid didn't know what to think now. She felt certain of one thing—the killer's rage had hit a point of no return. He would go after someone. The question at this point was, who?

She and the rest of the team had been outwitted. That much was clear. When it came right down to it, she knew she could never compete with the killer's technological savvy. It was time to bring him on level ground where she could find better footing.

"Drive," Reid said, buckling her seat belt.

"Where?" London asked.

"To your parents' house."

London was already peeling rubber.

"What's going on?" Boyle asked.

But Reid didn't answer. She was still hashing out the details of her new plan.

"Answer me, Sylver."

London braked to a screeching stop in front of the Gold residence. "What now?" she asked, turning to Reid.

"Get out of the car." Reid said. "Take Mug with you."

"Sylver, what the hell is going on?" Boyle said again.

"I said, get out. Now!" she barked when London made no move to exit the vehicle. "Gold's with you now, Lieutenant."

London searched Reid's face, her brown eyes full of questions, confusion, concern. Without a word, she nodded and stepped out into the dark night with Mug at her heels.

❖

Reid scooted over to the driver's seat and took a deep breath. Time to begin the next round of the game. She spoke directly to the killer, confident he was listening, "Matthew, I'm here. Whatever you were planning tonight, put a cork in it. I'm tired of chasing you. You win. By now, we've both realized my heart just isn't in the game." She wasn't expecting a response and wasn't surprised when none came.

"I'm done pretending to be one of the good guys," she went on. "You picked me because you know we're the same. I'm sorry it took me so long to admit it." She sighed, acutely aware that Boyle and the rest of the team were also listening. "We're both damaged goods. You know I have scars on my body from what my grandmother did to me when I was a kid. I still have nightmares about her locking me up in that damn dog crate in the basement. You know what I used to think about when I was down there?" she asked. "I used to imagine how good it would feel to sink a knife in her chest and stare into her eyes as she took her last breath. But I'm sure you know by now that I never had the courage to do it. When she died a few years back, I knew I'd lost my chance. I hated myself for being such a coward.

"You picked me to be on your team. I accept. To hell with the Good Guys—I'm ready to be who I really am. You and I will choose our victims together—people who deserve to die—and we'll kill them as a team. I'll have your back if you'll have mine."

There. She'd said everything she believed the killer needed to hear. She took another deep breath and mentally reviewed her list of checkpoints. "Meet me on the game board, where you made the first move." Seemed appropriate to end this nightmare on the playground where it all began. That location was especially poignant because she and the killer had both endured rotten childhoods. She knew the irony of joining up there wouldn't be lost on the killer.

"If I know you, Matthew, you're somewhere close by. I'm ditching the cell phone, laptop, and earbud. You'll be able to see them when I throw them out the window. All I'll have with me is the collar Mug was wearing, so you, and you alone, can track me."

She lifted the cell phone and laptop from the passenger's seat, withdrew her earbud, and chucked everything out the window. Satisfied her point was made, she put the car in gear and headed west toward Tadpole Playground.

❖

Reid glanced at her watch: 10:23 p.m. She stood from the swing and tucked her coat more closely around herself, wishing she'd thought to bring her hat, scarf, and gloves. Felt like the temperature had dipped into the twenties.

She'd been at the park for over an hour, silently wondering if she'd blown her cover somehow with the killer. Had he seen through her charade? Had she laid it on too thick? She thought back to London's face when she'd ordered her out of the car. All part of the act, yet she still felt twinges of guilt. She'd be sure to apologize—assuming they all survived tonight's events.

Apologize? She never apologized to anyone. Ever. London's lecture about taking accountability and saying sorry for the other person's benefit sprang to mind. She had to admit, there was some truth to that. Maybe she'd send Mrs. Alinski one of those edible arrangements with a note. On second thought, food might not be such a hot idea. Maybe flowers. Everyone liked flowers, right? They smelled good, looked pretty, and made you smile. How could Mrs. Alinski hold a grudge with beautiful, good-smelling flowers? Reid shook her head. The rookie was definitely rubbing off on her.

A voice called out from the darkness behind her. "Detective Sylver?"

She turned, her hand over the gun in her coat pocket. She'd traded her usual firearm, a Glock 22, for the much smaller and more easily concealed Glock 27. "Here," she said.

"A man asked me to meet you and give you this." Wrapped in winter garb from head to toe, a middle-aged woman with a beagle on a leash handed her a cell phone. "You okay?" the woman asked.

"Fine," Reid replied. "Are you?"

Nodding, the woman looked at her quizzically before letting the dog lead her away.

Reid looked down as the cell phone vibrated in her hands. She accepted the call and put the phone to her ear.

"Your former boss and the rest of the team just left the Gold residence. They're looking for you now."

She replied, "I ditched the car. It'll take them a while to find it. But it's only a matter of time before they figure out I'm here."

"I've already arranged for an Uber to pick you up. He'll be there shortly."

Her heart raced. "Where should I tell the driver to take me?"

"To the Gold residence. There's a unit posted out front, but that won't be an issue."

"Seems too risky. I thought the point here was *not* to get caught."

"That's the beauty of it," he explained. "They'll never expect us to return there tonight. It's the perfect plan."

He was right. No one, including her, would expect such a brazen move.

"How many times did adults turn their backs on you when you were a kid? They knew what your grandmother was doing. Am I right? But they didn't lift a finger to stop it. Brad and Patricia Gold are no different. They turned their backs on their daughter. That kind of sin just can't be forgiven."

"They need to pay," she agreed.

"And we'll show up tonight to make sure they pay in full."

Instincts told her to follow his lead. "What's the plan?"

"I'm already inside the house," he whispered. "The Golds are upstairs getting ready for bed. All you have to do is show up. I disarmed the security system and left the back door unlocked for you."

A minivan pulled up to the curb in front of the park entrance. "Uber's here," she announced, her heart pounding.

"See you soon, partner."

Showtime. She looked in the front and back seats of the minivan, then asked the driver to pop the tailgate just to be safe. Satisfied no one was lurking inside, she climbed in and recited the Golds' address from memory.

They drove in silence. She wondered where London and the rest of the team were. Close, no doubt. And hopefully safe.

Reid leaned forward, scanning the street signs as they drove. "Drop me here," she instructed. They were still a block from the house. A patrol car was parked up ahead, just like the killer had said. She paid the driver, climbed out, and jogged across the street, ducking through several backyards until she came to the Golds' eight-foot wooden fence.

The killer had neglected to mention this formidable obstacle. It had admittedly been a while since she'd scaled something of this magnitude. On second thought, she'd never scaled an eight-foot fence. Was it even possible?

Since the wooden slats were on the inside, there was nothing for her to grab hold of and use to hoist herself up. Best way to climb over, she knew, was to get a running start.

Epic fail. She slid down the fence like a snail. Something told her London would've scaled this fence with minimal effort and would have done so with the grace of a leaping gazelle.

After two more unsuccessful attempts, she activated the flashlight feature on the phone and started searching the ground nearby for a boulder or tree stump that would give her the height she needed. That's when she spotted the step stool. It was propped against the fence a few feet away. There was a note taped to the top: *Welcome to the party. Matthew*

She doused the flashlight, slipped the phone into her coat pocket, and finally ascended the wooden barrier, still sweating from her failed attempts. Good thing none of the guys were here to see this. She'd never hear the end of it.

She stepped onto the grass and half expected a floodlight to announce the intrusion, but none came on. An expensive house like this would likely have state-of-the-art security with integrated outdoor lighting, which the killer had already proven himself adept at disarming.

Alert to signs of an ambush—she wasn't ruling out the possibility that the killer had figured out her scheme and was just playing along—she crossed the backyard in silence and ascended the porch steps. The back door was ajar, just as the killer had promised.

❖

London tried to keep her mind focused as she ran. She and Boyle were in the lead with Marino, Boggs, O'Leary, and Garcia behind them. They'd had to abandon their unmarked cars and proceed on foot because traffic lights were malfunctioning all across the city, and traffic was gridlocked. She had a feeling that wasn't simply a coincidence. The killer had no doubt hacked into the MassDOT's traffic management system.

Keeping a steady pace with Boyle beside her, she read the street sign up ahead. They were still at least two miles from her parents' house. Her heart raced. There was no way they'd make it there in time to help Reid subdue the killer. It looked like Reid was on her own.

❖

Reid stepped inside a dark living room and paused long enough to let her eyes adjust. Shadows of the Golds' furniture fell into focus as she made her way through their house.

"You made it." The killer's voice sounded over speakers nearby. "Come upstairs. We've been waiting for you."

Apparently, he'd already started the party without her. She just hoped the Golds were still alive and unharmed.

Reid found the staircase and quietly made her way to the second floor. She wasn't sure if it was her imagination, but she swore she could feel his eyes on her the whole way. When she reached the top, she paused to let her vision adjust once again. A glowing door crack up ahead caught her eye. She felt her way along the wall down a long hallway and pressed her ear to the door.

"That's the one," the killer announced through another nearby speaker.

With a deep breath, uncertain as to what awaited her on the other side, she pulled back from the door and withdrew the Glock.

"You don't trust me?" The killer sounded disappointed. "Understandable. It'll take us both some time to adjust to this new partnership."

The gun felt reassuring in her hands. She didn't care if the bastard could see her. It wouldn't stop her from blowing a hole in his head at the first opportunity. She turned the knob and cracked the door open just enough to peek inside.

CHAPTER TWENTY-FIVE

The killer was standing over a king-size canopy bed. Mr. and Mrs. Gold were bound and gagged with expensive-looking silk ties, just like Bill Sullivan. Reid inwardly sighed with relief. No blood. No visible injuries...yet.

She pushed the door open the rest of the way with the toe of her shoe. The lights were low, but she could see Matthew clearly now. He was holding a knife against Mrs. Gold's throat. The massive scar covering the right side of his face was even more disturbing in person. He was surprisingly short—something she hadn't been expecting. He was at least a few inches shorter than her. She could've sworn the man Bill Sullivan showed her was much larger. But Matthew couldn't be more than five four and probably weighed a buck twenty, if that. She was surprised he'd had the strength to move the bodies of his first two victims, let alone subdue two large men.

"As you can see, our guests are prepped and ready. I've never been a fan of guns. Too fast, too easy, and not enough blood. Knives are my weapons of choice." He nodded toward several leather satchels that were spread out neatly on the floor near the foot of the bed. Knives of every shape and size were evenly displayed. "I brought some of my collection to show you. Put the gun away, and pick your poison."

Mrs. Gold winced as he dug the knife deeper into her flesh. Blood trickled down her neck and onto the white sheets.

The threat was clear. Put the gun down, or Mrs. Gold would die.

Reid stepped across the room and set her firearm on the dresser.

"Also, as a side note," he went on, "I've taken the extra precaution of scheduling an email to be sent at midnight tonight. It'll go out to everyone at the BPD. Can you guess what's in it?"

"A kick-ass pumpkin pie recipe?" she joked. The holidays were fast approaching.

"Your secret. I took the liberty of attaching multiple audio and video files as proof." He sighed. "I did this for the same reason you came in here with a gun—we don't trust each other yet. Had to make sure you're not trying to pull a fast one on me, pretending to be my partner just to turn around and haul me off to jail."

She hoped he was bluffing. Having an email fired off to the entire BPD revealing her aptitude for talking to the dead was definitely low on her bucket list. "Not to sound ungrateful," she said, trying to change the subject, "but why do *you* get Mrs. Gold?"

He regarded her. "I'm happy to trade. This was just the easiest way to get her husband to cooperate."

"If you don't mind, I prefer her."

"This is your first time. It should be special." He nodded in understanding. "Gil," he called out. "Can you please confiscate Reid's firearm?"

Surprised to hear Gil's name, she turned and watched as Gil stepped out from the master bathroom, head bowed.

"You didn't tell me there was a third wheel," she said, doing her best to sound offended.

"Relax. Gil's not a true partner—not like I know you and I will be. He just does the heavy lifting. Think of Gil as a very strong, very obedient dog. He's done everything I've ever asked of him since we were kids. He trusts me. He knows I'm the only person alive who has his back."

She hadn't anticipated having to take down *two* grown men on her own. The little guy, she could handle. But the big guy looked, well, big. She needed to stall for more time so she could come up with a plan. "You know my life story, but I don't know yours." She squinted. "Who did that to your face?"

"Show me your scars, and I'll tell you."

Reid shrugged out of her coat and let it fall to the floor, glad to be rid of it if things turned physical. Without hesitation, she lifted her sweatshirt and held it aloft, turning in a full circle.

"Not bad," he said. "Cigarettes, huh?"

"A few cigars. Some lighters. I swear she would've used a blowtorch if she'd had one."

He lifted his shirt to show her his life story. She wanted to look away but forced her gaze to remain steady. Instinct warned her this was some kind of test.

She took a quiet breath. Matthew was studying her reaction. It seemed he was trying to outdo her scars with his.

Instead of drawing back, she stepped toward him, reached out, and ran the tips of her fingers over his scars. His skin had been assaulted repeatedly by the same iron that stole half his face. The scars were truly disfiguring on a level she had never seen and, before now, could not have imagined.

"I don't iron much," he joked.

"Wow," she said, feigning wonder, admiration. "Make mine look like a sunburn. Who the hell did this to you?"

"My foster parents." He pulled his shirt back down. "My foster dad owned a funeral home. Taught me the trade growing up…and taught me a few other things he probably shouldn't have. Sick bastard." As he talked, he kept the knife firmly against Mrs. Gold's neck. "But my foster mom was the bitch who burned me. Said it was my punishment for taking her husband's attention away from her in the bedroom."

Reid found herself feeling sorry for Matthew. He'd obviously never had a chance as a kid. She believed everyone started out innocent and pure. What he'd turned into, the man she saw standing before her today, wasn't entirely his fault. What had made them lead such different lives, she wondered? How'd she end up on one side of the law, and he, the other?

She stood in place and searched for something to say but came up empty-handed. As if in answer to her dilemma, Kelly Clarkson's song sprang up from the dark recesses of her mind like ill-timed tulips on a wintry day. "Well, you know what they say. What doesn't kill us…"

"Makes us stronger," he finished. "I *knew* we'd get each other, Reid." He lowered his shirt and gazed at her hands. "Go pick your blade." His eyes twinkled mischievously.

"I already did." She nodded at the knife in his hand. "I want that one."

He glanced at the knife.

"It has a serrated blade," she went on. "It's the one you used to saw off Bill's fingers and toes, right?"

The Golds' eyes widened in terror.

"That's very observant of you, Reid."

"Since Bill was their friend, they should share the same fate. Kind of brings this thing full circle, don't you think?" Reid could see the skepticism dying in his eyes. Was he actually falling for this load of crap?

"Have to admit, I had other things in mind for these two," he said wistfully, studying each of the Golds on the bed with unconcealed lust. "But seeing as this is your first time, I'll leave it up to you. The secret to sawing digits successfully is finding a good set of earplugs. You want their screams to be muffled enough so your eardrums aren't damaged, but not so muffled that their screams are drowned out completely. Because, let's face it, where's the fun in that?"

"I didn't bring earplugs," Reid said, pretending to look disappointed.

"As your mentor, it's my job to think of these things. Here, I brought you a pair." He lowered the knife from Mrs. Gold's throat and reached into his shirt pocket.

This seemed as good a time as any to tackle him and confiscate his weapon. She hadn't yet devised a plan for the other guy. Looked like she'd just have to improvise. Maybe she could talk to Gil, convince him not to retaliate on Matthew's behalf.

She waited until Matthew's hand was in his pocket before stepping around behind him. In one fluid motion, she grabbed his wrist, swiped her leg in front of his, and shoved him down hard, face first, onto the floor. Caught totally by surprise, his arm was still across his chest with his hand inside his shirt pocket when he landed. It was his forearm, she guessed, that broke the impact of his fall with an audible crack. He howled in pain.

Unrelenting, she dug her left knee into the center of his back and pinned his arm to the ground with her right knee, sliding the blade from his grasp with ease. Without handcuffs—bringing them would have undoubtedly blown her cover—she had no way to restrain Matthew and protect herself against Gil, who had emerged from the bathroom and was now charging like an angry bull.

❖

London sprinted to the front door, ahead of Boyle. Locked. She jogged down the steps and scanned the ground. There, tucked against the house, was the same fake rock they'd been using to hide keys in since she was a kid. Nice to know some things never changed.

She was already unlocking the door when Boyle caught up and set the skateboard down in the grass. They waited as Marino, Boggs, O'Leary, and Garcia jogged over. Everyone—save for London and the lieutenant—was winded, red faced, and sweating profusely from the three-mile trek. Boyle set his hand over the top of hers. "Wait," he whispered. He turned to the men behind him. "Catch your breath before we go in."

"Let me go in. I'm fine," she whispered. She couldn't wait one second longer. Reid was in there alone with the killer, and the lives of her parents were on the line.

"We go in as a team," he said sternly. He waited a beat and pointed to one side of the house. "Marino, you take the right. Boggs, left. Meet around back. O'Leary and Garcia, you're with me."

"What about me?" London asked, feeling a rising panic to do something.

"You stay here until I tell you otherwise." He pointed to the earbud.

Still breathing hard, Marino and Boggs jogged away and disappeared into the darkness.

❖

She kicked the knife under the bed, stood, and yanked the killer to his feet, holding his body in front of hers as a shield. He was small, weak, and—like a rag doll—easily maneuvered, especially now that his arm was broken.

She slipped her arm around his neck, effectively putting him in a chokehold. "Come any closer, and I'll break his neck."

Gil stopped in his tracks, obviously perplexed as to how to reach her. He met Matthew's gaze, beseeching. "What I do, brother?"

"Kill her," he replied through clenched teeth.

Gil shook his head. "But she'll kill Matthew, and then Gil will have no more brother." Tears were already coursing down his cheeks. "Gil will be sad without Matthew."

"Gil, go sit in that chair." Reid nodded to a tufted chair in the quaint sitting area of the bedroom. "You sit there and stay there. Do *not* get up. Do you understand?"

"Gil understands," he said, still crying as he obediently followed her instructions.

Boyle rounded the corner, gun drawn. Boggs, O'Leary, Garcia, and Marino entered the room on his heels, breathing heavily and soaked in sweat.

Reid looked from one sweaty face to the next, hoping she wouldn't have to administer CPR to a fellow detective. "Took you long enough," she said, frowning. At Boyle's insistence, each member of the team had strapped a department-issued GPS tracking device to their ankle. She'd thought it was overkill at the time but now appreciated the wisdom behind Boyle's decision. "Were you guys taking a nap or what?"

"The minute you arrived here," Boyle said, "all the traffic lights between here and downtown went haywire. Traffic was at a standstill, so we had to come on foot."

"From where?" she asked. "Tahiti?"

Oddly enough, Boyle was the only one *not* out of breath. Until very recently, he had also been the only one in their group who smoked a pack a day.

"Hillcrest Street."

Hillcrest was over three miles away. She studied Boyle suspiciously.

Marino was bent over with his hands on his knees. "Our selfless leader cheated," he explained between breaths. "Stole a kid's skateboard...Got Mug to pull him and coasted the whole way here. Rest of us...had to run...to keep up."

"Barely broke a sweat," Boyle added proudly, holstering his firearm.

O'Leary, red faced, turned and threw up in a potted ficus tree.

"You guys should really think about joining our morning workouts." She handed the killer off to Garcia, who appeared a smidgeon less close to cardiac arrest than the other three. "Where's Gold and Mug?"

"Downstairs." Boyle withdrew his handcuffs and brought Gil to his feet. "Told Gold to stay put. Didn't know what we'd find up here."

"Speaking of the Golds," Reid said, turning to Boggs and Marino. "Can you two untie these nice folks and see if they need us to call a bus?" Brad and Patricia Gold appeared unscathed, but sometimes it was hard to tell with old people. They could be fine one minute and then dropping dead from a heart attack the next.

Marino and Boggs nodded in unison. O'Leary, however, was sprawled out on the floor, facedown.

"Maybe we should call a bus for *him*." She pointed to the floor as she stepped over O'Leary's body.

"I'm good," came O'Leary's muffled response as he gave her a thumbs-up. "Just need a minute."

Beatrice and Marge appeared just a few feet away, shoulder to shoulder. *You got him, dear*, Beatrice said with a wink.

"We got him," Reid confirmed with a nod in their direction. "And the Good Guys take the lead," she went on when the other detectives cast questioning glances in her direction.

Marge smiled. *Thank you, Detective Sylver.*

"You're welcome."

"Welcome for what?" Garcia called out behind her.

She locked eyes with Boyle. He was studying her intently from across the room. "For holding down the fort until you got your lazy asses here," she replied.

Coat in hand, Reid stepped into the hallway, switched on the lights, and jogged down the stairs. She found London waiting in the foyer. Mug stood obediently by her side. "He's in custody," she said with a reassuring smile. "Your parents are fine."

Mug trotted over to greet her and bounced around excitedly, his signature tennis ball lodged firmly in his mouth.

"Thank God." London sighed, visibly relieved. "I wasn't sure we'd get here in time."

"You can go upstairs and see them if you want."

London set her hands on her hips and gazed up the staircase. "You're sure they're okay?"

"Positive." She glanced at her watch: 11:46 p.m. The killer had warned her that her secret would be revealed at midnight. The dreaded hour was fast approaching.

"What's up?" London asked.

She shrugged into her coat. "Tell you in the car."

"We don't have a car. We left it on—"

"Hillcrest. Yeah, I know." Damn. She couldn't be around Boyle and the others if the email came through. One way or another, she had to get out of here.

"We'll call a squad car to come get us and drop us at the precinct," London offered.

But Reid just shook her head. She felt like a caged lion and started to panic.

"Did you happen to see the carriage house out back?" London asked.

Unable to think, Reid just stared at her.

"My parents can spare a car for an officer in need. Come on," London said, already heading toward the kitchen. "I know where they keep the keys."

CHAPTER TWENTY-SIX

A Rolls-Royce?" Reid asked. "You want to steal a *Rolls*?"

London set her hands on her hips. "We're not stealing it. We're borrowing it. It's my father's all-time favorite car."

"All the more reason to borrow a different car." She lifted a plush fabric cover to peek at the second car in line—a sleek silver Aston Martin Valkyrie. Nope. Still too expensive. Next up was a canary-yellow Zenvo TS1 GT, a car so expensive she'd never even heard of it. Last in line was a candy-apple-red Mercedes-AMG One. Shaking her head in disbelief, she walked back to London. "Don't your parents have any normal cars?"

"My parents aren't normal, so the answer is no."

Reid checked the time again: 11:54 p.m. Felt like a bomb was about to go off.

"We have no car of our own here, you don't want to call a squad car, and you keep checking your watch like you have somewhere to be." London opened her arms, gesturing at the insanely expensive cars around them. "Lookie here: cars. Problem solved."

Reid shrugged. "We did just save their lives."

"That's the spirit."

"And I'm sure they won't mind if my drooling hundred-pound mastiff rides in the back seat of their million-dollar car."

"Who doesn't love a little drool? Besides, I never rebelled as a teenager, so this is my chance to shine." London grinned broadly. "Gotta love karma."

❖

This was the one time—the only time—in her life that Reid refused to get behind the wheel.

London dangled the keys. "You sure?"

"Yup. Your rebellion. You drive." She opened the rear passenger's side door and motioned for Mug to jump in, which, of course, he was all too happy to do. She winced as he climbed atop the moccasin-tan leather seats. "Don't burp, fart, or sneeze. And keep the drooling to a minimum," she ordered, shutting the door like it was made of eggshell.

The moment her body made contact with the passenger's seat, she fell head over heels for the car. It enveloped and supported her in all the right places, like a warm embrace from the Pillsbury Doughboy himself. "Oh. My. God."

"Right?"

"It even smells like fresh-baked cookies in here."

"Every Rolls-Royce Phantom is custom-made," London explained. "No two are alike. My father loves the smell of cookies coming out of the oven, so the manufacturer teamed up with Yankee Candle. They wove the scent into the fabric of the car." She inhaled deeply. "Still just as fresh as the day he bought it."

Mug farted loudly in the back seat.

London cracked the windows. "Mr. Irvington, if you'd be so kind as to open the door, please." The carriage house door instantly slid aside.

"Who's Mr. Irvington?" Reid asked, confused.

"That's the name my father gave the carriage house. Each car is equipped with voice recognition. And the carriage house door is programmed to respond to *Mr. Irvington*."

Reid rested her arm on the cushioned armrest as London started the ignition. "How many miles are on this thing?"

London glanced at the odometer. "Eighty-six."

"Thousand?"

"Eighty-six miles."

"And he's had this car for how long?"

"Twelve years."

"Holy shit."

"Please do not use foul language in my presence," said a woman's voice with a British accent over the car's speakers.

Reid sat up. "Who the hell is that?"

"Mrs. Fitzpatrick." London pulled out of the carriage house and glanced at Reid like she was a total idiot. "The car."

"Your father named the car Mrs. Fitzpatrick?"

"Of course. Doesn't everyone name their car?"

"Not everyone." She shrugged. "But when they do, they're usually more common names like Fred or Betsy."

"Mine's Mother Trucker," London admitted with a mischievous smile. "I drive a Silverado."

"What if your parents think the car's stolen? We should let Boyle—"

"No need. I left a note."

Curious what such a note would say after they hadn't spoken in ten years, she asked, "What'd you write?"

"Borrowed Rolls. London."

Well, if the killer didn't give Mr. Gold a heart attack, maybe that note would do the job.

Reid's watch alarm started beeping as they drove from the carriage house. It was now 12:01 a.m. Her moment of truth. She withdrew the phone from her coat pocket and logged into her email account. Nothing. Guardedly optimistic, she let out a breath. Maybe the killer had been bluffing.

"What's going on?" London asked, suddenly serious as she waited at the end of the driveway.

"Do me a favor, and check your email." She handed the phone to London. "Your work email."

"What am I looking for?"

"If it's there, you'll know it when you see it."

London put the Rolls in Park and tapped on the phone as Reid looked on from the passenger's seat.

There, at the top of the list, was an unopened email from Matthew T. Killer with a subject line that read: *Det. Sylver's Secret.*

"Open it," Reid said, feeling her face flush with anger. "Please," she added, reminding herself it wasn't London she was angry with.

London tapped on the message.

To Everyone at the Boston Police Department:
    As I'm sure many of you know, the average BPD homicide detective has a success rate of about 47 percent a

year. Detective Sylver, however, has managed to solve 100 percent of her cases every year for the past thirteen years. What accounts for this discrepancy? Follow the links below to find the shocking answer.

"Reid"—London looked over at her—"I'm so sorry this happened."

"Can you send me a copy?"

London tapped on the screen and then handed her the phone. "What now?"

"Just drive."

London put the car in gear and pulled onto the street. She reached across the seat for Reid's hand and held it tight. "Might not be as bad as you think."

"I can't wear those rose-colored glasses right now, London."

"I'm just saying, you haven't even watched the videos yet."

To prove her point, and maybe to satisfy her own morbid curiosity, she slipped the phone from her coat pocket, brought up the email, and tapped on the first link.

It was an audio clip of her conversation with London in the parking lot of the animal hospital, just after Mug was taken.

"You want to know how I solve every case?"

"Okay, I'll bite. How?"

"I talk to the dead."

The clip went on for several minutes, revealing all the personal details of the visit from London's nana.

When the clip reached the end, Reid sat there, stunned. "I'm sorry you got caught up in this."

"It's nothing we can't handle. We'll both be fine," London assured her.

"Should I play the rest?"

"Might be a good idea to scroll through both the audio and video files," London said, composed as ever. "See if there are any of us from last night."

Reid swallowed hard. Shit. She hadn't even thought of that. "How about we come up with a game plan first?"

"What kind of game plan?" London asked on the seat beside her.

"If there's a video or audio clip of us, you know…"

"Having the hottest sex of our lives?" London finished, seemingly amused. "At least, it was for me."

"Me, too. If that's in here somewhere, and everyone from the department sees it, it'd make me feel better if we hatched an escape plan."

"Oh, I get it now." London nodded in understanding. "Like, fleeing the country and never returning so we wouldn't die on the spot from embarrassment."

"Exactly."

"Sure, I'm game. Can I go first?"

"Have at it, but I must warn you. My plan's good."

London raised an eyebrow. "You go, then."

"We get facial reconstructive surgery, create new identities—I know a guy—and relocate to England to assume our new careers as detective inspectors." Everyone had a pipe dream. Mastering the British accent and working as a detective in England was hers.

London frowned. "But isn't fleeing the country *and* getting facial reconstructive surgery kind of redundant?"

"It's to go along with our new identities. Can't have new identities with the same boring faces."

"Okay. That's true," London said perkily.

"You have something better?"

"Mine's easier, less expensive, and probably less painful."

"Lay it on me."

"We pack enough food and supplies to last us, hop aboard my houseboat, and sail the world. Mug comes, too, of course." He lifted his head from the back seat at the mention of his name.

Reid nodded. "Not bad."

"Thanks."

"If you threw in a skimpy bikini, I could be down with that plan."

"Done."

Reid lifted the phone from her lap and took a deep breath to steady herself. Another moment of truth. This time, however, she felt braver with London by her side and their backup plan in place.

One by one, she tapped all eighteen links and came up empty. Felt like they'd just dodged a bullet or, more accurately, a world-obliterating asteroid.

"Where do you want to go?" London asked in a chipper tone,

obviously just as relieved as she was. "Just name a place, and I'll take you there. Consider me your chauffeur for the night."

Reid sighed. "Home. I'm tired. I just want to sleep." She imagined that was how anyone would feel after discovering their career had ended overnight.

They drove in silence for several miles. "I have a better idea," London said finally. "Do you trust me?"

They locked eyes, and Reid nodded. "I do."

London slowed the car, switched on the blinker, and made a U-turn in the middle of the road.

London reached across the seat and held Reid's hand. Despite their playful banter, there was a heavy feeling in the car. She knew Reid was grieving for the career she thought was over. But London wasn't so sure it had to end that way. The beginnings of a plan were already starting to take root in her mind. She just needed more time to sort things out.

In the meantime, she intended to support Reid in the best way she could. By being with her every step of the way.

Back at London's houseboat, Reid climbed out of the Rolls with Mug. "Are we starting our pirating adventures tonight?" Her breath billowed like smoke in the cold nighttime air.

"You can dress up as a pirate and raid my treasure if you want." London winked. "I think I even have an eye patch inside somewhere."

Reid laughed as London walked around the car to join her. Actually, come to think of it, that could be fun.

London stood in front of her and leaned in for a slow, sweet kiss. "After everything that happened today, neither of us should be alone tonight. I'd like you to stay here. With me."

Reid pretended to consider the offer. "If you threw in that eye patch, I could be down with that plan."

"Done."

After she showered and changed, Reid lifted her watch from the bathroom vanity: 1:43 a.m. She'd been awake for nearly twenty-four hours. It was hard to wrap her mind around everything that had transpired in the course of a day. Her life, as she knew it, was forever changed. Not only was she starting a relationship and allowing herself to fall in love—neither of which she'd ever considered was even remotely possible—but she'd traded her career and reputation for getting a killer off the streets. All worth it, in her book. But still, it was a lot to take in.

Naked, she brushed her teeth with the spare toothbrush that London had on hand for guests—thankfully, still in the package. Not being able to brush her teeth before sex would be a deal breaker, no matter how horny she was. She paused, thinking. Would they have sex tonight? Maybe. Maybe not. They'd both been through a lot today. She'd let London make that call, knowing she'd be fine either way. The idea of snuggling intrigued her. It was something she'd only seen people do on TV but had never experienced for herself. She'd bet anything London was just as skilled at snuggling as she was at sex.

She slipped into the plaid pajama bottoms and T-shirt that had been left on the shelf for her. Smelling faint traces of London on the fabric, she smiled and shook her head. They'd come a long way in a short amount of time. Everything they'd been through during the course of the investigation had pushed the getting-to-know-you stage into hyperdrive. But she was okay with that. Something told her London was okay with it, too.

"Did you find the pajamas I left for you?" London called out from the other side of the door. She'd apparently already finished her shower in the bathroom on the opposite side of the boat.

Reid opened the door to find London standing there in a skimpy white bikini. Her natural blond hair was now a shade darker, still wet from her shower.

London grinned and held out a black eyepatch. When Reid raised an eyebrow, she explained, "From my Halloween costume last month. Glad I kept it."

"Aye," Reid said, snapping it in place. Guess that answered any lingering questions she had about the agenda for tonight. "Do ye know where I could score me some pirate's booty?"

Laughing, London led her to the bedroom and shut the door.

❖

Reid had barely fallen asleep when she awoke with a start. She sat up, plucked her watch off the nightstand, and checked the time: 3:57 a.m.

London sat up in bed beside her. "What's wrong?"

"Boyle."

"You had a bad dream about Boyle?" London asked sleepily.

"No. I'm supposed to meet him in thirty minutes"—she leaned in for a kiss—"for our workout."

"You're still going? But you haven't slept in, like"—London twisted Reid's wrist to steal a glance at her watch—"a really long time. My brain's too tired to do the math."

"I'm fine." She had always been able to function adequately for long periods on little sleep. "Mind-blowing sex and a catnap are all I need to get me through the day."

"What are you planning to say about the email when you see Boyle?"

"No clue." Reid sighed. "I'll work that out on the way."

London kissed her sweetly on the lips and then gazed at her with such tenderness. "Want some company?" she asked sincerely. "For moral support?"

"Thanks, but you stay and sleep. I'll catch up with you later." She stood, tucked the blankets around London, and kissed her on the forehead. London smelled so good at this early hour. Smiling to herself, she walked to the door, paused with her hand on the doorknob, and glanced back uncertainly.

London sat up. "What's wrong?"

"Can I take the Rolls? Just remembered my car's at the precinct."

London didn't blink as she nestled back beneath the covers. "Sure. Keys are on the counter."

"Thanks." She turned and hesitated at the door's threshold once again.

London sighed, poking her head out of the covers. "What now?"

"The eye patch," Reid said sheepishly. "Can I take the eye patch, too?"

CHAPTER TWENTY-SEVEN

R eid stepped off the elevator with Mug at her side and two muffins in hand.

Boyle was already waiting for her in his office, clad in bright orange basketball shorts and a neon-yellow tank for their first workout together.

She reached into the paper bag and tossed him an oatmeal muffin. "It's way too early for clothes that bright." Grimacing, she looked him up and down. "On second thought, there's really no good time to wear that."

"My five-year-old picked them out," he said sadly. He looked down at himself and frowned. "Made the mistake of taking her shopping with me. I tried telling her these weren't Daddy's colors, but she wouldn't take no for an answer." He met her gaze, unapologetic. "We'll just have to suffer through this together."

She pulled up a chair on the other side of his desk, surprised to see her battle-scarred travel mug perched on the edge.

"Cinnamon?" she asked, pointing.

He nodded. "Cap told me how you like it."

She took a sip of coffee, and they ate together in silence.

Finished with her muffin, she looked up. "You check your email today?"

"Yup."

"And?"

"And what?"

"Did you see the links to the audio and video files?"

"I saw them," he said, his expression unreadable.

Shit. Like pulling teeth. "Well, did you open them?"

"Nope."

"Why the hell not?"

"Didn't need to. Cap already filled me in."

Reid had never been so surprised in her life. "All this time…you *knew*?"

"Yeah. So?"

"You never let on. Never treated me any different."

"Why would I? You're the same kick-ass detective who walked in here thirteen years ago and set this place on fire."

She stared at him, still in shock. "Do the guys know?"

"They do now." He sighed. "But not from me, if that's what you're asking."

She'd had the last half hour to think about her next move. Thirty minutes didn't sound like enough time to make a life-altering decision, but she realized she'd started planning for this contingency a long time ago. She was clear on what needed to happen. "I'm taking that two-week vacation you offered."

Boyle paused. "Makes sense," he said finally.

"And I'm not coming back."

He leaned back in his leather chair and laced his fingers together behind his head. "Back where we started, huh?"

"Never really left," she said honestly. She told him about the governor's threat to expose her if she didn't return to mentor London. The killer had already made good on his threat, but she didn't feel the need to point that out.

"So you were damned if you did and damned if you didn't." He shook his head. "I wish you'd come to me sooner, Sylver."

"I wish I had, too, Lieutenant."

"Mug's going with you?" he asked glumly.

She nodded, realizing he'd probably miss the dog more than he cared to admit.

They sipped their coffee in silence, watching as Mug raided his stash, two tennis balls at a time.

"I'm glad we caught the bastard," she said finally. "I'd trade the job a hundred times over if it meant getting a killer off the streets. No regrets," she said firmly. She wanted Boyle to know she wasn't bitter about any of it.

"What am I supposed to tell the guys? They love you like family, Sylver."

She pierced him with her zero-tolerance-for-bullshit stare down.

"Okay." He put his hands up. "Maybe love was too strong a word. But just hear me out." He walked around to her and perched on the edge of his desk. "Not only do the guys in this unit care about and respect you, but they'd lay their lives down for you in a heartbeat, Sylver, no questions asked. Finding this out about you isn't going to change that." He shrugged. "If that's not family, then I don't know what is."

And that's exactly why she was leaving. Everything Boyle said was true. And the feeling was mutual. The guys here would defend her to the end. It was the rest of the BPD she had to think about—they didn't know her from Jane Doe. The one thing she'd learned over the years was that cops liked to talk. They stuck their noses in everyone's business. Busybodies with guns was how she often thought of them. Without a doubt, she and the rest of Homicide would be the butt of every joke. She wasn't about to let the guys face endless ridicule on her behalf. Her mind was made up. No matter what Boyle said.

"I'll be back in two weeks to empty out my desk." She was tempted to do it now and get it over with, but she was just too damn tired. She stood and extended a hand to Boyle. "Thanks for everything, Lieutenant."

"You, too, Sylver."

As she walked to the door, Cap stepped in front of her, effectively barring her exit. She considered ignoring him and passing right on through him, but that never ended well. Doing so was like getting zapped by a live wire that left her entire body tingling for hours. She wisely halted in her tracks and kept a respectable distance.

Tell him he's doing a damn fine job filling my shoes. Cap crossed his arms and looked at her sternly. *Go on. Tell him. He needs to hear that right now.*

She turned and leaned against the doorframe, putting her back to the captain. "Cap's here," she announced

"He is?" Boyle looked around the office. "Where?"

"Behind me." She threw a thumb over her shoulder. "He's being a pain in the ass."

Boyle craned his neck to peer over her shoulder. "I don't see him."

"That's because he's dead."

"What do they look like?" Boyle asked, appearing genuinely curious. "Spirits, I mean."

"The same as when they were here. Whenever I see them, they're always wearing the same clothes they died in. I'm not sure if that's how everyone sees them, but that's how I do."

"Then, for your sake"—Boyle gazed down at his radiant outfit—"let's hope I don't kick the bucket today." He looked up. "Is Cap trying to convince you to stay?"

She shook her head. "Wants me to tell you you're doing a damn fine job filling his shoes."

Boyle's somber mood instantly brightened. "Yeah?"

"Yeah."

"Hey, while you got him on the line, can you ask him where I'd find the key to the damn closet?" Boyle pointed to the closet in the corner of the office. "And what the hell's in there, anyway?"

She nodded at the clock on the wall. "He says it's taped to the back."

"Already looked there."

"Look again."

Boyle lifted the clock from the wall and set it on the desk, facedown. The black electrical tape blended in seamlessly with the clock's black backing. "Clever. Could've saved me a lot of time if he'd told me about that beforehand." He carefully peeled the tape back, revealing a silver key. "Do I even want to know what's in there?"

Confident her former captain had no secrets, she listened to his answer and started laughing. There were no skeletons, literal or otherwise, in Cap's closet. That was part of his charm. What you saw was what you got with him.

"What's so funny?" Boyle asked.

"You'll find some clothes, toiletries, a pillow, a blanket, and a blowup mattress in there. He'd sleep here whenever he and the wife were fighting. Says his best advice for a lasting marriage is for you to do the same."

Boyle joined in on the laughter, shaking his head.

As she straightened to leave, her lieutenant took a seat behind his desk. He looked good there. Even if he *was* dressed like a human glow stick. "Couldn't ask for a better co-parent for Mug," she admitted. "When I get back from vacation, once our divorce is finalized, you can have him every other weekend, if you want. Child support must be paid on the first of each month."

"Let me guess. Tennis balls in lieu of cash?"

She nodded.

"Deal." He taped the key back in place and set the clock aside. "And tell Cap we miss him."

"I already did."

Back at home, Reid packed enough clothes, toiletries, food, and paperback novels to last two weeks. She wanted to hurry up and hit the road before she was tempted to change her mind, before she found herself driving to London's houseboat and slipping back beneath the covers with the sexiest, smartest woman she'd ever known.

Mug pranced around after her, following her from room to room. He'd accompanied her on more than a handful of camping trips over the years and knew all the signs of an impending departure. She was never sure who was more excited. But there was a somber feeling in the air today that had never been there before. She realized she was going to miss London.

With one last look around the house, she locked up and climbed inside the RV. The sun was just beginning to rise, right on cue. Looked like they were going to beat morning rush hour. They'd be well on their way to New Hampshire before commuters even started honking their horns.

She and Mug always camped in Mount Washington State Park and spent their days hiking endless miles of trails. The fresh air and solitude never grew old. Because the area was so sparsely populated, she also rarely encountered spirits—a welcome reprieve.

She pulled to the side of the road a few miles from where she knew service was spotty and retrieved her cell from the passenger's seat. She quickly texted London, having already worked out exactly what she wanted to say: *Took Mug on a road trip. Will be out of service area. Be back in two weeks. Putting in my papers when I return. Sorry in advance for the flak other cops will give you because of that email. But I know you can handle it. Having me gone should make things easier for you and the rest of the Good Guys.*

Reid struggled with how to sign off. She didn't want London to think she was expecting anything from her. She wanted to give London room to breathe because she knew the coming weeks would be challenging. After facing countless interdepartmental questions—and, no doubt, being the target of unrelenting criticism and wisecracks from other cops—she wasn't sure if London would *want* to be associated with her anymore. She needed to give London the time and space she needed to decide what was best for her, both personally and professionally. She was already head-over-heels in love with London and only wanted what was best for her. Wanting what was best for someone, even if that didn't include her, was what it meant to truly care for someone. It was a bittersweet feeling but one she was happy to finally experience.

So, in the end, she simply wrote the truth: *Hope to see you soon.*

She hit Send and put the RV in gear. But before she could pull onto the road, her phone dinged to let her know she'd received a text. Couldn't be London. She was home sleeping. But who else would be sending her a text? Curiosity got the best of her, so she put the RV in Park once again and grabbed her phone off the passenger's seat. Sure enough, it was London.

You

You? You what, she wondered? Was London texting in her sleep? Maybe she'd somehow forgotten the word *fuck*, intending to type *fuck you*. She frowned. No, London didn't cuss. Maybe *suck* would soon follow. *You suck* made more sense. Perhaps London was angry. She was still trying to puzzle it out when another text appeared: *will*.

"*You will*," Reid read aloud. "I will what?" she asked the phone. She nearly jumped out of her skin when London knocked on the passenger's side window. She pointed to the lock and mouthed, *Let me in.*

Reid pressed a button to unlock the door and stared at London as she climbed into the passenger's seat. "You again?"

"Me again."

"Thought I left you sleeping on the houseboat."

"You did. But I'm fast in these." London gestured to her Adidas running shoes, the same ones Reid had made her change into when they first met. "If you were trying to lose me, you should've taken all my shoes and clothes and just left me with the bikini."

Reid glanced in the side-view mirror. There, parked on the side of the road behind her RV, was the Rolls.

"You brought the *Rolls*?" she asked in disbelief.

"I brought the Rolls," London replied with a smirk.

Mug trotted to the front of the RV for his customary greeting, giving London a gentle nudge and several licks for good measure.

"How'd you find me?"

"I called the lieutenant to let him know I was taking a personal day. He mentioned you were leaving town."

Reid frowned. She hadn't told Boyle about this trip. "How'd he know I was leaving town?"

"Said you had that look on your face when he saw you this morning."

"A look? What look?"

"He called it your need to get the hell out of here now face. Said you always hit the road with Mug and head north whenever things get stressful at work."

Reid shook her head. Working with a bunch of detectives definitely had its downside.

"So I hopped in the Rolls and headed north, figuring I'd catch up with you sooner or later." London pointed behind them. "V12 twin-turbocharged engine."

The sun reached through the RV's side window and grazed London's hair and cheek, casting her in a heavenly glow. God, was she beautiful. "Are you inviting yourself along on our camping trip?"

"Are you kidding?" London balked. "I wouldn't dream of interrupting your alone time. I just needed to make sure you were okay."

But the idea of London joining them for this trip suddenly filled her with profound joy, a joy she realized she'd never known before. And the fact that London had driven all this way just to check in made her feel cared about in a way she'd never experienced. "I'm still kind of in shock over the whole thing. I knew I'd retire eventually. Just didn't think it would be this soon."

"Then don't," London said, her brown eyes filled with razor-sharp resolve. "Stay on. Face this with me."

"I can't," she said firmly, certain her decision was the right one. "IA would scrutinize every single case I worked from this point forward. No one from the DA's office would want to touch my cases with a ten-foot pole, no matter how solid and irrefutable the evidence was." She shrugged. "I'm too much of a liability for the department now. They couldn't keep me on, even if they wanted to." After all was said and done, that was the final layer of truth. Like a giant sinkhole in the middle of a busy road, there was no way around it. Her career in law enforcement had come to an end.

CHAPTER TWENTY-EIGHT

So that's it, then?" London pressed. "You retire and spend your time…doing what exactly?"

"Maybe working as a PI." It was an idea Reid had been tossing around for years. "I don't have all the details hammered out yet. That's why I came up here. I needed someplace quiet to plan out the next few chapters."

London gazed out the window and nodded, her sadness palpable. "Makes sense."

"Would you like to join us?" she asked, hoping to lift London's spirits.

"For what?"

"For tonight's black-tie event at the Ritz." Reid rolled her eyes. "Camping."

"But you just said you needed quiet to plan your next move."

"I do."

"Well, we both know I like to talk. Having me there would be counterproductive."

"Maybe I could use a sounding board."

"That's okay." London offered her a reassuring smile. "You go do what you need to do. I'll be there when you get back." She leaned across the console, kissed Reid gently on the lips, and then opened the passenger's door. She was halfway out by the time Reid found the courage to speak her mind.

"Other than Mug, I've never wanted anyone to come camping with me. The whole point of this trip is getting away from people, both dead and alive."

"No worries." London glanced over her shoulder. "I get it—"

"No, you don't get it. I want you to come with us, not just as a sounding board but as a partner, friend, and lover." She took a deep breath. "I want you to come as my girlfriend." There, she'd said it. No matter how London responded, she could take comfort in knowing she'd found the courage to take a risk. "Obviously, that doesn't mean you *have* to come. If you can't or don't want to, that's totally fine." She found herself stumbling over her words in an effort to cushion her fall.

London took pity on her and threw her a rope as she plummeted into an abyss of self-doubt. "I'd love to."

"Really?"

"Really."

Reid sighed, thankful for this unexpected change of plans. "I realize there's a twelve-year age difference, but—"

"Eleven years and five months," London said matter-of-factly.

"You looked up my birthday?"

London nodded. "Before we started working together. I had to know if our signs were compatible."

London was nothing if not thorough. "You believe in that stuff?"

"Not really." London shrugged. "Maybe a little."

"What did it say about us?"

"We're among the most compatible signs in the zodiac."

Interesting. Her curiosity was piqued. "What are you?"

"Capricorn. December twenty-second."

She made a mental note that London's birthday was coming up next month. "The goat, right?"

London nodded.

"And I'm a Leo."

London sighed and nodded again. "Fitting."

"But doesn't the lion eat the goat?" Reid asked, frowning.

"Not if the goat headbutts the lion when necessary to put her in her place."

She laughed. That pretty much summed up their entire relationship to date. "The age difference really doesn't bother you?"

"Not at all."

"And the fact that I'm no longer a cop?"

"I'm not with you because you're a cop." London reached across the console to hold her hand. "I'm with you because you're *you*."

Now that her insecurities were out in the open, she felt both relieved and grateful to London for airing them out. "Service gets spotty just up the road." She handed London her cell. "You should probably call Boyle before we go any farther."

"Why?"

"To request time off. I'm sure taking down a dangerous serial killer has earned you some personal time."

"I already did."

"Did what?"

"Cleared time off with the lieutenant. He gave me a week."

"You planned on joining us this whole time?"

"I figured you might want some company." London shrugged. "But I was fine either way."

"Why didn't you just tell me that from the get-go?"

"Same reason you didn't invite me. Because I didn't want you to feel any pressure."

Reid laughed. At least they were on the same page and looking out for one another.

❖

A week later, heading home in the Rolls, London reflected on her mini-vacation with Reid. It had been the best vacation of her life. She'd met her soul mate. There was no doubt in her mind.

They'd left work in the city where it belonged and focused solely on enjoying their time together in the great outdoors. Countless hikes, runs, campfires, stargazing. Reid had even taught her how to skip rocks in the lake, something she'd never taken the time to learn before. And they had made love every night. Each time, she'd swear the sex couldn't get any better...only to discover it could.

An unspoken agreement to live in the moment had kept them from discussing Reid's plans to become a PI. But London's wheels never stopped turning during their time together. Her mind had a habit of not letting go until it found a workable solution.

Which she had.

Still driving, she glanced down at her cell phone as the service bars reappeared. She wasted no time and dialed the lieutenant's direct line.

❖

Reid decided to pack up and head home earlier than planned. London had stayed with her and Mug for a week before heading back to return to work. She and Mug had remained behind, intent on wringing out every drop of playtime and relaxation for another week. But after three days, it ceased to be fun and started to feel lonely. She missed London. Even Mug seemed to have a little less spring in his step.

She, London, and Mug had hiked every day and spent their nights making s'mores and cuddling by the campfire. She had no idea camping could be so much fun with another human being. Instead of growing apart and annoyed with each other after spending so much time together, which had been her fear from the outset, their relationship grew stronger and more intimate. They'd made love every night and fell asleep looking up at the stars. London's body was now as familiar to her as her own. Reid was even more in love after their time here together. She was confident the feeling was mutual.

She shoveled dirt into the campfire pit, dismantled the canopy, folded the chairs, and packed the last of the supplies in the RV's exterior storage compartment. She was on the road by seven thirty and decided to call Boyle en route.

He answered on the first ring. "You back?"

"On my way home now. I'm dropping by tonight to clean out my desk." She'd play it like a true coward and wait until the guys had left for the night. "Just thought you should know."

"Made it easy for you. Already cleaned it out. Everything's in a box. All you have to do is swing by and pick it up. What time will you be here?"

"Around eight."

"Fine. I'll wait up for you—"

"Don't. I'd prefer just to get in and out. Make it no big deal."

"Not for you, Sylver," Boyle said. "For Mug. This is my weekend with him. Remember?"

She laughed. "It's only Thursday."

"Well…can I have him a day early?" Boyle pleaded.

"Yeah. Okay. That's fine."

"Great." He hesitated on the other end. "But you know you can't just slink away without saying good-bye."

She saw where Boyle was heading and cut him off at the pass. "No."

"No what?"

"I do *not* want a retirement party. And if you plan one for me, I'm taking full custody of Mug."

"No visitation?"

"Nada."

He sighed. "At least meet me and the guys for a beer at Foley's tomorrow after work. Say, around seven?"

Foley's was their unit's favorite hangout. Garcia's nephew had been managing the bar for years. "I'll be there."

❖

London yawned into the phone. "You sure you don't want me to come with you?"

"No need," Reid said. "I'll be quick. Boyle already packed everything."

"Bet it'll be kind of sad."

"A little," she admitted. "I'll swing by your place after I'm done." Talk about presumptuous. She paused, giving herself a mental dope slap. "Or I could just go home," she offered, suddenly uncertain about how to proceed. Had London yawned as a signal that she was too tired for company tonight? Relationship etiquette was dizzying. "Actually, I haven't been home much, so I'll just go there."

"Then I'll come to you," London said without hesitation.

She laughed at herself. "Sorry, this is all new for me. I just assumed we'd spend the night together. Should've asked first."

"I assumed the same," London admitted. "And you don't have to ask. You're always welcome here."

Reid parked in her usual space as they ended the call. She walked around to the passenger's side and held the door open for Mug, quickly scanning the lot. Looked like the guys had already left. Only Boyle's truck remained.

She'd spent the last twenty years of her life working here. In many ways, this building felt more familiar to her than her own house. Hard to believe this part of her life was coming to a close. It was a huge loss that couldn't—and probably shouldn't—be glossed over. Like the captain's death, she knew she'd need time to come to terms with this unwelcome change.

As if reading her thoughts, Cap appeared as she entered the building's stairwell. Fortunately, no one was around, which was the very reason she'd chosen the stairwell instead of the elevator. She had a feeling he'd show up here tonight. "Hey, Cap."

Good work getting a killer off the streets. Even in death, he was a solid leader.

She leaned against the wall and smiled. "Thanks. It was a team effort."

I know you don't like surprises—

"I *hate* surprises." She glanced up the stairs, instantly pissed off at Boyle for betraying her. "He promised."

He promised not to throw you a retirement party. Cap slid his hands in his pockets, just like he used to do when he was trying to reason with her. *Not to worry. He kept his word on that.*

"Then what are you saying?"

Wanted to give you a heads-up. There's a gift waiting for you upstairs.

She eyed him with sudden suspicion. "What kind of gift?"

That's not for me to disclose. But it's precious. And a lot of people helped to make it happen. He stepped closer. *Your people* and *mine.*

Instinct told her, whatever the gift was, it wasn't to be taken for granted.

You can still do a lot of good work here, he said.

"Are you telling me I should stay?"

He glanced over his shoulder at something—or someone—behind him. Nodding, he turned back to her. *I can't advise you either way.*

"Right," she said, catching his drift. "Free will." She started up the stairs.

Sylver, one more thing.

She turned to face him.

My wife's in a tizzy. Water heater broke and flooded the basement. She thinks our wedding album was down there and got ruined. But she doesn't know I moved our box of memories to the attic. Can you pay her a visit and tell her?

"And just how do you propose I do that?" she asked, amused. "Excuse me, Mrs. Konigsbergdormenoffski—" She stopped herself. "No wonder we called you Cap. Your last name is way too long and hard to say."

I know. He shook his head. *Just call her Mrs. K.*

"Excuse me, Mrs. K," she went on. "Your dead husband informed me that he moved your wedding album to the attic. By the way, sorry to hear your basement flooded. He told me about that, too."

Perfect.

"With all due respect, sir, did you lose your common sense in the afterlife?"

My wife already knows about your gift.

Reid set her hands on her hips. "You told her?"

Not to worry. She's never breathed a word of it to anyone.

"Fine." She started up the stairs once again. "I'll drop by your house in the morning."

Mind if I come with you? He hurried up the steps alongside her. *I might've promised her you'd pay her a visit to pass along some messages from me after I, you know...*

"Kicked the bucket?"

Yeah. That. He frowned. *There are a few more things I'd like to tell her.*

She paused in the stairwell. She'd always promised herself she would never do that. Passing messages along to loved ones seemed like a tricky business. But Cap was different. Not only had he become a father figure in her life, she owed this man her career. "It'd be an honor, Cap."

Thanks, Sylver. Then, with one last smile, he was gone.

She had a feeling she'd be seeing a lot more of him for years to come.

When she reached the fourth floor, she set her hand over the door handle and hesitated. Whatever lay on the other side had better not make her cry. Being known as the crazy cop who talked to dead people was one thing. Being labeled as a touchy-feely cop who cried was another. She'd worked hard to earn her reputation as a hard-ass. She had a duty to uphold that image.

Steeling herself, she swiped her badge and yanked the door open.

There, lined up on both sides of the corridor, were patrol cops, detectives, sergeants, lieutenants, and captains from every precinct. They started applauding as soon as she stepped through the doorway. The applause grew in volume with cheers and whistles as she made her way down the center with Mug at her side.

"Nice job, Sylver."

"Way to get those bad guys."

"Best detective we have."

"Couldn't be prouder."

She rounded the corner and noticed the spot where her desk had once rested was now bare. Just four rust-colored stains remained on the tile floor, left behind by the desk's metal legs.

She looked up. London, Garcia, Marino, Boggs, and O'Leary were standing in front of Boyle's office. As they stepped aside, she noticed that a second doorway had been installed alongside the original. There were now two doors. A wall had been erected in the center of Boyle's office, making one office into two.

Her desk was now inside the second office.

The applause died down as Reid stepped over. Boyle was perched on the corner of her old desk inside the new office. "What do you think?"

She grimaced. "The walls are pink."

"Primer. Boggs and O'Leary are painting it this weekend. Didn't expect you back so soon."

She saw the nameplate on her desk. "This is for me?" she asked, stunned.

"You're still retired," he assured her. "BPD created a new position for you, as a civilian." He walked over to the newly installed door and gestured to the lettering on the glass: *In-House Homicide Consultant*.

"We come to you now with our cases," Garcia said.

"Not just us," London explained. "Homicide detectives from every precinct around Boston are already lining up, waiting to meet with you."

Unable to hold back any longer, the damn waterworks started. There went her reputation. "How'd you pull this off, Lieutenant?"

"All I had to do was show the commissioner your stats for the last thirteen years. They got on board with the idea pretty quickly after that."

"They'd be stupid not to," Boggs said. "The more cases we solve, the better they look."

"Hope you got plenty of rest on your vacation." Boyle slapped her on the shoulder. "You start Monday."

"First appointment's with me." Marino grinned.

"Then me," O'Leary said.

Boggs shouldered O'Leary aside. "And I'm after throw-up face here."

"You're booked out for a while," Boyle admitted. He pointed to the chair on the other side of her desk. It was one she didn't recognize. "Cap's chair," he said. "Pretty beat-up, so we had it reupholstered for you."

"What do you say, Sylver?" Boggs asked. "You game?"

Reid nodded and wiped her face, but it was no use. The tears just kept coming.

Boyle stepped outside to the waiting crowd. "She accepted the new position," he announced.

Another round of obnoxiously loud cheers and clapping ensued.

"We're heading to Foley's." Boyle shouted to be heard. "Beer's on the house!"

The applause grew impossibly louder. One by one, everyone filed out, and the room grew deafeningly quiet.

London poked her head inside. "Congrats, Sylver. See you at Foley's."

Pretty soon, she and Boyle were the only two left on the floor. Reid walked around her desk and sat in Cap's old chair. Mug curled up on his new dog bed in the corner.

"Gold had a lot to do with this, you know." Boyle took a seat in a chair on the other side of her desk.

She looked up, surprised. "Yeah?"

"When I told her the idea, she drew up an elaborate PowerPoint presentation for the commissioner. Charts, graphs, current stats, projected stats—the whole nine yards. Half of it I didn't even understand." He shook his head, clearly impressed. "Man, she kicked ass in the meeting that day."

Reid smiled to herself. Sounded like London all right. Her girlfriend was definitely going places.

Boyle gestured around the room. "The guys chipped in on their time off to make this happen."

"Family," she said, meeting Boyle's gaze across the desk.

"Family," he repeated with a smile.

CHAPTER TWENTY-NINE

Home again and already naked, Reid slipped off London's panties and eased her back onto the bed. They made love with a tenderness and familiarity that felt magical. Making London climax was her new favorite pastime. The way she cried out, threw her head back, and dug her nails into Reid's back was intoxicating beyond measure.

Not to be outdone, London flipped her over and returned the favor with a fierceness and confidence that she found equally intoxicating. As they shifted into a slower rhythm, London leaned forward and gazed into her eyes. "I'm in this for the long haul," she whispered. "You can count on me, you know."

"What about the dog?" Reid asked. She didn't dare say Mug's name for fear he'd come barreling in with his usual grace and gusto. "We're a package deal, you know."

"Trust me." London rolled her eyes. "I'm well aware of that."

"From now on, I promise you'll always have the front seat."

London kissed her. Sweetly. Slowly. Straddling her, she guided Reid's fingers inside. "I love you, Reid."

"Me, too."

"That's almost as bad as *ditto*."

"What, you want me to spell it out for you?" She laughed, knowing London could take the teasing. "How about this? I'm head over heels in love with you, London Gold. And I intend to make you my wife one day."

"Needs work. But it'll do for now." London arched her back and moaned as Reid increased the pace.

Their passion reignited, Reid readied herself for round two.

About the Author

Michelle is an author of lesbian romantic thrillers, a long-distance runner with no sense of direction, and a nunchuck-wielding sidekick to a pair of superhero sons. For more information, please visit: www.bymichellelarkin.com.

Books Available From Bold Strokes Books

A Love that Leads to Home by Ronica Black. For Carla Sims and Janice Carpenter, home isn't about location, it's where your heart is. (978-1-63555-675-9)

Blades of Bluegrass by D. Jackson Leigh. A US Army occupational therapist must rehab a bitter veteran who is a ticking political time bomb the military is desperate to disarm. (978-1-63555-637-7)

Hopeless Romantic by Georgia Beers. Can a jaded wedding planner and an optimistic divorce attorney possibly find a future together? (978-1-63555-650-6)

Hopes and Dreams by PJ Trebelhorn. Movie theater manager Riley Warren is forced to face her high school crush and tormentor, wealthy socialite Victoria Thayer, at their twentieth reunion. (978-1-63555-670-4)

In the Cards by Kimberly Cooper Griffin. Daria and Phaedra are about to discover that love finds a way, especially when powers outside their control are at play. (978-1-63555-717-6)

Moon Fever by Ileandra Young. SPEAR agent Danika Karson must clear her werewolf friend of multiple false charges while teaching her vampire girlfriend to resist the blood mania brought on by a full moon. (978-1-63555-603-2)

Serenity by Jesse J. Thoma. For Kit Marsden, there are many things in life she cannot change. Serenity is in the acceptance. (978-1-63555-713-8)

Sylver and Gold by Michelle Larkin. Working feverishly to find a killer before he strikes again, Boston homicide detective Reid Sylver and rookie cop London Gold are blindsided by their chemistry and developing attraction. (978-1-63555-611-7)

Trade Secrets by Kathleen Knowles. In Silicon Valley, love and business are a volatile mix for clinical lab scientist Tony Leung and venture capitalist Sheila Graham. (978-1-63555-642-1)

Entangled by Melissa Brayden. Becca Crawford is the perfect person to head up the Jade Hotel, if only the captivating owner of the local vineyard would get on board with her plan and stop badmouthing the hotel to everyone in town. (978-1-63555-709-1)

First Do No Harm by Emily Smith. Pierce and Cassidy are about to discover that when it comes to love, sometimes you have to risk it all to have it all. (978-1-63555-699-5)

Kiss Me Every Day by Dena Blake. For Wynn Jamison, wishing for a do-over with Carly Evans was a long shot; actually getting one was a game changer. (978-1-63555-551-6)

Olivia by Genevieve McCluer. In this lesbian Shakespeare adaption with vampires, Olivia is a centuries-old vampire who must fight a strange figure from her past if she wants a chance at happiness. (978-1-63555-701-5)

One Woman's Treasure by Jean Copeland. Daphne's search for discarded antiques and treasures leads to an embarrassing misunderstanding and, ultimately, the opportunity for the romance of a lifetime with Nina. (978-1-63555-652-0)

Silver Ravens by Jane Fletcher. Lori has lost her girlfriend, her home, and her job. Things don't improve when she's kidnapped and taken to fairyland. (978-1-63555-631-5)

Still Not Over You by Jenny Frame, Carsen Taite, and Ali Vali. Old flames die hard in these tales of a second chance at love with the ex you're still not over. (978-1-63555-516-5)

Storm Lines by Jessica L. Webb. Devon is a psychologist who likes rules. Marley is a cop who doesn't. They don't always agree, but both fight to protect a girl immersed in a street drug ring. (978-1-63555-626-1)

The Politics of Love by Jen Jensen. Is it possible to love across the political divide in a hostile world? Conservative Shelley Whitmore and liberal Rand Thomas are about to find out. (978-1-63555-693-3)